BROKEN LIKE ME

DALE ALLEN-ROWSE

Wolf Vision Publishing, LLC
Mountain Center, CA

Wolf Vision Publishing, LLC
P.O. Box 157
Mountain Center, California

www.DaleAllenRowse.com

ISBN (book): 979-8-9873971-0-7
ISBN (ebook): 979-8-9873971-1-4

Editor and Interior Design: Micah Schwader
www.inspiredlifepublications.com

GRATITUDE

For John. My husband. My Thad.

TABLE OF CONTENTS

"A dream you dream alone is only a dream.
A dream you dream together is reality."
~ Yoko Ono

PROLOGUE

Heading south on Canada's Route 37, Jack kept experiencing a buzzing sensation in his head. *Ugh. Why? What now?* he thought. It was a lot for Jack to process, given the fact that he still hadn't figured out where he and Yolo the crow were going to land. They had no home base other than the trusty and rusty Blazer, but even that was showing the pangs of old. Yolo flapped next to Jack, swatting him in the head with a wing.

"Yo…Yo, Yolo. Settle down, girl. What's up? You need to go outside or something?" Jack's voice conveyed annoyance, but it didn't hide his fears over her ever-growing restless state. It was a state that most likely signaled that she might be a bit mature for his coop and that perhaps it was time she went on her way. She was old enough to know how to care for herself, and Jack knew this day would come. However, he was surprised it arrived so quickly. They had only been together two and a half weeks.

Jack often stood in sheer amazement of the lessons this bird had taught him, but of course, the second half of that equation was that Jack stood before her daily, asking to be taught. Through this, he found an openness that was neatly hidden behind the thinnest of veils that required just the slightest touch to open. Internal channels are funny that way. The hardest part is finding them; the rest is simply allowing.

"Scraw!!!" shrieked Yolo while turning in the passenger's seat. The volume of the screech was headache-inducing in the enclosed space. If Jack rolled down the windows, the crow would flap her wings because the air moved around her too quickly. It was a no-win situation. Jack pulled the truck over and got out of the vehicle. Letting the fledgling bird emerge after him, Jack somehow knew it was time. This feeling of "knowing" something had been sitting with Jack the entire trip south. While he didn't exactly know where they were going, Jack knew his life was about to take off in ways he couldn't have foreseen several months ago.

Jack closed the car door and gazed at his reflection in the window. Today he was okay with what met his eye and mind.

"Yolo!" Jack yelled into the sky, unsure of where she had gone. He waited and turned in the other direction. "Yolo!" The long waits between her reappearances were the final signal that she needed to take flight toward a life of her own making. Jack knew he would miss her, but she deserved a family of her own.

"Where the hell is that damn bird?" Jack asked himself while noting that he should have inquired about a tracking device because it seemed a shame to say goodbye forever. The bird had come to mean a lot to him. *Great,* he thought. *One more thing to try and not be sad about.* He shrugged and looked skyward again. *But I guess we all have to be as intended.*

Jack got back in the truck. His head was still pounding from the bird's screams, and searching for her in the bright clouds wasn't helping. *Maybe she's already gone,* Jack thought. He had hoped for a more formal goodbye, and what he was feeling being solo, well… he needed a minute.

Jack pushed his driver's seat back and exhaled, thinking, *Now what?*

CHAPTER 1

ARTERY

"Hey Thad, how are you?" Jack smiled into the phone, trying to come off cool despite the butterflies flapping at his nerves.

"Well, hello, mate," Thad replied. "I was hoping to hear from ya."

"Oh yeah? Why's that?"

"May I quote you?" Thad asked flatly.

"Ooh. Yep, ya. I certainly always enjoy people honoring my good name with my pearls of wisdom. So go on." By now, both men were trying to stifle a subtle laugh.

"Ah, yes then. The gems of foresight and knowledge as bestowed upon us by the one and only, Handsome Jack."

The phrase "Handsome Jack" met his ears as the deepest pool of crystal blue gratitude. Jack had never known himself as handsome, and somewhere inside, it fed him to hear those words. He knew he was enough. He got that, but for someone to say those words to him from the place that Thad did could emotionally bring Jack to his knees. Very few things in his life thus far had felt so good. It was as if Thad was giving him permission to believe it about himself, and that was a place he had been hoping to get to for a very long time. This new lush ground Thad lent him was summer grass that slipped soothingly through Jack's toes. He exhaled.

"Yes, yes… go on, Thad. If you're quoting me, I already know it's going to be fucking brilliant, so out with it."

"You are a bloody lunatic, Jack. You know that, eh?" Thad said through a chuckle.

"Not exactly news… but go on." Jack laughed.

"Just wanted to make sure I got the phrasing correct, but I believe your exact words were…. wait, let me get to the exact text.

Ah yes… here it is, and I quote….” He paused for dramatic effect, then cleared his throat. “‘That's nice, but I just want to fuck your brains out.’” There was a beat of silence between them before they both laughed while Joy barked in the background.

“Oh! How's the little puddin'-head?”

“Sorry?” Thad said, slowing his laugh.

“Puddin'-head. Little Joy-Joy. Joy to the world! Joy.”

“Ya, don't call her that.” Thad laughed, teasing.

“K. How about Miss Smoosh-your-face Pickle-Pack of Joy-Joy?” Jack managed, laughing harder.

“WHAT is WRONG with you?!” Thad sent back in a chuckle while they settled back into themselves and regained composure. “Oh my God, Jack, thanks. I needed that. It feels good to laugh.”

“Indeed, it does. It feels good to laugh.” Jack wasn't sure he wanted to follow through with his sentence but did anyway because he and Thad were done with missing their opportunities to show up for one another, so Jack shored himself up. “It feels good to laugh with you.” Upon saying the words, red instantly flashed to Jack's ears, but he was willing to take a chance, and hot ears were the price he could easily pay.

“Awww…,” Thad said. “It's funny. As a handicapped person, I don't often get the chance to have conversations like this, let alone have someone flirt so openly with me.”

“Well…,” Jack started but wasn't sure how to follow up. “I guess we'll learn together then.”

“Ha!” Thad laughed into the phone, making Jack shrink in his clothes. “C'mon, mate. You must have had all the dates you ever wanted.”

Jack was feeling a bit off-guard. “Well, that hasn't been my experience.”

“Seriously?” Thad said in disbelief.

“Yes. I'm not sure exactly why you'd think otherwise. We're both not exactly Grade A beef.” Jack regretted this the second it left his lips. “It's just that…. Ah damn. I'm sorry, Thad, that came out weird. I didn't mean it like that.”

"Ya well, not a new sentiment to these aging ears. I only meant that with your body and all, I couldn't imagine that you haven't been successful in the dating department. Am I right?"

"I've done okay, I guess." Jack just wanted to change the subject. He didn't know how honest he could get with Thad yet. Telling someone you were a sex worker for almost a decade was never easy, and it was usually at this point when new potential partners stepped off the platform to head down the tracks to a different life – a life without Jack.

"I've just passed Iskut and expect to be in Prince George in two days. Got any plans this weekend? I figure I could be there by late afternoon Friday if you're around."

"Sure thing, and Jack." Pause. "And… I'm sorry if I assumed something about you that wasn't true. I just think you're very handsome and can't imagine anyone saying no to going out with you."

Jack leaned back and listened while resisting his rising walls because that behavior no longer served him. He understood that, but moreover, he was done with the constant prison of loneliness that his sense of safety required because it was an optional prison and one that asked much too much – walled off from the world, trusting no one, sipping on fear with his back against a wall of safety.

"I get that, Thad. It's just that I haven't always been the best person, and I don't really trust people, so I'm usually alone. It's easier that way."

"My brave boy."

Hearing this from Thad, a tear sparked in Jack's eye, then rolled hotly down his cheek. Jack didn't know why he was experiencing Thad's words in this way.

"Those who live on this side of okay are seldom experts at dating, love, and relationships. It's much of what my book is about. Ooh! Did you have a chance to read it yet?!"

"Yes," Jack lied, hating himself in the moment. "I'm working on it. And I can't wait to talk to you about it in person."

"You haven't read it yet," Thad said without emotion.

"Bleh! Ya… oh, God. Give me a few days. I really want to, but Yolo." Jack stopped. "Oh my God. I didn't tell you that Yolo, my crow, she flew off!"

"See!" Thad said enthusiastically. "You're terrible at relationships," sending them into laughter. "But seriously, Jack. I'm sorry. You said she was young. Did you have her long? Were you close?"

"We were together a few weeks," Jack thought quietly out loud. "We had a special connection."

"Well, again. I'm sorry. It must have been tough losing your friend."

"Ya. It was unexpectedly difficult. I just want to know she's okay. You know?" Pause. "We went through a lot together. I just wish I could have had a proper goodbye."

"What? She just bloody up and flew off? Not so much as a goodbye?"

"Pretty much," Jack confirmed, snickering.

"Well, that's fucking damn well bloody rude now, ain't it?"

Jack laughed.

"Can crows be skanks?"

Jack laughed harder.

"Bloody no-good kids, ain't it? Always the taking and such. 'Can I borrow the car,' they say. Well, it'll be state schooling for her from now on, won't it? So you can stop saving for her college now, I guess."

Jack was in hysterics. Thad's Liverpool accent somehow made his jokes even funnier.

"Well, my friend, I need to scoot. I just wanted to check in to see if we can meet this weekend," Jack said after recovering his breath.

"Sounds good. Call me Friday morning, and we'll make plans." Pause. "And Jack…." Pause. "I'm really looking forward to seeing you again."

Jack smiled and replied, "Me too, and give Miss Smoosh-your-face Pickle-Pack of Joy-Joy a kiss from me."

Thad laughed and shook his head.

"You're really something else, mate."

"Bye, Thad."

"Talk soon, Handsome," Thad said. "And Jack...?"

"Ya?"

Silence.

"Well, never mind." Jack could sense there was a story there. "We can talk about it when you're here. Bye."

Jack refocused on the road ahead. "Okay, mate," he joked. "Talk soon."

Chapter 2

Hunker

Jack had been on the road for a few hours after hanging up with Thad. The nuances and words from that conversation were being picked apart internally with each passing mile. Directions? Life? Where was he? Where was he going? What next? He didn't know, and in the cab flying solo, Jack felt very alone.

His thoughts were soon broken by a percussive racket coming from under his hood. *Damn it.* He thought about trying to find a place to pull over. Steam began to pour out from the vehicle making it more and more challenging to navigate the road at highway speed, and eventually, the Blazer came to a crawling and unsettled halt at the edge of the road. Jack pushed himself back into his seat, resigned and exhausted from the fuckery of the moment. He got out of the truck and popped the hood, sending clouds of oily gloom heavenward while he searched his pocket for his phone to see where he was.

"Meziadin Junction," Jack read aloud, seeing that was the nearest and only mechanic's shop. He dialed, hoping someone would answer.

"Harrow's Motel and RV."

"Uh. Hi," Jack said, confused because he was expecting to reach a mechanic. "I was looking for the mechanic's shop. Perhaps I have the wrong number?"

"No. This is the place. I just didn't realize you had wrung through on the other line. Hold on."

Jack heard a click then the same voice came across the line with, "Dinty's Garage at Meziadin. How can I help you?" Jack had to quickly suppress a laugh at the simplistic weirdness of the guy, but given he was in dire straits, Jack was happy to have reached someone.

"My car broke down. I'm just up the 37 a way, probably twenty kilometers or so toward Iskut. Any chance you can send a tow?"

"Oh, sure. But it'll cost ya."

Jack tumbled in mixed emotions over the answer. He was extremely relieved that there might be help sent, but the idea that this exercise might empty his bank account wasn't exactly welcome news. It was a tough situation.

"Well, please send someone. I'm on the southbound side near...." Jack looked around, trying to fix on a landmark of some kind, but there was just the road and the trees, same as there'd been for miles and miles and miles. "Hold on...." Jack flipped through his phone to the compass app and found his exact coordinates. "I'm at 56.404134 & -129.339977."

Jack heard an old typewriter in the background plunking away at something — a sound that felt detached from the expected. Then, from somewhere in the background came a young woman's voice. "Mr. Harrow, I need to speak with you about the unwanted guests that arrived late last night."

Mr. Harrow covered the phone, but someone with a rather terse tone could still be heard.

"I said I will speak to you later, Poppy! Silver needn't worry. The authorities won't be here for another twenty hours."

None of what Jack was hearing was making sense.

Then, the muffled voice gave way to a clear-toned, "Now where was I, young man? Ah yes." More plunking at a typewriter in the background. "Says here your coordinates put you about twenty-seven minutes north of us. I can have Gren there in about an hour."

The muffled voice continued. "Gren! Gots a run for ya." There was a big deep unintelligible voice in the distance that Jack couldn't hear clearly.

"Ya, about an hour. Sit tight. Gren'll be there. And I suggest you keep in yer car there. The willows'n such be out this time of year." Click.

Jack repeatedly blinked in rapid succession to jump-start meaning to anything he had just heard. Nothing rational came to mind.

Willows'n such? Jack thought, looking into the face of his phone as if it might somehow offer up more information to clarify what that all meant. Regardless, Jack was grateful that help in the form of a 'Gren' was on its way. He kicked back in his driver's seat and exhaled.

Fuck, Jack thought to himself. *No place to go. No place to call home. No companion… and now no car while I'm also hurdling toward the possibility of no money.* He had to figure out his next moves fast.

"Jack?" The voice he heard came from within. "Are you there, Jack?"

Oh, fuck off, Jack sent back in response. *I'm seriously not in the mood right now.* He reached for his mokee pipe, which he stuffed with hopes of chemical stillness, lit, and dragged on it with newfound desperation, hoping to replace his current reality with a new weird world. Jack exhaled as his jaw clicked and punched smoke rings into the cab, skewing the outside world, which was precisely what Jack needed.

"Fuck," he repeated to himself, exhaling again as his shoulders dropped another half inch. He just needed time to settle, adjust, and see where he was in terms of location, energy, mindfulness, and alignment. Pressing pause on a noisy brain was the best Jack could do at the moment. He reached for his cowboy hat and lowered the brim over his eyes. This wasn't walling himself off but more like cocooning, the quiet of an enclosed space appropriate for denning and thinking.

Just then, Jack's gut pushed *D a n g e r* into his brain.

Jesus of Las Vegas, Jack thought. *Now what? Danger?* Jack looked out the smoke-filled cab at the ridgeline while the shine of the day waned, giving the air of the place a newfound sepia, the blues giving way to the grounds of earth browns. Jack saw nothing of concern, so he closed his eyes to rest.

Crack! The noise tore through the silence, bringing Jack fully into the present. *What the…?* Jack thought, realizing he had fallen asleep. He could tell by the tilt of the world's light that he was somewhere he hadn't been just ten minutes ago.

Crack! Jack heard, making him spin around, searching for the source of the resonance, but the down valley echoes made any identification impossible. He was on high alert now. Jack lowered himself cautiously from the truck to not disturb the source of the thing while he noted the complete absence of thought in his high alert mind.

I'm in. Jack noticed. *I'm back up here. I know this place. I know the silence and lack of a second voice here.* He realized he had involuntarily accessed the mind of his consciousness, the observation deck to the mind, the seat of his soul. This place was not that of the gut, which is *knowing*, but rather the higher self of *being* that could sense and tap into everything around him.

Later in the day, Jack would recall the moment and find it very curious that this was done without his thought or effort. It was as if the clarity required in this tense moment was automatically met by the best and most appropriate part of his system. Effortlessly, it had presented itself and stepped forward to meet the moment. Much like digestion, it was something done without Jack's consent or attention – an odd sensation that Jack internally filed under "items to revisit while in the in-between."

A tow truck appeared, heading toward him on the opposite side of the highway. Jack prayed it was his help sent up from Meziadin Junction. He watched it pass him and noticed the driver's long hair whipping in strange straggly strands out the window. *I guess that's Gren,* he thought as the vehicle crossed into the median and then swerved back around to head for his Blazer.

"Oh, thank God," Jack said aloud, forgetting the disturbance in the woods. He waved his arms as the recovery truck positioned itself ahead of him, then backed into position. The driver got out and outstretched a thin pale hand.

"Gren," the man said.

Jack shook his frail bones and introduced himself. "Hi. Jack. Thank you so much for coming."

The skeletal man with ribbons of hair that seemed to lack an understanding of gravity eyed Jack up and down. Jack instantly noted that Gren, too, only had one eye. There was no attempt at covering up his truth, however. His vacant, orb-less mar gleamed a disturbing brownish pink in the dimming light. His response to Jack's appreciation was a silent wave meant to convey that Jack was to get out of the way, which he did.

Gren then set about hooking up the tow while classical music was heard tinkering out of the strange man's cab.

"Is this Camille Saint-Saëns?" Jack perked up, recognizing the orchestration from his playlist of favorite classical tracks. The creep and timber of this particular work were instantly recognizable because Jack would spend time, like he did when he was a teen, lying on the floor and embodying the resonance while losing himself in the world the vibrations presented in his mind. Jack's question about the composer was met with silence, making him question whether Gren even spoke English.

"Peux-Je vous aider, monsieur? Can I help you with…." His question stopped short when Gren passed him and pushed his Chevy keys into Jack's chest with far more force than necessary. Jack was taken aback by the aggressive move. The skinny man waved an arm in the air, hopped in, and started the tow truck. Jack understood and begrudgingly put himself in the stink of the cab as well, where he quickly rolled down the window while Gren dialed up the current sound of a timpani as they rolled onto Route 37.

The ride to the motel and RV park set Jack's mood for the day. A disquiet, an uneasiness, a sliver of dark that wasn't big enough to be parsed from ordinary things. It was a taint that couldn't be showered off; it reminded him of the moods he would fend off when he was a new arrival in Vancouver's seedy West End.

"Hey. What's your name? You new here?" a handsome guy in his late twenties asked. At the time, Jack was huddled in a pile of dirty clothes with stains that ran down one pant leg. Jack didn't answer.

"I'm James."

Jack remained silent. That's the thing about trauma and the experience of being an object or used trash; the teachable lessons aren't something one can forget despite what we tell ourselves about detaching.

James leaned against the bricks of the place and lowered himself to sit next to Jack, who, in the moment, was too afflicted to speak.

The tow truck slowed around the final corner while the crescendo of an opus in a faltering minor found its way back to sleep in the truck's buzzing speakers. Gren cut off the radio and finished parking in front of Dinty's Garage as Jack jumped out of the vehicle and looked around.

"Where in the actual fuck?" he said to himself quietly while taking in the surprisingly stagnant air and the wriggle of the place that unnerved Jack to his bones. That's the thing about old places; if something new was never introduced, the old simply fettered on. The schizoid nature of this place had clearly never been disrupted despite what might be seen as normal or appropriate.

Gren stood at attention, a move that caught Jack off-guard. The old scarecrow of a man then pointed to the neighboring building, which was separated by an old playground in tragic disrepair. The decaying wheels of abandoned hope creaked as the wind moved the parts that hadn't yet been caught up in the web of frozen rust. Above the neighboring motel fizzed a neon sign reading Harrow's Motel. Below it, a failed DIY attempt at a hand-painted sign offered visitors "And RV Park!" but it was a sales pitch that no one seemed to be buying. Even at first glance, the "RV Park" was just a painted-off section of the parking lot with a few picnic tables.

"Allez!" Gren barked, snapping Jack to attention. They headed up to the main entrance of the motel lobby. Jack stepped inside, willing to check in, but he was unnerved that his departure date could not be foretold.

CHAPTER 3

SINK

Stepping into the dank lobby of Harrow's Motel, Jack had to take a second and blink away the corners of light that remained in his working eye to adjust for the darkness. A "How ya now?" greeted Jack as was customary in rural B.C. Jack blinked a few more times, searching the room for the innkeeper while an overly expressive piano concerto seeped from the dilapidated speaker that sat in the corner.

"Yep. Just fine now. Thanks for sending someone to get me. I appreciate the tow." Jack closed the door behind him yet still hadn't found the source of the voice, and his working ear couldn't help but think that Rachmaninoff might be the composer of the expressive piano battle being waged in the air surrounding him.

"Well, don't thank me yet. That'll be $375 for the road service, and you'll be spending the night then?"

A response Jack confirmed with internal dread. "Ya. Just 'til I can get the Blazer up and running again." Even while saying the words, he desperately searched for confirmation from the man that this would be just a quick stopover. Then, much to his surprise, a tiny man found his way up a set of small steps that lead to a platform, allowing him to meet Jack eye-to-eye. Jack pushed his weight back onto his heels taking in the Kafkaesque scene. Mr. Harrow then turned the volume knob on the stereo, allowing Jack to exhale and gather his twisted twits. Then, as if the scene weren't surreal enough, Gren entered the lobby.

"La voiture, la...." The three stood silently, waiting to see if Gren would finish the sentence. Simple saying, 'the car there' left them hanging mid-thought.

"Oui?" Jack prompted, but again, Gren seemed to be adrift while his gaping eye socket puckered at the air. He offered no further direction or insight. Again, Jack repeated. "Oui, Monsieur. Quisque a?"

Gren broke from his daydream, shifted his stance, and trained the voided socket on Jack. Stepping forward into Jack's personal space, the tall man punctured a "Voulez-vous que." into his face. Once again, Gren simply stopped talking mid-sentence.

Now Jack was getting a bit frustrated. He just wanted to get to his room and shower off the ludicrousness of it all. He could feel the Frenchman's breath on his face forcing him to step back. This prompted Gren to again break from his fantasy. "Je traville sur la voiture, monsieur?"

"Oui. Merci." There was plenty more Jack wanted to convey to the man, but he figured keeping it brief might grant a break from the hover he currently found himself under. Gren turned without confirming and then was gone.

Jack exhaled as he heard laughter from behind him. "Seems between yous, you might scrape together one set of decent peepers." This comment sent Mr. Harrow into gales of self-amused guffaws.

None of this amused Jack, and the longer they stood there while the stripped bare piano pluck-fuckery concerto scored, the more side-kiltered the space around him spun. He had had enough.

"So, how much do I owe you? I'd like to check-in, thanks."

Eventually, Mr. Harrow regained his composure, righted himself, and cleared his throat. "Let's see now...," he said as dead Liberace laid waste to another epic scale run. "Seems we only gots room 54 left." A comment that greatly surprised Jack.

"Room 54?" Jack turned this way and that as if moving in this manner might right the world and explain the warp of rooms that seemed to be missing or were currently off-grid. Yet, even at first glance, one could tell there were no more than a dozen rooms.

"Yep. Don't recommend it, but that's all we gots."

Hearing this, Jack's exhaustion grew tenfold. He just wanted to be somewhere warm and safe, but unfortunately, that was a bar that probably couldn't be met in Room 54. Nonetheless, Jack forced himself to remain curious. "Um… is there a problem with the room?" Jack asked as Mr. Harrow turned to start plunk-plunking on an old typewriter as if to write up an order of some kind. The tiny man again cleared his throat, then adjusted his spectacles to focus more clearly in the dimming light. Dusk was now upon them, and Jack noticed that the dingy antiseptic-smelling place grew more peculiar in the fading light.

"Like I said," Mr. Harrow continued, "It's all we gots. It's $54 for the room."

Jack dropped his head in resignation as he fished out his debit card and placed it on the counter. He just wanted to escape from the moment and end the pangs of hunger and future regrets that were now accordioned in concert with the warbles of the rapid-fire piano concerto. "Fine."

Mr. Harrow finished typing the flimsy receipt, ran Jack's card then handed him the yellow slip from behind the white. "Here's the key." Jack took it but recoiled given how greasy it was. "Last door down. No monkey business, and you re-up or are out by noon. Capiche?"

Jack stood there taking it all in but was propelled into movement by Mr. Harrow's parting words. "Pitter-patter, son." Jack found the phrase as annoying as it was familiar in this part of the world.

Jack exited, noting he only had possession of his backpack and might need to get a few more things from his vehicle. But first, he wanted to check out the room.

Leaving the lobby of the beat-down motel, Jack took in several gulps of fresh air as if to cleanse his lungs from the fetid tint of the Harrow hall. *So awful!* Jack thought as he let the stench ramble through his nervous system. *Bleh… gross. This place has truly been forgotten by time. Hell… off-grid is one thing but this? This is tinker-town insanity.*

Jack then snickered with his next thought. *I guess it's where those who don't fit in elsewhere come for community and employment.* Jack took a left down the pedestrian alley between the abandoned playground and the motel as the gentle mountain air continued to find its voice. It came in padded gales that crept under swing sets, setting the blue and abandoned steel into motion.

Suddenly, a few lights began to flicker around him. "Get me outta here," Jack said under his breath. He just wanted to escape it all, so he picked up the pace. As he did, he felt something at his heels. He turned. Nothing.

D a n g e r. Jack's gut offered to his mind. *D a n g e r.*

"Fuck." He picked up the pace even further.

D a n g e r. Jack heard it internally again. He shoulder-checked his surroundings for the source of the cold presence that poked at him yet could not be seen. Finding nothing, he burst into a sprint toward his room.

Reaching the door that read "54," Jack threw his back against the door. He paused just long enough to scope out the parking lot and assess the current situation. Jack saw nothing other than the scattered folding chairs and picnic tables in the "pedestrian only" area in front of the rooms. They backed up to the chain-link fence that separated him, and the reliquary of past joys now set to rust in this place of the unwanted.

Jack noted his internal feelings of misalignment. He simply felt "off" and all he had was a mindset full of misses. It was always confusing when the external failed to meet the internal. It was a moment that was more disturbing because it meant that either his internal was off or, more likely, something in his external world. Jack had yet to put his finger on what exactly was amiss here. He exhaled and quickly let himself relax by keeping his back to the door frame.

"What the...?" Jack said under his breath as he took in the room. It was typical in its cheap motel decor and furniture placement. It was the last room of the row. However, room 54 had windows on two sides instead of the standard single-paned window by the door. At first glance, one might think this was an added benefit or upgrade, but that's not how things worked here in this place, the Junction of the Meziadin.

Inside, Jack turned around and around, assessing the room. The dinge of the carpet and soiled stains of the ceiling only added to Jack's uneasiness. Turning one last time, he pressed into the bonus window. The one that didn't face the playground. The one that was there where it shouldn't be. His breath splashed into fog on the cold pane as Jack used one eye to see the thing and the other to feel it. His expression dropped.

Right below him, just inches on the other side of the wall, was a massive sinkhole with yellow caution tape chasing the perimeter of the chasm. "Holy shit!" Jack exhaled, stepping back from the window where the void opened up just beyond him. Jacked noted how internally upset he was. He flopped onto the bed, sending clouds of dust flowering into the last streams of light now softly penetrating the room.

Chapter 4

A Void

Knock. Knock. Knock. The harsh sound rapped into the room.

Hearing this, Jack realized he had fallen asleep, and the world was now deep into nightfall. He reached for the bedside lamp and clicked it to life. "Hold on!" Jack shouted in the direction of the door. He quickly met himself in the mirror above the rickety desk before letting in the intruder.

It was Gren, who yet again seemed anxious to invade his personal space. Without a hello, he took a half step into Jack, saying, "Tu as des problèmes." Which made Jack burst out laughing. It wasn't every day someone stated so succinctly his lot in life.

"Ha!" Jack laughed. "You got that right. Mais… j'ai des problèmes ou la voiture?" His jocular ride of mental amusement was not to be shared by sweet old, dead-staring, smells-of-farts, Gren. Jack noted that the tall man had no facial arrangement labeled "expression B". There was an awkward silence.

Gren punched a yellow slip of paper into Jack's chest and walked off. "Ow," Jack complained and then yelled after the Frenchman, "Nice chatting with you, Monsieur!" Jack's tone conveyed that he didn't appreciate how this news of "problems" was being relayed. Next, he held out the paper slip and read, "VOITURE MORT," written in all caps. Beneath that, several lines in thick black ink underscored and emphasized the deadness part. Jack walked back to the bed and slowly lowered himself onto the less dusty corner.

"What now?" was what he could manage as his face slipped into the position of those without much hope or direction.

"Jack? Are you there, Jack?" hit his mind making his mood worsen.

"What?!" he said, covering his head with his arms. "I can't do this right now. Just fuck off!" There was silence, then he continued, "I just need a minute." He laid back and stared up at the stains on the ceiling as his mind fell silent again. He didn't wake again until morning.

As the first rays of morning met the earth, Jack awoke with an uneasiness. He reached for his phone and checked for battery life—54%. *Weird,* he thought but then was interrupted by what seemed like men scurrying around just outside his room.

"BAM!" his door dislodged from its hinges and blew open from an unknown force or explosion. Within half a second, several armed policemen were on him, hitting and wrestling him onto his back and handcuffing him. They flipped him over and started screaming his rights while also firing off multiple commands to the other officers, who ran off in various directions.

Jack gained his bearings as he was being flipped onto his back. His hands locked under him as the cop sat-straddled him, pinning him in place. The rights reading was then quickly followed with "You're not getting away this time, Mr. Silver."

"My last name is Daw!" Jack protested. "Get the fuck off of me!"

Then two cops popped into the room. "That's not him. We found Silver. He's just made a run for it. C'mon. Hurry!" All three then bolted out of Jack's room, leaving him trying to catch his breath as he lay with his eyes closed. He could feel the metal of the cuffs scratching at marred marks of old scars still present on his wrists as if to mock his return to a place that felt a lot like rock bottom.

I'm a person, Jack thought mournfully, wanting just to disappear. And yes, while he was a person, his personhood wasn't seen in the same manner relative to the gold standard of western society. He was a minority person, not a straight white person; a thing that didn't grant him a full 100%. Jack couldn't meet that. He fell short of that. Was born short of that and would be raised and reminded of that by family and friends. The best he could hope for hovered around forty or fifty percent, but this wasn't something that could even be seen by the majority of folks. Selective. Blindspots. Chosen and taught by the rulers and Christ-keepers. Their tally and tolls are not open to reason and are simultaneously devoid of love. Things have a purpose, and the purpose of this standard has been evident since they invented the rules.

Jack closed his eyes. *Maybe the room can fall into the abyss on the other side of the window,* he thought. *Maybe this world can swallow me whole.* Jack's mind slowly wandered with pain as he rolled over and resigned himself to the moment. Lying there handcuffed and battered, he briefly recalled a time before his wrists were a thousand highways of mistakes sliced into his flesh.

"You speak English?" James asked, offering Jack a cigarette while again doing his best to prompt a response. Jack continued his silent vigil as the two sat on the frozen pavement. The gaze at his feet was the only thing he was capable of right then. "So…," James continued. "I'm going to assume you're an Anglophone and that you do speak English." Long pause. "You look like a Colton to me. Sound good?" Pause. "Listen. Do you need a place to stay or something? Is there anyone I can call? Gots a new phone 'n everything."

Jack was impervious to it all, his system body-slammed and inert. A space reserved for those whose hearts had been recently lacerated and then removed without the precision of tools. The void advertising that he had already relinquished life.

It seemed James was about to give up when an old man approached him. "I've been looking for you, James."

"Uh… this is Colton. He's new, and I think he needs help. He's not responding." James then dusted himself off while backing away from the elderly gentleman. "I gotta go." James took off running down the alley.

The elderly man knelt before Jack, forcibly raised his chin to look into his eye, and said, "You'll do nicely." He then stood and made a phone call.

CHAPTER 5

BEGGARS

The only thing Jack remembered of that night long ago was being loaded into the back of a car, being driven to some unknown location, and walking into a room with no furniture aside from a few mattresses on the floor.

"Rest up," the old man said, as he turned to leave the room. "Someone will be here in the morning to get you started." Jack didn't know what that meant, and he didn't care.

Later in life, Jack would learn the truth of not caring and what that means to someone who is all care, all feelings, and who links with affinity to everyone and everything around them. When that's gone, when the caring part is gone, the light is out. And that's the most dangerous place for someone like Jack to be. A quiet detached fossil inhabited by none. I don't care. *Jack lied to himself as he closed his eyes and slid into a deeper unconscious state.* None of this is real.

The next morning, Jack woke with a start. Wide-eyed, he searched the dingy room. He noticed a figure lying on a mattress on the other side of the space. Jack quickly ran through what to do next when his thoughts were interrupted by a single, unfamiliar word: "Colton." Jack turned to see who was speaking.

"Hello?" Jack said quietly. The person across the room then stood and approached.

"Colton."

Jack was confused. "I'm sorry?"

"It's me, James."

Jack's mind ran. "I'm sorry... I don't...."

Suddenly, the guy sat next to him. "Listen, I ain't seen you here before."

A silence fell between them as Jack noted more sadness than fear rising in him.

23

"Right?" James said, nudging Jack in a manner that brought both young men to full attention. "Right?" Another nudge as Jack sat silently, processing what he was able.

"Dude. You need to start getting it together. Cut the silent treatment. We don't have time. Major will be back after sunrise." But, of course, this statement made no sense to Jack. It only sent his mind spinning further.

Jack repeated. "Major will be back after sunrise." But even after he said it, he felt no attachment to it and no need to launch discovery into why this guy was calling him Colton.

"What do you have on you?" James fired off.

Jack was unsure. "I don't know," Jack confessed. He hadn't taken inventory of what he had on him when he left his parents' home. He wasn't thinking that consciously, not then, not now. "Why?"

"Seriously, dude?" James looked at Jack in disbelief and then started snapping his fingers in his face. "Dude! Wake up. We don't have time for..." The man reviewed the space around Jack then finished with, "...this. Major will be here soon."

Jack still didn't know what any of this meant, but again, he didn't care. That switch was now welded into the off position. A place it would remain for the better part of a decade. "I don't know...." Jack repeated, trailing off again.

James was now rushing to his feet and pulling Jack up with him so he could begin shaking him down. "Did Major take anything from you last night?"

"I don't know...."

James continued swatting at Jack's clothes to see what might be hidden. "Ah!" James said in delight. "Yous fucking do have something."

He lifted a wallet from Jack's pocket. "Excellent. Here." James pulled anything with Jack's name from his wallet, noting Jack's real name. "Yous gotta hide this. Better yet, throw it away." Jack stood there untethered from any sense of understanding. "Go!" James yelled, handing Jack his library and ID cards.

In Jack's state, he couldn't think clearly, and the only thing propping him up was this command. Somehow, this stranger named James seemed moored to a reality that Jack knew he needed to share regardless of how fucking absurd it was. None of it made sense.

"Why?" Jack finally managed.

"Listen!" James pulled up close. "I'm about to hand you the keys to this castle, but we ain't gots time for this little game of yours. I need you to listen quick." James grabbed the ID cards back from Jack and headed for the kitchen. By the time Jack caught up to him, the garbage disposal sound was already filling the room.

"Damn it!" Jack protested. "C'mon. Why?" He was fully awake now and lunged at James, who turned around and then pinned Jack up against a wall.

"We ain't got time for this. Listen!"

Jack slowed his body and stopped struggling.

James took a step back and shook Jack loose, saying softly, "Listen." They both were catching their breath. "I'm trying to help you out here. You can get a new library card, and I feel that school of yours is not in your future anymore."

They both took a second to breathe more and calm down. "You're in the crash pad for guys like us. Yous're lucky there ain't more guys here right now, but they'll be in soon. I ain't supposed to be here anyhow, but I kept a key after I left." James laughed. "Not supposed toos." His thoughts wandered off, which made him laugh even harder. Unfortunately, Jack wasn't in on the joke. James re-trained his focus on Jack.

"Ya, gotta lose the name, buddy. Only yous and mes knows about it so let's let it die there. You will understand in time. We gotta wipe your ID clean off the records. Otherwise, you'll be tracked home, or people will be called, and if Major likes us, that can't a-happen. Cool?"

All of this new information was making Jack nervous. He didn't know why. James continued. "Just trust me. In the long run, this is your best option. Also...." Someone unlocked the front door. "Shit!" James grabbed Jack's hand and ran into the bedroom, switching out lights as they went. Reaching the furthest mattress, James threw himself down and pulled Jack on top of him.

"Anyone home?" came from the front door.

"Please, Jack, I mean Colton," James said nervously in a hushed tone. "Hide me as your trick. I'm not supposed to be here. Tricks have a right to some privacy here. I just need time to slip out. Say you're new. That Major is meeting you here soon."

Jack was so nervous he could barely speak but managed in the direction of the front door.

"I'm here. Major's meeting me here soon."

"Okay." Pause. "You alone?" the figure said, peeking into the room.

"Ya, kinda busy here. Little privacy." The guest excused himself and left the apartment. Both men exhaled in relief hearing the door close. James grabbed his things and headed for the door.

"See if the coast is clear," James whispered loudly.

Jack popped open the door slowly to check. "We're good," he said, confirming to James, who then leaned in and kissed him.

"Thanks. You'll do well here." He pulled the door open and said over his shoulder. "They can't make you do anything you don't want to, but you have to make a living. The choice is yours. If you get into trouble, my number is on the back of the bathroom door." He gave a parting wink and was gone.

Jack closed the door and tried to plot his next move. He ran to get his things from the bedroom and then checked his face in the bathroom. He looked like hell. Hell, he smelled like hell. Jack searched the backside of the door, verified that James's number was there, then quickly undressed to shower, which severely called out that putting his dirty clothes back on was not going to be pleasant. He lathered quickly with the scraps of soap and shampoo that had been discarded. He tried desperately to be grateful for that, but the massive tumble that was his innards made reaching that place impossible. He was all nerves, and he shook involuntarily, making cleaning himself more difficult. As the warm water cascaded over Jack's skin, his mind kiltered and bobbled.

"Nothing is real." His only mantra. He hurried.

Click, went the front door.

Hearing this, Jack froze as the sound of the shower continued.

Footsteps. "Hey, Colton?" It was Major. Jack heaved but not having eaten for a while, there was nothing to come up.

"Colton?" the old man said gayly. "So glad you're settling in." Jack's heartbeat was thundering in his ears. "At first, I was going to send my assistant… but then… Colton?"

"Colton?" the old man's hand opened the door. "I have a surprise for you." Jack didn't know knees could have the sensation of knocking until now. It took everything he had to arrest himself and say, "Hi, Major." He heaved again silently. "I'll be right out."

"Fine!" the old man said in delight. "I'm so glad you're here." Jack could hear what sounded like a brown paper bag. "I thought you might need some clothes. Come out when you're clean, and we'll try a few things on."

Jack managed an "okay," but he was dying inside. This was the most nervous he had ever been in his life. His insides shook, but there was only so long Jack could delay. Finally, he gathered himself, grabbed a towel off the floor, and dried off.

"Come!" Major said from the living room. "I have a few things laid out for you." Jack headed toward the sound of Major's voice.

In the living room, there were indeed a few different outfit options. The fact that this was true made Jack relax a bit. The first thought that this guy might be trying to help crept in. "Come, come," Major repeated, waving his hand toward himself. "Which do you like?" He said pretty gleefully for a man of his years. Jack paused and looked around, unsure what would happen next. Major, however, suddenly noticed Jack's scarred face more clearly. "Ooh… a tough guy!" Major said, drawing in closer to Jack's right side. "So butch."

He paused, anticipating that Jack would move or say something. "So…?" Major said, gesturing toward the outfits.

Each outfit had its unique style, but Jack was so shut down and nervous that he wasn't speaking or moving. "Dunno," Jack said, not looking up.

"Well, come on now," Major said, pulling up next to him to assist. "You need some clothes, and I need you looking good." Jack backed away from the man.

"Listen, I appreciate being able to stay here, but I gotta go."

Major laughed under his breath. "Do you now?" Pause. "Where you off to?" Jack was walking backward into walls and fumbling to the bathroom to collect his things.

"Looking for these?" Jack heard from behind him. He whipped around to see the old man holding his stained and dirty clothes. Major laughed a bit under his breath. "Listen, Colton. I know you're new here. I know you're scared shitless, and I know you have no options, so I'll make you a deal."

He walked back out to the living room, waiting for Jack and his towel to follow. "Come." He waved Jack back over to him. "Relax, would ya?" Jack didn't move. "I promise I won't touch you, okay?" Jack relaxed a bit and took a step toward Major, noticing for the first time that the man only had one arm. He then noticed the empty sleeve wasn't quite empty. The more Jack noted one deformity, the more he saw the next. His one hand had no thumb but five fingers that all faced the same way. The sheer bizarreness of it was like a trick of the mind that Jack couldn't process — even as he watched the five fingers sway in unison, opening and closing in a deranged hello.

"Come, come... come, boy, my God, you're a lump."

Jack took another step.

"Which do you like?" Major held them up one at a time.

"I dunno," Jack repeated.

Exasperated, Major said, "Fine. I will choose for you, which I was hoping for." He laughed and then grabbed the one that Jack thought looked like a motorcycle jacket and matching pants. "What size shoe are you?"

"Uh, ten."

Major went to a closet and fished out black boots. "Here," he said, handing them to Jack. "There are socks in the bedroom drawers if you want." Then much to Jack's surprise, Major collected the other clothes that were laid out and headed for the door. "I'll be at work all day. My number is on the back of the bathroom door. I need you ready by 9 PM. So wear those clothes, hang out with me tonight, and no, nothing will happen without your say-so, so fucking relax already. I'm just paying you for your time. That's it. Here's a key... and this'll help." He dropped a front door key and a pack of white powder in a small baggie into Jack's hands and then left.

CHAPTER 6

CONDUIT

Knock. Knock. A female police officer entered Jack's motel room as he lay there resigned, fighting off bad memories and wondering, what next?

"Officer Jensen," she introduced herself while uncuffing Jack. "Thanks."

"Sorry about the mix-up. May I ask you a few questions?" Jack knew he had nothing to offer and agreed with a nod. "Says here you were resisting arrest." Jack clammed up even more, wanting to disappear. He said nothing. "Are we going to be good? Or are we going to have a problem?"

This was the no-win situation for minorities when they "accidentally" arrest you. Then, when you protest because what they're doing is not correct, you're seen as a problem. A problem they grant themselves the right to fix. "I'm happy to assist in any way I can." He smiled fake enough for her to read its expression. She paused, unimpressed.

"Good." She grabbed for and flipped through a pad of paper. "Just a few questions then."

Twinge.

Holy shit, Jack thought, feeling the stress explode inside him. He knew what happened to people like him who had a medical emergency in front of a cop. In Jack's experience, this could be bad. If he didn't have control of his body and could not comply with an officer's demands, he would be arrested and probably beaten again. *Fuck,* he thought, trying to slow his breathing.

"May I grab a few medications. I need to take them." The contractions slinked down his spine, curling him.

"You a drug addict or something?" she asked, assessing the interior of the cheap motel.

"No, ma'am," Jack choked. "I have a disorder that's causing me some trouble right now. She turned to face him as half his face untethered and drooped, the surprise registering on her face.

"I see," she said, heading for the door. "Again, sorry for the mix-up. We'll be in touch."

With the click of the door closing, Jack dropped onto the bed to curl up in a ball — not that he had a choice in his position. He waited for the contraction to subside enough to stand, then raced for his meds. He found Paula's little white boxes, which is precisely what he wanted to take. But seeing as how it was morning....

Wait? Jack thought. *It's morning, and I'm having an attack?! Not good. Not good at all.* Once he had a second to process everything, Jack realized that this was a horrible turn of events. In the past, he could always count on being fine for most of the day, but it seemed recently that was a less and less reliable rule. *Not good.* he thought again. He reached for the phone in the room to dial 0.

Ring. "Dinty's Garage," Mr. Harrow said.

"Hi," Jack said quickly. "It's me, Jack, in room 54. It looks like I'll need to stay another night. Can you just charge the card again?"

"Oh, Jack," Mr. Harrow noted as the clickity-clack of the typing began. "So glad you called. It seems...."

"I'm sorry, sir, but I have to run," Jack sped. "Please just charge the card again."

"But your car!" Mr. Harrow complained as Jack hung up the phone. He moved across the room as he was able and gulped down meds while arranging himself on the bed.

"Stay in curiosity," presented to his mind. "This doesn't have to be scary. Just let it be what it wants to be." Then Jack had a brand new thought. *Let me await its gift.* The full expression of himself softened.

The neurological connections popped to life and cracked through Jack's brain, stormy with electric cognizance. The whirl of it let Jack know he didn't have long on the conscious side and would soon be pulled to another plane.

Jack readied himself and switched to *Let me await its gift* as he closed his eyes and gave into the drag to the otherworld. This time it didn't seem as terrifying. This time, he just let go and observed what was.

Chapter 7

Dangling

As is the hallmark of those who live with Jack's condition, he dropped behind the wall of his mind. He detached from this world to be one with the other. He let go and allowed himself to feel the air rushing past him, almost stinging his face. Then, slowly opening his eyes against the whirling energy surrounding him, Jack tried to wave his hand in front of his face.

What could he make out here? Anything? Could he see his hands? Could he feel them? The torrent of energy whipped at him while he laid back into it to see what was available. Jack quieted his mind and took a step deeper into curiosity. He seemed to slow his descent, which served to calm him even further.

While his last several times visiting this place were medically induced, Jack wanted to discover the difference of the place when he was still, conscious, and fully aware. He slowed to a float. The surface of his physical body relaxed, and the gnarl slowly unwound.

"Is this zero?" he asked with a chuckle, feeling pretty sure that he was at the point where he could begin to use his mind instead of the other way around.

It was just after 11:00 AM when Jack began returning from his attack. He rolled over onto his back and assessed how he was doing physically. Mentally, he knew he'd have a storming hangover for the balance of the day. He closed his eye to meet himself gently where he was. No need to push. Not today. His room was already paid for; it would be okay to collect himself and figure out his next move. He grogged slowly to life and reached for his phone. In this state, he was incredibly tender-hearted and blue. It just felt like a lot he was dealing with, but that was Jack's normal. Everything was always too big, too much, too extreme, too fast, and too rocky a road for peace.

"Why can't my life be normal?" he asked himself. Jack knew he was a failure at anything normal. Always had been.

He opened his phone.

Hey Thad. You there?

Hey handsome. What's up?

Ugh. Don't ask.

Yeah?

I'm not going to make it
to your place this weekend
My car died, and I'm stuck
here in Meziadin Junction.

Oh no. That's where exactly?

It'll take me at least 20 hours
to get to you if I can get my car fixed.
The mechanic says it's dead.
Not a total shock, I guess.

Well damn.

I was looking forward
to seeing you this weekend.

Me too.

Well, let's think of reasons
why this is perfect. You
game?

For you, sir, always.

Grrrr. Don't say that.

It's been a long time since
anyone flirted with me like
that, and I might explode.

Lol. Well, we don't want that.

Do we?

Let's just take it as it comes.

Maybe we can still spend the
weekend together, just
perhaps not as we had
hoped.

Where are you planning
on staying?

I don't know.
I don't know what I'm going to do.
I feel stuck with no options.

Okay. Can I help?

I don't know
What do I do?

Let's see if the car can be
fixed.

Is there another garage you
can take it to for a second
opinion?

No. I'm in the middle of nowhere

You really are stuck. You
okay tho?

I don't know

Maybe we should talk

Jack's phone rang.

"Hey," Jack said quietly into his phone.

"Hey, Jack. You okay?" Silence. "Can I help in any way?"

"I don't know, Thad. I just need to figure this out." Jack was too embarrassed about his cash situation, and there was no way he was going to be a burden to someone he had only run into three times in his life. There wasn't enough of a relationship there to get into something like this. Jack knew he had to figure this out on his own.

"I'd offer to come to get you but, not sure if you know this, I don't drive. But maybe I can help you arrange something?"

Jack hated that he needed help. "I need to go."

"You're doing it again, Jack, making me feel bad." This was news to Jack's ear.

"Doing what?"

"Each time we have a moment to talk, you run out on me."

There was a long silence while Jack discovered this truth about himself. "I know."

"Why? The signals you send are super confusing, and it's frustrating. One moment you're asking me to come and share a meal with you. The next, you're collecting your things and taking off again."

Jack was growing smaller in his clothes, and he was retreating. "It's just that...."

"Yes...?" Thad prompted after a pause.

"It's just that I like you," Jack said quietly.

"And so logically, you move away from me. Explain that... and I'm not judging, but rather trying to understand."

Jack didn't say anything. He simply laid on the horrible bed and felt small and tired and wrung out. He wanted to share with Thad. He wanted to open up, but this relationship was quickly becoming important to him, and in showing Thad all his scars and ugliness, he, well, nothing in his past said this would end well. "Jack...," Thad continued.

"Yeah," he replied in a whisper.

"Take a chance," Thad said. "Take a chance that I'm someone you can trust."

Silence.

"I like you, scars and all, Jack. And I promise you there isn't anything you can tell me to scare me off so long as it's true and that you, in return, continue to be trustworthy."

Silence.

"Is that a deal we can make?" Thad asked. "Are you, or can you just be open with me?"

"I'm just not good at this stuff," Jack said with his eyes closed.

"I know, and we've talked about this, but maybe we can be terrible at it together."

"Maybe we can," Jack said, relaxing.

Chapter 8

Conjure

For the balance of the day, Jack stayed in bed. He wicked away the daydreams that showed him the potential outcomes of his current situation. His embarrassment in front of Thad, his perilous financial state, his broken car, his loneliness, made only worse by the decrepit motel that played the abandoned Merry-Go-Round song as it creaked and scraped in the frigid air, its voice a rasp sung in the key of rust. Jack did his best to block out the constant chirrs and groans of the place, but it was ever-present, and the winds had no choice but to deliver their wanting cries.

Around dinner time, Jack reached for the fliers on the bedside nightstand. "Let's see what they're serving in this town." He was at least hopeful for a pizza or a Chinese delivery. Opening the drawer, he noted that the fliers weren't take-out menus as he had assumed. Instead, one was for a biker's club, another for Ju-Jitsu, one for an AA meeting, and a pink one for a ladies-only workout facility. The pieces of this puzzle weren't making sense because there were no other buildings or facilities here in the Junction of the Meziadin that might hold such events. As far as the eyes could see, there was only the motel and the garage. That's it. He grabbed the gym flyer to check where these events were taking place.

"Dinty's Garage, Upper floor." This was information that did little to answer Jack's follow-up questions. He grabbed the karate flyer and again, Dinty's Garage, Upper floor. Next, he read the AA flyer. "Sobriety in Time!" was the name of the group. A name that Jack couldn't make sense of. "Sobriety in Time?" He let it roll around in his head. No further clarification was offered, but the location was Dinty's Garage, Upper Floor.

"Huh," Jack mused, noting he hadn't seen a second floor to the building on the other side of the playground. The last one he reached for was titled "Hell's Detour." It read, "Don't fear dying, fear not living."

However, the meeting club location wasn't Dinty's Garage's upper floor but rather something else. Jack double-checked with his working eye, reading slowly.

"Harrow's Motel, Room 54." Jack sat upright in bed, eyes wide as he searched the room and surroundings, realizing that he was, in fact, in the location of the Biker's Club. Jack was wide awake, and adrenaline forced out the last whispers of his dystonic lag. He grabbed the phone.

Ring. "Harrow's Motel," Mr. Harrow said into the phone, which was immediately followed by a grumble of a voice in the background urging, "And RV Park. You always forget that part."

"Not now, Poppy!" Mr. Harrow could be heard through a muffled receiver, giving Jack the impression he wasn't supposed to be hearing this part. He returned to Jack in a clear voice. "How can I help you?"

"Mr. Harrow! This is Jack in room 54," Jack said quickly into his phone. "I just read the flyers on the nightstand, and they seem to indicate."

He was cut short by yet more muffled talking. "Told you he'd be looking for the AA meeting," then a laugh.

"No, sir. It's not that." Jack injected quickly. Mr. Harrow continued his side conversation.

"Damn it, Poppy, go clean out the meeting ashtrays. The meeting starts in an hour, and we need to get them to pay rent this time." Jack could hear laughter in the background. "Go! Go."

"Sir," Jack continued, with upset in his voice. "Sir!" Mr. Harrow returned to Jack's attention.

"Yes, Jack. We have you covered. The meeting starts in an hour. Good-bye." Click. Jack hung his head feeling invisible and defeated. He chucked his phone into the nightstand drawer and punched it closed.

Aaaargghhhh.... Jack thought, pulling a pillow over his head. *Fucking AA. Been there. No thanks.* His mind then returned to that first morning at Major's crash pad. The morning he was first handed a baggie of "Major's Mix," as the boys called it.

Chapter 9

Fusillade

Jack's nerves collapsed immediately as he watched Major leave the apartment. It had taken everything in him to merely stand and get through that first interaction. He reached for his phone to call James.

Ring. "James! It's Jack," he said quickly into the phone.

"Who?" the voice replied. "Ooh. Colton. Hey, seriously, yous gotta get with it."

Jack had no patience and quickly blew a fuse.

"Damn it, James! What the fuck?! Why are you pushing this agenda on me? What gives?! Why can't I have my own name?!" The voice on the other end was silent for two seconds before being met with, "ANSWER ME!?"

"Colton. Are you really this fucking stupid?"

Jack waited for more information, hoping something would be sent to his mind to offset the kiltered world he now seemed to inhabit. "If you want to make it out here on your own, you CAN NOT be tied to a searchable ID. Period! How is that hard to understand? Your ID says you're not yet 18. Correct?"

Jack turned around in the apartment's living room, trying to clear his head. "Yeah."

"And so, smart guy, yous will wash out and be on the next bus back to whatever tundra-town you leaked outta. Got it?!" Jack was silent. "You wants more of what's your running from or a nice place to live and an opportunity to get ahead of this?"

"I'm sorry, it's just that...." Jack's sentence was cut short by an agitated James.

"Listen, Colton. I'mma just trying to help yous out. There ain't nothing in here for me. I left that place for a reason. Don't wanna work for Major no more. I gots my clients, and Imma gunna keep my cash but yous? Yous ain't

gots a place to land and no way to make a living. Your passport to this new life is your God damn fucking name. Got it?"

Jack was silent. He didn't know what to think or ask.

James continued in a more relaxed tone, "You're gunna be okay. Just watch what the other guys do, find what works for you, be nice and be patient. You'll do well here. Men like a guy who looks like he can take a punch. That's your ticket. Work that angle. With your face and body, it won't be long before you run the place." Jack was still silent, "IF that's what you want." Jack flopped onto the sofa in the living room and tried to come up with something to say but found nothing. Then James asked with concern, "Is that what you want?"

"I honestly don't know," Jack replied, resigned. "What if it's not what I want?"

"Well, you're not old enough to get a job without your parents being involved, and you have no address, so whatcha gunna do? Apply at The Bay to sell shoes or some shit?"

"Are there Provincial services or something? You know, like for run-aways."

"Step 1, fingerprints, which equals a record with the police. Yous got your prints on file yet?"

"No."

"So nothing that'll tie you to your real name?"

"No."

James exhaled. "Good. Keep it that way. If they do fingerprint ya, again, DO NOT tell them your real name. Anytime they get that, they gets it for goods, and your candy ass will be on a one-way ticket back to your old life. That's your options."

Fuck, *Jack thought, closing his eyes.* These are my options, *he thought, then asked,* "What's this baggie Major gave me?"

"Oh, he gave yous that just open-handed like?"

Jack didn't know what that meant, then responded, "Ya. I mean, he gave it to me as he was leaving."

"Very odd," James said.

"But what is it? I mean, I assume it's drugs, but what kind?"

*Jack could hear James twisting on the other side of the line. "It's....
Well... it's Major's concoction of speed, boner pills, and some rare Chinese
shit he gets down dockside. The boys will fight you for it. You need to hold
that close. Use it VERY sparingly. A little goes a long way. It's the guys that
lose sight of that that gets thrown out. Do not let it get you messy. That
slippery slope will eat you alive. Trick I learned, if it ever makes me do
things I'm not choosing to do, it's time to cut the shit. Promise me that
you'll keep your wits about yous, or you're dead."*

*"Understood," Jack said, flicking at the baggie to check its contents. He
hung up the phone and searched for his old clothes, which he discovered
Major had taken with him.* Fuck, *he thought as he heard the front door
open.*

*"Oh, hi," a tall black woman said, stepping into the room. Jack wasn't
sure what was happening. She stepped toward him and his towel with an
outstretched hand. "I'm Harlow."*

"Uh... hi. I'm new here. Just trying to...."

"Yeah yeah... same old. Did Major leave you clothes?"

*"Oh," Jack said, surprised that there was a continuity here that seemed
normal to this person. "Ya... clothes. Just, umm... these," he pointed to the
black leathers on the coffee table, making Harlow smirk. A reaction that
unsettled Jack deeply.*

*"C'mon," she said, heading into the hall where she opened a closet. "This
is the lost and found crap. Mostly left behind by tricks flying outta here for
some reason or another. See if there's something there you can wear during
the day."*

*Jack's first instinct was to grab an outfit and just run. But where to? He
didn't know anyone in the downtown area, and he sure as hell wasn't going
back to "God's going to get you" Mom and "let me teach you about God's
will" Dad. There was now a rage in Jack that even just their memory sparked
to life.* Not a chance in hell, *he thought to himself.*

*Jack found a grey pair of sweatpants and a Canucks t-shirt that fit; he
fished out a pair of flip-flops or "thongs" as they're called in this part of the
world. "That'll have to do," he said to Harlow, coming out of the bathroom
where he had been dressing.*

"Nice," she said. "Anyhow, I just wanted to check on you. Major normally has me greet people and get them started first, but apparently, he's already been here." She stopped. "He must like you. I have to get on to school, but he wanted to make sure you got this," she pulled something black out of her purse.

"I'm sorry, that's what now?" Jack was confused.

"Come," she said, heading him over to a mirror. The woman put Jack in front of her, and with a move like when you're putting an expensive necklace on someone, she gently put the black cloth up over his head to settle it into position. She tied the black leather cords behind his head and stepped back to admire the adornment. The thrill on her face was unmissable because it lit up the room. Jack turned to look at himself wearing an eyepatch, but it was a version of himself he didn't know, at least not yet.

Jack stepped back where, in his infancy of adopting this new world, he chuckled about truly being a one-eyed Jack, but the joke landed more depressing than funny. It was going to take some getting used to.

"Major wants me here at 7:00 to give you your makeover. Then he'll be here at 9:00 to get you and take you to the club."

Jack took the eye patch off and turned to face Harlow. "What am I supposed to do all day? I don't have any money or anything."

"Have you eaten?" she asked, making Jack look at his feet and not respond. She continued, "When was the last time you ate?"

"I'm not sure," Jack said, not looking up.

"Ah," she said, reaching for her purse, "New, new," she said. Then, "Here."

Jack didn't know what to do. "Here, fucknut. Take it. You will need to provide for yourself, but Major will be super pissed if I deliver you to him in...." She didn't finish the sentence. "Take care of yourself, but stay outta sight and stay outta trouble. If you do fuck up, call me first. My number is on the back of the washroom door." She turned to leave.

Jack found desperation, "Where will you be?"

She turned unimpressed. "As I said, I have classes all day. So I'll be back at 7:00."

Jack pursued the line of inquiry with more desperation, "Where's Major?"

"He's at work?! God, give it a break. I'll be back in a bit."

Jack couldn't let it go. "Where does he work?"

"He's an English teacher at St. Patrick Regional Middle School on E. 11th, but for God's sake, DO NOT call him there. He'll throw you out if you do that." She paused, then calmed herself. "Just give it a chance." With that, she was gone.

Jack sat on the edge of the sofa. The realization that Major was a middle school teacher made it all the sicker. I don't belong here, he thought, then a voice inside him said, "Never know, buddy. Could be fun." A thought that produced a devilish grin on his lips.

It was rounding half-past 6:00 PM, and Jack could feel his opportunity to run slip away. Was he going to see this through? He wanted to run, but where to? What else? Where else? He simply couldn't figure it out. Maybe he should just run up to someone in the grocery store or something and spill his guts. But every imagined scenario like that always ended with him getting sent home — a thought that paralyzed him. Finally, at 6:55, Harlow stepped through the door.

"Had a nice day?" she asked. Jack was stunned at how fly she looked. She was drop-dead gorgeous. Her flat chest taking center stage of a dropped neck V-line damn near down to her mystery parts.

"Damn!" Jack said. "You look amazing." She crinkled her nose in a manner that meant, 'I know.'

"C'mon. Your turn to get dolled up." She pulled a black box from her purse and pulled out a chair, indicating that he was to sit. He did. She then pulled up a chair for herself and leaned in. "Listen...." Pause. "I know this might all seem very odd to you, and you're probably understandably freaked out, but I got you." She messed up his hair with a tease. "You seem like you have a good heart. Just hold onto my number if anything gets out of control for you or if you just need someone to talk to." Jack sat silently. "How about a little make-over to lift your spirits?"

Jack smiled. "Okay." Then he added, "But nothing too crazy, okay?"

Harlow just smirked and put a cloth around his neck to start cutting his hair.

By 9:00, Jack's make-over was done, and they celebrated with a few drinks. "Ooh...," she said, reading a text. "He's here. Come get your shit."

What shit? Jack thought. He had nothing other than a fairly empty wallet and his phone… and his drugs! He ran back to the bathroom, where he had hidden the baggie. Pulling up in front of the mirror, he didn't even recognize himself. He looked badass and was shocked that who stared back at him was him. An eye-patched version of him, but it was him nonetheless. He turned his head back and forth, noting that the eye patch covered most of his skull disfigurement. He was shocked at how much more sexy and whole it made him feel.

"C'mon!" Harlow yelled from the other room. "He doesn't like to be kept waiting."

Jack broke his gaze from the mirror, tucked the drugs in his leather pants, and raced out. Harlow locked the apartment and then offered Jack her arm, which he took. They laughed and got in the limo that awaited them.

"Well, don't you look nice?" Major said, putting his five-fingered hand on Jack's thigh. "I had a feeling you'd clean up nicely. And yes. Yes indeed, the eyepatch does the trick." He leaned in and whispered, "Best not to upset anyone. However, I need your story to be legit. That's a fake eye, right?" Jack nodded, then Major continued. "I need you to take it out."

This made Jack super uncomfortable. "Take it out?" Jack said, the nerves evident in his voice.

"Boy, don't question me. Things here are done for a reason. Give it to me!" Jack looked to Harlow in desperation, which was met with a reassuring gesture. He consented and took out his eye.

"I'll hold onto that," Major said, taking it from him and pocketing it. Jack started to protest, but Harlow squeezed his knee hard, signaling that he needed to settle down. He did.

Twenty minutes later, they were heading into a packed club, where the music not so much thumped as shook the souls within the place. Jack was grateful that he was partially deaf. Finally, they reached a far booth that was elevated in the corner. A spot from which the rest of the floor could be easily viewed. Major made introductions to all in this VIP area, and Jack couldn't help but notice how fucking sexy so many of Major's friends were. One guy, in particular, caught Jack's attention. A curly-headed blond Adonis type, wearing nothing but low-slung pants and an armband. Damn,

Jack thought to himself. Harlow then grabbed Jack's hand and led him through the club.

"This way...." She opened the door to a bathroom, pulled them in, then locked it. "Here," she said, putting smokey black eye makeup on him, then pulled her baggie out of her purse. "Snort this," she said, leaning into Jack with a small pile of Major's mix on her fist. Jack stopped short.

"God...," she retracted her arm. "New, new. You guys are always the same." She snorted the fist's bump and then poured out more, offering it to him. Jack knew he was at an essential intersection of his life, but he leaned forward with no one else to chime in and snorted the drugs. The earth-shaking reaction was instantaneous. Jack felt a rush and a flush, unlike anything he had ever known. The response of it sent shock waves of power through Jack. His legs and butt gained strength a thousand times beyond what he had learned. His torso rippled with adrenaline and strength while his cock involuntarily hardened and throbbed. His heart was the beating hooves of a thousand horses, and the sense of power made him feel invincible, unstoppable, and ready to take down the world if necessary. He had never felt this alive, and it flushed him with a sense of immortality. Jack grabbed onto the sink's counter and shook. A shake not of the weak or scared but of a fantastic monster coming to life after being held prisoner for a lifetime. The immense power that pulsed through Jack's frame and dick was fucking intoxicating.

Still holding onto the counter, Harlow opened the private bathroom door where the curly-headed shirtless guy stood alone, waiting to come in. He pulled up behind Jack and pushed himself teasingly into his hip.

"You new here?" he whispered into Jack's good ear. "I'm Tristan." Jack continued to hold the counter as he thundered new atomic energy. "What's your name?" Tristan teased.

Looking up from under his eyebrows, he said into the mirror at his reflection, "I'm Colton."

CHAPTER 10

CROSS

For Jack's part, the morning's neurological storm kept washing him onto shores he did not care to revisit. He had to force himself to rouse and shake off the webs of bedevilment. As Jack walked over to the window, he felt deep pangs of hunger. He had already eaten everything he had with him. The sky over the playground ahead of him grew darker with each minute. The shadows were growing longer with age, their edges black and reaching. Jack stood still in the window and watched them advance. He closed his eyes.

A little help here? Jack asked himself.

"We're here, Jack, if you need us," his conscience offered. He exhaled, hoping to sink into himself deeper. A place he'd retreat to when times were uncertain or challenging.

"Uh. Hi," he said under his breath with his eyes closed.

"Jack?" was put forth quietly into his mind.

Uh, ya?

"Why do you continue to talk to us from that vantage point rather than ours?"

Jack was perplexed. *Do what now? Sorry?*

"You are there."

Yes, Jack replied, uncertain of where this was all going.

"And we are here."

Again Jack confirmed the point internally. *Ya...?*

His conscience slowed its input of information. "Tell us where those two places are. Teach us the difference."

Jack closed his eyes to search for an answer to the question that a part of him had just asked himself. "Tell us where those two places are. Teach us the difference," he repeated aloud. "Tell us where those two places are. Teach us the difference." Jack let it roll over and over in his mind.

You're there, Jack finally said.

"Yes," met his mind. "Where is here?"

Well, that one's easy. Ha! Jack lit up, delighted that he finally got a slow ball pitched at him. His mind meandered on... *And I know where that is because I've been there a few times now.*

"Correct," was the response rising from within. "Now define it."

You are my higher conscious. You are not so much 'there' as I am here.

Jack did a quick gut check on his internal response, "y e s" he heard and *knew* all simultaneously. In doing this, he put a pin in this thought. The somehow knowing part. He'd file that away to work on next. Jack was curious.

"Yes," Jack said under his breath in the voice of wonder. "Yes," he repeated. There was an air of delight now in Jack's words. *You're not so much there as I am here.* The process of Jack working through this within himself was creating energy. His other channels started to open, sensing the shift. Jack could feel them, and he welcomed their glow. He stood his ground against the approach of the dark and reached inward to buzz and pistol and pop. This uncommanded opening filled the corners that needed to be filled as his mind connected and continued.

You're there. Pause. *I'm here.* He then used his memory to find the channel back to his higher level of consciousness. He immediately returned to the seat of the soul. *I'm here,* his voice thundered within him, *and....* He flipped back down to have Jack say, "I'm here."

His insides now felt like they burst with yellow light as he repeated the exercise.

I'm here, Jack said, then repeated from his upper conscience, "And... I'm here!"

"y e s," his gut confirmed.

"So...," Jack said aloud, his breath and presence crystalizing on the frigid glass in front of him. "I'm here...." Then, like a visit to the eye doctor where differing lenses are put in front of his view to choose from, "And I'm here."

He came back to the moment to see the fog smashing into the window before him from both sides. He exhaled deep from his guts, blasting the air from the deepest parts of him. "I am both." Jack's mind got stuck on one point, so he asked, *So why do I mostly only know how to perceive from the lens of Jack? Why, when I wake up, am I Jack? I assumed once one achieved access to higher places, you'd just kinda live from that perspective.*

"Jack," his higher conscience said, "you were born you, and you will always be you, but you have accessed us, and we hope you're beginning to see the purpose of that."

I do, Jack replied.

"Tell…," was put forward in his mind, but he cut it short.

Ya ya… tell me why, or teach me why or some such shit. Jack exhaled.

His upper awareness chuckled then prompted with, "Go on…. You know how to do this." Jack settled into himself, opening the channels that best receive information from beyond him; he *allowed* himself to be open to the answer.

The purpose of my higher conscience is like a tool or a lens in which I, Jack, can elect to view the world.

"Yes. As you sensed before, the hardest part is finding that access point. The rest is simply an allowing. Tell us more about allowing."

Bleh, Jack tumbled. *Allowing. What is allowing? Why is it allowing? Not choosing or directing.* The window before Jack was now crunchy with freezing moisture that crept its way at him from the pane's corners.

"Whatcha got, Jack? Whatcha got?"

He blanked his mind, as was his new nature. To be clear, it was the nature of the storm where he internally lived. He rumbled on with an internal tidal roll chasing the answer he put into his mind's eye and, by extension, into the all. He let go. His eyes softened as his slack muscles opened their channels. He flipped up into the seat of his soul and boomed his energy outward, reaching to connect to what was, accepting the things that he saw as he journeyed – his voice from this place a belt that thumped against the solid parts and flew through everything else.

The allowing is not a doing. All the other words to describe this action are doing words, and that's not how one gets there. The access to portals is feminine. So feminine energy, the yin, must be called forth to get there.

Jack's encircling vortex of the moment pushed at what was, the room slow wagging massive energy as it rolled back and forth with the force of felled trees repeatedly falling on either side of him. Jack thundered with the thing. Slow wag. BOOM. Slow wag. BOOM. The back and forth of the universe, the undulating, the song of what was. All of it met him simultaneously, and he stood, unwavering in his commitment to this moment, the moment when what is meets the blank mind. Then it happened. Like it had happened so many times for so many years.

Jack's brain went 'click,' and although he remained standing, he was no longer ov him. He no longer inhabited him. He no longer had access to his thoughts, body, mind, or consciousness. He crossed over. It was bright air. It was brilliant — the void of nothing and the presence of everything. Jack internally hummed and quieted himself even more, to receive as was the ultimate power of twin-sided feminine Jack.

He opened his eyes and glanced at his feminine heart's reflection in the now frozen window, repeating words she had said to him from the other side of a loving lens. "Hello."

Chapter 11

GRUMBLED

As Jack stood in the window's reflection, he watched his lens of the feminine fade back to Jack. It was momentary, but he couldn't help but sense that he was discovering something.

"y e s," his gut offered.

Ah. Thanks for confirming? Jack questioned into the universe of his guts. He reached for the motel room phone and dialed 0, hoping for a different outcome this time.

Ring.

"Dinty's Garage and RV Park," Mr. Harrow said into the phone as the piano background music accompanied the whackety-whack metronome of the typewriter.

"Mr. Harrow…," Jack said quickly into the phone, not wanting to be redirected into some new weirdness with this guy. "It's Jack, in room 54…."

He was cut off by, "Well, thanks for not making the meeting." Jack stammered for a second, then Mr. Harrow continued. "We made coffee this time and was hoping to see you. Gotta be committed or get committed." He then laughed hysterically, his voice lending a lofty gale to the tune of pianos and vintage office machines currently in full swing.

Oh, my St. Francis of Olivia Newton-John! Jack internally screamed. *This guy is completely certifiable.* Then he doubled down on his reason for calling, desperate not to get knocked off-course again.

"Mr. Harrow. I am very hungry and haven't eaten in a while. I've been struggling today with a medical issue, and I'd like to find something to eat. Can you please help me?"

The room Mr. Harrow inhabited seemed to quiet as his voice softened out of hysteria. "Well now, Mr. Daw…." There were muffled voices in the background as Mr. Harrow continued. "Why don't you join us for supper?" Jack was not expecting this response. He flustered.

"Uh…."

Mr. Harrow came back to life with, "Not a worry. Bring some wine if you have any. Room 44. Thirty minutes." Click.

Jack hung his head and wanted to cry. Everything here was difficult and off and messed up, and he just wanted to escape it. Jack flopped back onto the bed and exhaled the fuckery of it all. His next thought was, *Wine? Did that midget just scold me for not making the AA meeting then also ask me to bring wine to dinner?* Jack processed the information again, and yes, that is what just happened. "Ugh…," he let out with frustration. "Why is Meziadin Junction so fucking dense?" He cupped his hands over his head and closed his eyes.

His phone buzzed with a new text from Thad:

Hey, Handsome.

        OMG kill me

Lol. Why?
Are you being funny, or u ok

        I don't know.
        It's messed up here
        The owner of the motel
        invited me to dinner
        it's so weird
        The guy is maniacal
        or something
        He gives me the creeps

But you ok?
Might be nice to meet the locals

        I dunno.
        Just wanna get outta here
        but I'm so fucked

Say more about that

        About what

You said you're so fucked.

Why?

Jack slowed himself to try and figure out how best to respond.

I guess I don't feel
safe right now

Say more about that

Lol. Are you my therapist
or something?

C'mon mate
We said we were going to try and
trust one another, and you rarely
just volunteer information, so
You still game for that?

Hearing this, Jack could feel how he would do anything to be with Thad right now, how he wanted to be with him, how he wanted to connect with another human right now on that level. He fell into himself and exhaled, trying to right the staff of the mast, a move that meant shifting from fantasy to reality.

I am

Good
So tell me more
What's making you feel unsafe?
Let's get honest

Jack froze at the sense that he was being asked to be vulnerable. He had to get honest with himself about his willingness to go there with someone he knew so little about, but perhaps that was the point of the exercise.

Ok

This motel is so gross, and
there is nowhere else to go

I have no idea how I'm
going to fix my car

There's no restaurant or anything here, and I'm starving

And we haven't talked much about my neurological situation, but let's just say today was a very bad day.

That's a lot

Are you scared yet? Lol

Not in the least
I wish I were there

I wish you were too

Thad and Jack texted for a few more minutes when Jack heard a knock at the door.

"Uh… coming," Jack said, confused, then texted Thad.

Hey, someone's here. Brb

Jack opened the door to see a short girl who had an outfit that could only be described as harlequinesque. His greeting stopped short at the sight of her. "Oh… hi."

"Listen." She gum-popped as she pushed a plate of food into Jack. "Dinner got canceled. Harrow's concerned about the Willows 'n such down valley. He said best to stay in tonight. You know." She then just turned and walked off.

You know what exactly? Jack thought to himself. "Uh, thanks," he shouted after her. He then added quickly, "You're Poppy?!"

"Poppy," she said, not looking back while offering a peace sign overhead.

Jack grabbed his phone and set his plate on the cold metal desk in the room.

I'm back

What was that about?

The owner canceled dinner
but did fix me a plate

Well, things are already looking up

Care for company
while you eat?

Like how?

Jack's phone rang.
It was Thad.
Jack answered, "Well, this is nice."
"I thought we could have dinner together over the phone," Thad replied. The two men ate their meals together and talked for hours. That night Jack went to bed grateful. It might not have been where he wanted to be, but he was becoming ever more thankful for small mercies in such a dense place.

Knowing, he said to himself as he drifted off. *What do I know about knowing?*

CHAPTER 12

BESET

The following day Jack lazed in bed. He was drifting between this world and that, an exercise he was becoming more comfortable with over time. His phone buzzed.

Hey handsome.
Here's your morning coffee ☕

OMG Thad.
You are very sweet
You a coffee drinker
or a proper Brit?

Proper eh?
Been called lots of things in
my time, but this is a first

The phone in the room rang.

Hold on

"Hello?" Jack answered.

"Votre voiture. Monsieur," Gren grumbled.

Jack grabbed his phone to sign off with Thad.

Listen. It's my car.
Gotta run. Talk soon.

He picked up the landline again. "Oui?" Jack was curious now. Maybe there was news.

"Ton Voiture est mort."

"Yes!" Jack said with more tone than was intended. "This is now a well-established fact. Je sais. Je connais. Je Vous Compendre Monsuir." Jack sat exasperated. "Est-ce cue ca peut etre reparare?"

He said this last part very slowly and clearly to not let Monsuier
Gren miss any of the words' meanings.

"Je n'sais pas?" Gren noted flatly, deflating Jack all the more.

Jack took another deep breath and blinked hard, repeatedly
saying, "Qui saurait, Monsieur?" More hard blinking like one does
who's on the verge of losing their shit. "Qui? Anyone?" A question
that was met with dead air on the other end of the line. "Monsieur,"
Jack repeated after several beats. "Is there? Y a-t-il?" Beat. "Anyone.
Un personnel." Beat. "There. La." Beat. "Who can help me? Qui
peux m'aider?" Wide-eyed BLINK. BLINK. BLINK. Silence, then…

"Je n'sais pas," Gren delivered, then hung up the phone.

Jack hung his head and forced himself to breathe through it.
Several minutes later, he reached for his phone and searched for
what else was around. Surely there had to be another service station
within a few miles. His phone coughed back an answer of Gitanyow
B.C. 134 k.m., which sent Jack back into his lamazesque labor
breathing exercises.

Once the painful stupefaction of his current predicament
cleared, Jack stood and grabbed his runners. He needed to clear his
head and assess where he was. He laced up and headed for the main
highway.

One, two, one, two. Jack felt the rhythm internally as he slowed
his breathing to that of his feet. One, two, one, two. He settled into
the right rhythm for access to clarity, which in Jack's experience,
was found in two places. One access point was at the metronome of
a slow run; the other was the "smooth air" zone accessed at
maximum velocity — the place of being forced into the present. The
place where one cannot afford to make mistakes. "The Zone,"
athletes call it. And today, such a thing needed to be accessed.

With this thought, Jack took off and ran faster, full tilt, his inner
self mindfully alive as he flew. His force on max, his chest wide
open to not just greet the day but to be one with it. Again, he forced
himself to go faster.

Jack ran south on the highway, daring cars to swoop and swerve and kill him. Such is the dare of one in the throes of a bad case of "fuck this shit." He lowered his vision and pushed into it harder.

"Jack?" He knew this was coming whether he wanted it or not. "Are you there, Ja...." His conscience was cut short.

"What?!" He swatted at their webs.

His higher self smiled at the childish response, making Jack more pissed off. He was done with his level of frustration at a world that refused to form itself into something reliable, helpful, or meaningful.

"Jack?" he heard again.

"Fuck off," Jack fired back. "I don't want to do this right now. I just need to clear my head." The fact he couldn't put these conversations into an off position would be a torment he would endure for the balance of his lifetime. The one access point that eluded him most was the off-position of his noisy brain. He internally screamed and threw his legs into a higher gear, punching his open presence into the trees as he ran beside them.

His mind drifted mid-flight back to when he mattered to people. Back when he wasn't *this* fucking crippled, *this* fractured a mind, or *this* disturbed. He slowed his gait, unable to keep up the pace. He slowed and coughed and sputtered and cramped and stopped, breathing harder than he had in a very long time. He knee-grabbed with all his focus, just trying not to pass out. He spat as he stood, feeling his system pulsing and wishing he could fuck it up some more.

"Jack?" his innards forced into his conscience. "Jack?!"

"Fuck. Off," Jack said as he pulled up and then broke into a sprint, still heading south, the opposite direction of the hotel. "Fuck me." He slammed into himself. "Fuck me up. Let's go." Jack sprinted and pushed and bulldozed and destructed. He pushed himself until he felt it. He was ready. He didn't know why he was ready to fuck himself up again, but he was.

Twinge.

"Good." Jack fired back, pushing himself into freezing, ankle-deep puddles. He screamed some more internally. "Let's go!" In another ten minutes, he was a roadkill lump on the side of the road. As he was losing consciousness, he thought he heard tires screeching to a desperate halt.

CHAPTER 13

FACULTIES

Jack awoke several hours later. No one had found him. No one had stopped. He just laid there on the roadside, his face peppered with grit and gravel. He righted himself to search his surroundings.

"Jack?" met his stream of consciousness. He just wanted quiet. He needed a minute, and he felt no need to answer the call in his mind. Regardless, it continued. "What was that all about, Jack? Your need to self-destruct is a curious trait of yours. That you seek to end your life by whim or casual happenstance is messy. Your passive consent to dark things seems to fly in the face of conscious living and decision-making."

Jack was silent.

"Jack?"

He didn't answer as he curled into a ball, feeling the stone-cold asphalt beneath his face. Its oily slick and fumes only added to his heady state.

CRACK! He heard in the woods to his side. Jack sat upright, eyes searching for a sign of what was happening. Then he heard it again. CRACK! It was the sound of trees being snapped like twigs. Jack slowly stood, brushing himself off while checking that his nervous system was back online. *What the...?* he thought, turning in slow circles with his feelers on max. Jack once again quickly checked his system to see if anything was still off-line. Legs. Check. Back. Check. Arms... meh... mostly on board. He could tell by the brain drag that this wasn't too horrible of an episode. *Not too bad,* Jack thought while the word *drama* pushed into his consciousness.

Jack started the long walk back to the motel, his good ear and eye trained on the woods beside him. He searched for any sign of life, roadside services, or anything that might serve as a Plan B.

There was nothing. Mile after mile after mile, the road meandered treelined and unchanging. More trees, more trees, more trees. The road was deceptive in its sameness. Had he gone one mile? Two? Five? The scenery was set on repeat and offered nothing apart from what was. Jack could feel sadness rising within him. His newfound awareness *knew* this was a lesser version of himself, but he just let himself be sad for right now. That was the paradox of his personality type. At times he seemed to be happiest when he was the saddest. The tragic romantic, the blue, the pained.

Why? he asked himself as his feet padded back toward Meziadin Junction. *Why can't things just work out?*

He forced himself to walk faster. His legs were communicating with him at a decent 70%. Unfortunately, the last missing percentage was becoming more evident with the tire of the exercise. He let his mind drift then he heard it again in the trees. CRACK! His pulse quickened. He walked faster as the air around him swirled in a tight circle. Jack's eyes widened as he volleyed his gaze searching for the thing. The trees to his left then ran-rustled, a path made by some unseen force. Jack picked up the pace into a slow run. An access point at times, but Jack's mind swirled too fast to connect to it. One, two, one, two. There was no finding new information with adrenaline pumping from fear.

"d a n g e r," his gut offered.

Fuck. he thought, desperately searching for any sight of the motel on the horizon. Jack pushed on, extremely aware of the shift in his life perspective from feeling suicidal to being vulnerable.

By the time he reached the motel, Jack had a quiver in him that he couldn't quit. It was a sliver of knowing that what was tracking him in the woods was a thing, yet a thing he couldn't define. Somehow he just *knew*.

That's it! he said, internally lighting up. He entered his room and threw himself on the bed to catch his breath and review the inkling. *That's it. That's mother-fucking it.* He tried to slow his breath to think more clearly. He sat upright, putting his legs into an akimbo position beneath him.

I know what I felt out there. I know that I sensed its presence. That's it, isn't it?

"That's what, Jack? Say more about that. What do you *know*? Teach us about how you internally know something as true."

He slowed his breathing more. *That's the knowing that I've been trying to grasp and understand.*

His consciousness paused, then returned, "Partially but not as you articulated. You're close. Focus there."

Close? Jack slowed himself more, which signaled to his other facilities that they should flower. Their openings reaching out softly as they put their antenna out to receive that which the universal winds might speak to.

"Close," he repeated out loud. *That's the knowing that I've been trying to grasp and understand.* His senses reviewed the position. *Damn*, he thought with a smile. *The edges, the intention of the seeking is off.* Jack was lighting up with the realization of his mistake. "Ha!" he let slip verbally, his mind still training on the exercise. "That's it. My mistake was in *how* I was searching for the answer."

"y e s," was confirmed from within his second brain. A gut check that doesn't lie even when Jack tried to deliver untruths to himself.

My intention was off. It's not the knowing that I've been trying to grasp and understand, but rather the knowing that I've been trying to allow and understand. I've been approaching it from the yang when access to new information and understanding of this manner is only found through the yin. He understood, then internally reframed himself to meet the quandary anew. Jack's feminine heart consciousness then stepped up. Her love radiated sunshine, which added to the midday sunlit experience she was having. She beamed a hello into him, which immediately burst Jack out of his trance. He ran to the bathroom to look at himself in the mirror to see if she'd appear again on his face.

"Holy shit!" he said to himself. "What was...?" Pause. "Or should I say who?" but her radiance was gone, and it was only Jack staring back at his damaged face. He splashed cold water on his face to shake off the weirdness.

Aaarrgghhh, Jack thought. His inner world made him exhausted and reckless. *Why can't I just be fucking normal?* He returned to the bed to flop as the room phone rang.

He picked it up and heard "Harrows Motel and Garage." The usual orchestration of piano and typewriter played on in the background.

"Um… hello?" Jack said, his voice tired and confused.

"Yes, sir. How can I help you?" Mr. Harrow inquired.

"Hello?" Jack retried to make it make sense.

"Yes, sir. How can I help you?" Mr. Harrow repeated. "Are you calling to re-up the room?"

Jack paused, then confirmed. "Yes… please just rerun the card."

"As you wish," Mr. Harrow said but quickly slid in, "Ju-Jitsu starts at 6:00 PM."

"But…," Jack tried to interject.

"AND don't be late this time." Click.

Jack looked at the phone's receiver, then smacked it into his forehead several times, clubbing himself with the madness of it all. He then rolled onto his back and exhaled.

Chapter 14

Succor

Ring. "Hey Dennis, it's Jack."

"Oh wow! Hi!" Dennis's voice radiated through the phone. "How's it going?"

"Meaaahhh…," Jack muddled, trying to land the right words. "Not amazing, actually, but okay. How are you and Wendy? What's the latest with the baby?"

"Ya, we're good. Wendy and the baby are doing well, and the place is looking great, and I found work at your old lumberyard. Thanks for the intro."

"You're very welcome." Jack paused to gather his words. "So listen, Dennis, I'm in a situation." Silence.

"Ya…?" prompted Dennis. "What's up? You okay? Is it your brain thing? You need help?"

Jack wasn't sure what piece of bad news to share first. "Well, that situation hasn't been great, but that's not why I'm calling. My truck broke down. I'm at a garage in the middle of nowhere, and the mechanic keeps saying it's dead and can't be fixed. I'm not a car guy like you. Speaking of…." Jack's thoughts redirected to a happier memory, "How's the canoe thing going? Making any new sales?"

"Well, the guy from Colorado came and got his, which was really fun. I have another person from the mainland who says they're interested, but you know… it's getting going. Oh! And I enrolled at some lady's house who does cooking classes and stuff. She even teaches you how to… you know… like, put them dishes and stuff on the table. She makes it look real nice. I think you'd be impressed by the dinners I can make now."

"No more burned pan-fried trout, eh?" Jack teased.

"Well, c'mon…. A guy's gotta start somewhere." The men's spirits were being lifted just to be near each other's presence once again. "But seriously, Jack, you okay? Mellie reached out when you were...." Dennis wasn't sure how to say the dying part, but the silence that hung in the air made clear his meaning. "You really had me scared, dude."

Jack exhaled and stared into the ceiling. "I know. It's been a crazy few months, but I'm fine, well... other than the car situation. Any thoughts on how we can fix this one or get me a new set of wheels? I'm at a complete loss, and the motel where I am is super creepy and messed up. I gotta get outta here." Silence hung in the air for a second, then he added, "I'm getting strapped on cash. I'm worried my workers' compensation from the Province is going to run out. I dunno."

"Where are you exactly?" Dennis inquired.

"Bleh. Meziadin Junction."

Dennis sputtered a chuckle. "Da fuck is that? Never heard of it."

"Ya, well, it's right at the intersection of shoot me in the head and get me the fuck outta here." Jack paused for the joke to land.

"Oh ya!?" Dennis laughed. "Didn't I live there for most of my 20's?"

"Not sure... but it sounds like a typical place to live after your baby is born." They both flew into laughter, enjoying the moment.

Dennis then asked, "But seriously, Jack. How can I help? We got your August payment ready to send. Maybe that'll help?" Jack did the math quickly in his head. Their $500 will get him less than ten days here at the motel, and the remaining $430 he had in the bank... well, those ends were not going to meet to get him through the month, but then where does the money come from to spend on fixing the car? It was becoming clear that survival mode was upon him.

Fuck, Jack thought to himself as his math met the real. *I'm so fucked.* He hung his head, hoping his tone wouldn't change as he said, "I was hoping maybe you could scoot up here and help me fix the thing? Unfortunately, I'm kinda running out of options."

"Are you close?"

Jack hard squinted and held his scrunch, saying regretfully into the phone, "It's about a 24-hour drive."

A silence punctuated the air. "Damn, dude." More silence. "It's just that with Wendy… she needs me here right now."

This was the moment that Jack knew was coming. He knew he would regret asking and that Dennis couldn't make it, but he had to try even though he knew his effort would fail. What other option did he have? It still felt too big of an ask for Thad.

What the fuck am I going to do? Jack thought to himself, the worry frowning on his face. He noted the subtle absence to the present and returned with, "Oh, ya, of course. I totally get it. I don't know what I was thinking…." Jack trailed off. His mind chased after the whispers of regret.

Noting the discomfort hanging in the air, Dennis picked up with, "Jack…?" Silent pause. "Can I tell you something?" Jack was silent but sent a smoke signal exhale into the phone. "You're one of the bravest dudes I know."

This information caught Jack very much by surprise. He regained himself to train on what Dennis might offer next. "I mean, you were super kind to help me when I needed help, so ya… I kinda owe you one, but I just can't right now. Wendy is having a bit of a tough time with the pregnancy. If there were anything I could do, I would."

"I know, Dennis."

"But seriously, Jack. Unlike anyone I've ever known, you got this. You've always had that way or karma or whatever to work things to your advantage. I mean, hell… who else got out of Kelsey? No one. You… and now me, and that was all because of you. Don't forget that, Jack. Don't forget that's whatcha got inside you." There was a loving silence that hung in the air. It was the unique gift of their friendship, the affection. "I believe in you, Jack."

"Thanks… I gotta go."

"Okay…."

"Bye."

Chapter 15

TREK

Jack lay on the bed for a while, trying to recover from the call with Dennis. Finally, he closed his eyes and let his mind trail back to the days in the trailer with Dennis and even before that, back when it was just him and Em. The simple, early days, challenging days, sure, but in hindsight – and compared with now – they almost seemed good.

"Oh, excuse me, sir," a young woman with shoulder-length blonde hair said, walking up to Jack. "Excuse me?"

He put down the towels he was considering buying. "Yes?" He was confused.

"How much are these?" She was a whirlwind of purses and shopping bags and packaged sheets. She shoved them toward Jack while trying to answer her phone.

"Uh, Miss...," Jack said, trying to get her attention. She waved him off, indicating she just needed a second with her newly important call.

"Excuse me."

Jack tried again but then quickly tired of the exercise. He put down the items she had handed to him and walked off. A move that very much enraged the already blustery young woman. She chased after him.

"Excuse me?" she yelled, trying to sign off from her call. "Excuse me!?" The last one was more of a verbal swat than a question. Jack spun to stop her in her tracks.

"What is your problem?" he asked.

"What is your name? I need your name?"

"Jack, but...."

She cut him off, clearly perturbed. "Listen, Jack...." She searched for his name tag. "I do not think your...."

Jack walked away from her, knowing full well that this would piss her off all the more. He grinned, internally girding himself for the explosion.

"EXCUSE ME!" she demanded as Jack just kept walking right out of the store. Oh sure, she flap-yammered for a bit, but once Jack got closer to the store exit, her error became apparent. She was mortified.

That was their first encounter. A story that would bring laughter to many a drink and toast. How they met, and again when he saw her buying coffee and how they both pretended like they had never met. Then again when they found themselves trapped in a doctor's waiting room.

Emily couldn't take it any longer.

"Hey...," she said softly across the room. "It's Jack, right?" Jack's response was a raised eyebrow. She continued. "Listen, I wanted to apologize to you. It was unfortunate what happened back a week or two ago in Winners. It had been an awful day for me, and...." She stood to cross the room and sit next to him. "Anyhow, I apologize for being a complete maniac." Jack just shrugged. "My name is Em. Well, Emily, obviously, but most people call me Em."

"Hi, Em."

"Are you here to see Doctor Bentine?" she asked.

Jack flushed with the frustration of being forced into a conversation with the woman. "Ya. Just, you know... a check-up." He shrugged again in discomfort.

"Ah." Then to keep the conversation alive, she asked, "Is it because your...?" She nosed in the direction of his busted-in temple. "Or... Oh, sorry. That's probably super...." She needed to get her foot out of her mouth, a situation Jack was quite good at handling by now.

"I believe the word you're looking for is complicated. And yes," Jack said, turning a shoulder in her direction. "It's complicated." She then noticed his Daughtry concert tee.

"Oh! Hey." She came back to life seeing an in to make up for the fact that, up until this point, she'd been a total dumpster fire. "Did you see the last Daughtry concert on the Mainland?"

He turned to her flatly. "I'm wearing the t-shirt." Jack squinted, which was meant to convey "you stupid, stupid woman" as she burst out laughing while falling into him like she was drunk.

"Oh my God," she laughed and screamed. "I," more laughter, "am so sorry." She laughed more and then returned to herself. "Oh my God. Yes, you did, and you're wearing the t-shirt." She chuckled once more. "But listen." She tried to get Jack's attention back. "What night did you go?"

"Dunno. I think it was, ya, it was a Friday night because I have to take that half day to make it. Why?"

She lit up. "Oh my God. So the Friday night he was playing was when I got pulled up on stage?" Hearing this, Jack blinked, churning his memory wheels. Remember?" she said excitedly. "The dumb blond that tried to dance with him then fell? It made the news!" She laughed some more. There was something about her character that Jack was starting to find disarming. Ya, she was a total disaster but so fun about it that you stopped caring just to be in the circle of her laughter. Jack softened up a bit and asked her about it.

Jack's phone buzzed with spam bringing him back into the motel room. His heart was tender with the early memories of them. His last solid relationship, as always, ended in disaster. He rolled over, noting that this was the first feeling he had allowed himself from that compartment. The warehouses of them. The rows and endless rows of unopened compartments. He glanced one last time into the one with Emily's name on it, then sealed it up again.

God, he thought to himself, *that feels like a lifetime ago.* Jack had a pang of wanting to go back, but back wasn't a direction people travel in life when they're on a path like Jack's.

His phone buzzed again. It was Thad.

The two men spoke again for hours. Then, Jack took Thad on a motel tour as he pulled dinner from the vending machine.

"Hey, fuckhead," said a pair of ponytails from behind a door that bobbled and popped out of Room 44. It was Poppy. Jack turned around with an expression that read, "What the fuck?"

"Fuckhead," she repeated. Jack told Thad he'd call him later and hung up his phone.

"I'm sorry, but...."

"Shut up," she interrupted in a loud whisper, which honestly confused Jack about what she was doing. He looked around to see if he was trapped in some colossal joke. "Come here." He walked to her door while looking around for witnesses again, wondering why she was reducing her voice to that of a loud whisper.

"Can I… uh, help you?" Jack asked, making it clear he was super confused about what was going on.

"Listen fuckhead…," she grinned. "You wanna get outta here?" She searched the walkway in front of the rooms. There were too many back and forths for it to make good sense, and Jack momentarily sensed she was miming watching a tennis match. She then suddenly burst with "SHHHHHH!!!!" She then quickly pulled Jack into her room. Her shushing continued. "SHHHHH!!!" Jack had once again been caught in the web of the place.

Fuck, he thought to himself. *Why is this place so much work!?* Jack looked her in the eyes. "Listen, I gotta go.…"

"NO!" she screamed, pulling him from the door. He pushed her off and opened the door as a locomotive of air blasted past them. Jack was pushed by the blast of air back into her.

"Ummm…?" Jack said, frozen. "What was that?" He eyed her in a manner deadly serious.

She clapped her hands and danced in a small circle. "They're here. They're here." Jack couldn't understand her cause for celebration. Instead, he damn near walked into something that he couldn't define. He made his way back to the doorway and stuck his head out, searching back and forth for whatever that was.

Poppy grabbed at Jack again. "You should come and meet the locals." He didn't answer. She bounced with excitement some more. "That's your ticket man.…" She lolled on the 'man' part, making Jack very uncomfortable. She laughed and clapped and pixied some more. "Come! Let's all have supper. You can meet the locals." She then close-eyed an inspection of Jack, saying, "Tempting isn't it… to meet the locals?" Her eyebrows then bounced up and down on repeat as her smile creeped, startling in its intensity.

"I gotta go. Another time for sure." Jack bolted for his room at the end of the corridor. However, something stopped him in his tracks just before making it. The barometer changed noticeably, and he felt like he was being watched from beyond the abandoned junk in the neighboring lot. Jack turned slowly in its direction. *Stay in curiosity, Jack,* he told himself, but the skulk of it felt wicked, cold, and without life.

Jack had met and hugged the angel of death. He knew her touch. He knew her warmth, and unless this was that, he refused to be afraid. His skin crept as his arm and neck hairs stood while his internal antennae piqued on max. He listened and felt for what he knew about the thing. He could sense its presence. *Let's go,* he thought as he marched in its direction with a fiery curiosity.

Chapter 16

Sketch

Jack made it as far as the fence of the abandoned lot before halting, pulling up short with a feeling that wouldn't allow him to go further. He searched the playground for clues of the thing that could be felt but not seen in the last seconds of the day's dusk. He felt something to his left and turned in its direction. It was Gren. *Oh, perfect*, Jack thought. *Just when I thought this moment couldn't get any creepier.* The tall Frenchman pulled up next to where Jack was standing and stood there, eyes trained on the unseen.

"C'est la?" Gren finally asked.

"Qu'est-ce que c'est?" Jack asked, not fighting the intrusion of the man. He had questions about what the thing was. Questions only a local might be able to answer.

Gren stood like a statue against the night wind, then offered, "C'est terrible." He then let out a long slow sigh. "C'est la douleur." Jack didn't interrupt. "La douleur des hommes."

The pain of men, Jack translated in his head as the two watched the thing grow in size while the final collapse of the day was enveloped in darkness. Jack's thoughts were cut short.

"Ce n'est pas prudent. It's not safe," Gren grumbled, side shuffling Jack back in the direction of his room.

"But what is it?" Jack managed not to take his eye off the thing whose presence still hung like a black void of pulsing freakish consciousness swirling and slithering around the children's abandoned joys and toys.

The tall man continued to shuffle Jack back to his room, then opened his door for him to get back inside. "C'est du tourment, c'est de la folie et il cherche à t'habiter."

As Gren closed the door, Jack reviewed his words. "It's torment. It is madness — and it seeks to inhabit you." The words living in Jack made him nervous, but he couldn't help but shake his curiosity of the thing. He moved to his window to continue to stare in the direction of the apparition, its presence and call haunting him.

Jack got himself ready for bed but couldn't escape the uneasy feeling that rattled through him. He knew the thing by its sinister presence, yet that wasn't a thing that one could name or verbalize. But this was precisely the portal Jack had been seeking. It was his toe-hold of understanding to things that were somehow only identified as *knowing*.

Jack knew the creep of it. He could sense it clearly. He knew that it was real despite having no physical or tangible proof beyond feeling and knowing that what he felt was true. Every human has experienced a sensation in the presence of an evil place. It's the walk of the empath through Auschwitz; it's the haunt and creep of spaces that the radioactivity of terror and death has forever atomized. That's what Jack knew of it. He knew that to his core, and that place was an entry point that weirdly excited him — an entry point into understanding things that defied actual substance and, therefore, typical comprehension. Jack willed himself to sleep as the thing wriggled and slipped into the sinkhole on the other side of his wall, leaving ice crystal trails.

The following day Jack woke in a sweat. He swung his feet onto the floor and sat on the edge of the bed, adjusting to the moment. With the previous night's disturbance still coursing through him, the cold morning air meeting the sweat on his back added to the feeling of being sick and muddled. *What am I going to do?* Jack asked himself. *Wait*, Jack's mental train halted. *Let me ask myself again.*

That was the one thing Jack knew about himself. Eventually, when he put a question into his mind, some perspective or lens of himself would offer an answer. It was often just a thread of a reply, but he knew that if he worked and pulled at it and tugged from curiosity, eventually, the case would unravel into an answer. He knew that as the truth about himself. It was this inkling, this knowing that beleaguered and pestered him. If he could just get to a definition, he could work with it. Maybe even give it purpose.

Jack grabbed his jacket to wrap himself in, then forced his question back into himself. *What am I going to do? How do I escape this place?* Jack closed his eyes and set himself adrift. *Show me how I get my life back on track. Please. Let me be on my way again. I miss the open road and the freedom that it brought me. How do I do this without the money to buy a new car? What is my path forward?*

His phone lit and buzzed with a text.

Morning, handsome.
How'd you sleep?

> Not amazing
> How about you?

Same. It was weird.
I felt restless somehow

> Ya, me too
> My brain kept struggling
> with my current situation
> I just feel stuck

So can we talk about
that for a second'?

Jack felt uneasy, as if this was a trap.

> Okay

Long pause.

Ya, mate, this is the part
where you say things

> Lol. I know.
> I'm sorry
> I don't know what to say

Is there something
you're not telling me?

> Like what exactly?

It's just starting to feel
like you're not letting
me in on what's
going on there on
purpose. It feels like you're
hiding something from me.
We said we'd take a stab
at being open and honest.
I'm not here to judge you
Jack, just help.
Just let me know.
 I want to know what's going on

I'm embarrassed about
my current situation
so it's hard for
me to talk about.

Hey, I get that. We all find
ourselves in that place.
But maybe if you let me know
what's going on, I can help
somehow.
Jack?
Talk to me

Pause.

Hello?

Jack took a chance at vulnerability.

Thad. Let me level with you.
I'm stuck, and I have
no idea how to get
out of my current situation
I don't want to involve
you in this mess
I'm sure I'll figure
it out somehow.

Okay. That's a start.
What's the biggest stumbling
block for you right now

Well…

I'm running out of money to
just stay here at this horrible
motel, and that doesn't take
into account any funds to
either fix my car or get a new
one. I probably won't even
last the month here until I'm
homeless.

I had enough money to do
my trip, but I didn't factor in
replacing or fixing my truck.
The nearest town is over an
hour away.

Maybe I just hitchhike there
and abandon my car?

Well, I'm sure if you pulled
up roadside and flashed that
smile of yours, you'd have a
ride in no time. They'd probably
give you a thousand dollars to
sit next to you. Lol.

Ummm…
Where you see a nice smile
others see a deformed scary
guy. Perhaps you haven't
been around me enough
to see how strangers react to
my face.

People don't trust someone
who looks like me
Dunno. I just know I have to
get outta here.

But even if I can catch a
Greyhound or something,
where do I go?

I've rented my house back on
the Island. I don't have
anywhere to go

Well, you could come here for a bit
Til you figure it out

                                        I don't want to be a burden
                                        And I know you have your
                                        writing to get done

Jack, I want to see you
Please come be with me for a bit
We can figure it out together
Don't shut me out.
That's all I'm asking for.
Just bring me along on your journey.
Let me see what I can work out.

The two men let hang in the air the unsaid. The 'I'm falling for you' part had yet to be articulated. Putting away his phone, Jack was heavy-hearted. He grabbed for his runners.

Reaching the highway, Jack headed north this time. He was more determined than ever to discover something – anything that could help him move on with his life. He padded into connection. One, two, one, two....

He reviewed Thad's words again, unsure of why he found them sticking in his brain. *"They'd probably even give you a thousand dollars to sit next to you."* Hooking? Jack searched. What am I getting here? Why is this gnatting at me? *"They'd probably even give you a thousand dollars to sit next to you."*

Jack found it impossible that Thad's deluded mind thought he was attractive. *The guy must be fatally flawed,* he thought. *"A thousand dollars...."* Pause. *"Just to sit next to you."* Jack chaffed at Thad's bizarre look into a reality attached to nothing. *Who?* Jack thought. *Who will give me a thousand dollars just to sit next to me?* His mind cycled back to Colton's rise as he accomplished what he was promised – owning the Major Manor. The shit-stained, furniture-less apartment down on 3rd.

CHAPTER 17

MEMBERS ONLY

New Year's Eve was always a week-long blowout for Colton and his crew. However, the upcoming year would be different now that Major was gone and he was in charge.

"Harlow, for God's sake, get in the limo," Colton yelled at the still vacant doorway.

"Coming," she said, finally stepping out into the night.

"Damn. As always, my love, you look amazing." Once inside the vehicle, he pulled her onto his lap, gave her a little bounce and a wink, and then settled in for a kiss. She reached for her purse as the limo headed for an unusual destination.

"Got ya a little something." She winked, clearly perking with excitement at the announcement. Colton sat back in anticipation, clearing his throat and adjusting himself. "Here," she said, giggling while handing him a small wrapped box.

Colton's patchless eye bounced between her smile and the gift he cupped in his hand. "You...."

She put her finger on his lips. "Shhh... I wanted to." She sat back next to him and opened her compact to check her make-up and nose. He opened it and started to laugh.

"An engagement ring?" he asked, pulling the silver-studded cock ring from the box. "Love it!"

"Put it on!" she screamed, laughing. Colton smiled, then smoothly moved next to her and grabbed her perfectly tucked dick.

"How about you first?" His words were that of steel, his eye unmoving from hers. He pushed up onto her more, just the way that made her crazy. He could feel in his hand her response.

"Now c'mon," she laughed, pushing him off of her. "Later. We got plenty of time for that once we get home." Colton sat back on the seat, loving the

moment between them. She put her head on his chest, and the two were silent for a moment. "Big night tonight?"

"Ah, you know... the usual." He thought about it further, then mystery twinkled as his internal demons side-shuffled, waiting to be brought to light. "Actually... I'm kinda looking forward to the date I have tonight."

"Oh ya?" She pulled up next to his good ear. "Better not be more fun than me," she teased.

"Not even possible," he said, touching her nose with his index finger.

"Another finance guy?" Harlow asked.

"Kinda. He's super hot. Some power banker from Montreal." Pause. "He's just got that look, you know." He knew Harlow knew what that meant. She clapped her eyelids together and bowed her head.

"Just be careful, Colt."

"I can handle myself. Don't worry, dear heart." Harlow then stared out the window and was silent as he said, "I'll be fine."

"I just worry...," she said, lightly touching the remaining bruise on his face from last time.

"Babe," Colton said, getting in front of her eyes. "These big guys like to play rough, but that's where the money is. You know that." They were both quiet for a second. "It's what funds all of this," Jack gestured at their limo, "and we got a good thing going."

"I just don't like how you pull complete strangers into this. Just wish you'd keep to your regulars, like the rest of us." She was getting emotional. "It's just...," her voice caught. "How do you know these guys aren't dangerous for real?"

"Babe...," he said sternly, "I got this. Let me do my thing, and then we can enjoy the rest of the night." Colton checked his phone for directions and then said to the driver. "Up here. This one on the right." He kissed Harlow and then stepped out into the night air.

"Just please be careful," she said as the limo pulled away. Colton winked and turned to enter Mr. DuBois' building.

CHAPTER 18

RIPE

After Jack's morning run, he returned to his motel room, vending machine breakfast in hand. He showered and then grabbed his journal. The one with the singular entry in it. *I am not awesome at this journaling thing.* Jack internally chuckled. *Ah... a fresh page, on...,* he lingered for the joke, *page 2 right after my list of things that make me happy.* He puzzled and paused, trying to find an entry to the connection point that did his higher thinking and problem-solving.

He drew a line down the center of the page. Then, at the top on the left, he wrote in all caps, PROBLEM, and then ANSWER on the other side. *Easy-peasy,* he thought. *And magical answers come to me now!* he jokingly willed into his brain. He then settled himself to focus on the left column. *Problems would be...*

Cash shortage

Car

Jack then blinked into the stained ceiling tiles. *And...,* he waited for more. Blink. Blink. *C'mon, Jack, whatcha got?* Blink... but nothing was being presented to himself. He moved to the bed to see if adjusting his position might offer more insight. Blink. Blink. Nothing. *Cash and Car. That's the list? That's it? Well... sure... dystonia is possibly getting worse now that it's presenting itself at all times of the day with far greater frequency, but... we're not going to think on that. Not today, probably never,"* Jack told himself. *What else? Thad.*

Well, that's not really a problems/solution item. Jack smiled with the memory of his voice, saying, *"Well, I'm sure if you pulled up roadside and flashed that smile of yours, you'd have a ride in no time. They'd probably even give you a thousand dollars to sit next to you."* He couldn't shake the feeling that something was there. A thousand dollars to sit next to you... what was the kernel of truth that he sensed lived there? *The money part. The money part is tied to the Jack part.*

His inner workings kept hitting the worn paths of the past, but Jack *knew* something was there, and it wasn't trading his flesh for cash. He was done with that, and the souvenirs he had in scars weren't a collection he wanted to add to anymore.

Money and me, Jack thought. *What's there? Why is there no bridge? What separates these things, and what brings them closer together?* Every imaginable combination was presented to Jack's mind. The internal static and noise of his frequency fighting to find its tune.

And that's the part Jack kept asking of himself. How does one tune the static of the noisy mind to a channel or frequency to bring in actual information instead of just the white noise and blur?

Later in life, Jack would look back at this moment. The moment when he lay on a crappy motel mattress and searched for a clarifying frequency. That's the portal part. The connection part of hooking up the noise of the mind to the clarity of the universe because those two are a match. A noisy, static-riddled mind is simply not tuned into a station yet, but stations of all kinds are available to those who understand this part. It's like the concept of success. It's something that can only be found by those who believe it is there.

Jack busted out his feelers on max and let the winds of change breeze through his senses, tuning the fuzzled into form. Clarity coalesced — the static hum finding words and forms and images that made sense to the human mind. Jack flung himself open more, seeking to catch new meanings. *Whatcha got, Jack? Hey!* Jack put into his mind. *Little help here?*

"Yes, Jack, we're here, but why are you calling us?" Jack was dumbfounded as this was not the response he was expecting.

Umm..., Jack muddled. *A little help here?* he tried again, hoping it would land in a manner more to his liking.

"Yes, Jack, and we've been over this. I shouldn't be here while you're there." Again Jack deflated a touch.

Oh. We're doing the, 'you're there, and I'm here' thing again? There was a long pause that Jack couldn't help but feel was a moment his higher consciousness *probably* needed to facepalm at his simpleness. Jack chuckled with the thought.

"This exercise is no longer valid when you hold the answer and yet somehow refuse to integrate it into your perspective. It is time you graduate. It is time to evolve. We will no longer allow you to use us in this manner. Trust what is and what is inside of you. Trust that what you are ov is that which you seek. Goodbye."

Jack sat up. *What in the actual fuck kind of response is that?* He searched for the upper channel again, but it was gone.

Hello? Jack pushed into his upper mind. *Hello?!* There was only silence.

Jack laid back down thinking, *You little bitch.* He pushed but then gave up. He knew he couldn't goad the upper voice into saying more. His connection to his upper source was gone.

"You're there," Jack reviewed, "and I'm here." He sunk deeper into himself. "Me and money." The static murmured more, seeking a clarifying port. Jack did his best to arrange his senses to catch the breezes of new information. "C'mon, Jack," he encouraged.

Then he felt it. It was as subtle as a hair landing on the palm of your hand. It was barely perceptible, but Jack *knew* what he felt. He chased the source to define further its location, and once that was done, he switched gears from the yang of the chase to the yin of the welcome. He tuned into it, further adjusting frequencies as needed because it's just noise and more noise until the noise's true words can be clarified. His noisy brain settled and fizzed. He flattened himself and his senses, allowing what was sought to be known to rise. He confessed the truth of the exercise to himself and opened further. The world kiltered and slid as Jack was taken into himself deeper. He allowed their divinity to be known to him as he spoke to the most powerful force within: the love, the truth… and the feminine. "Jack… come," she whispered to him from his heart center. "I welcome you."

Jack smiled, saying, *Show yourself so we might make new decisions and see this world anew.*

She smiled and answered, "You, my very brave boy. Look at what you've done. You are remarkable to find your connection to me."

Tears streamed down Jack's face. His forehead trembled as the avalanche of 'try' slipped softly into its truth. She held his mind in her hands for a few moments, then she was gone.

Jack rolled onto his side and heaved sobs of a thousand scars. Such is often the case when one is in the truest presence of self-love for the very first time.

CHAPTER 19

CATECHIZE

Not knowing what to do next, Jack reached for Thad's book. He had been meaning to get into it, but there was a catch in his intention that he couldn't quite verbalize. Maybe he was scared to see Thad as a great man. Maybe seeing Thad as a powerful human with successes of published books and thoughts and writings that people wanted to connect with was too big for the Jackness of him because him being who he is, in comparison with Thad being who he is, might not be good math. Jack feared that 1 + 1 in this relationship equation would equal one and a half and not three. He struggled to measure up to his love interest's power. Jack began reading and didn't look up again until almost dinnertime.

Knock. Knock. "Ya?" Jack shouted from the bed, but no one answered him back. "Bleh...," he said, rousing himself to a standing position. "Pcoplc. Why?"

Jack opened the door, and there wasn't anyone there. "Are you flipping kidding...." His annoyance was interrupted by his mind picking up a visual cue from the floor. He discovered a brown box addressed to Jack Daw, Harrow's Motel Room 54 Mezedian Junction, British Columbia, Canada. "What the...?" He was confused, but he noticed the return address when he picked up the box. It was from Thad.

"OMG!" Jack said, jumping back into his room and reaching for his Leatherman knife set. He tore into the box and found packaged meals of all kinds, snacks, some iced tea packages, and lots of instant coffee. "Oh my God, I love this man." Jack let it slip but then, out of fear, corrected himself. *Wow,* Jack thought, sitting back. He felt seen, and he was so touched by his new friend's attention to helping him out of his current situation. It felt like a lifeline. His heart was full as he reached for his phone to see if Thad was available for a call but hearing it go to voicemail, Jack resigned himself to leaving a message.

"Hey, Thad. Wow. I'm so touched that you helped me out. It's, well, it's just really nice to… you know, have someone help you out. I just wanted to say that I appreciate it. Give me a call later if you have time. Kiss to Joy."

Jack flopped onto the cold metal, unforgiving desk and started into a few snacks while doing his best not to relive the voice message he left and whether he said the right thing.

"Bleh…," Jack sputtered, leaning back to stare at the ceiling some more. "Okay… so… what the fuck, Jack? Just here. Just here in the God damn woods. Like a tool. Too afraid to ask for help. So what's the plan? C'mon… God." Jack stopped trying and let it go. "I got this," he said. However, he didn't 'got' this. Without his guide's voice, he didn't have much.

"Damn it, Jack," he cursed at himself. He could feel his usual worn path of frustration, and he wanted to get comfy in it, but he pulled himself up short. "Nope. Not going down that rabbit hole. But Jesus, this is weird. Just me. Just me in my head. Talking to someone who left. Nice. I'm sure that would make great sense to others. Ha. I'm sure they'd understand." Jack laughed at his joke. "Ugh." Jack exhaled. "The other voice. My conscience is gone." He hated that he missed its voice and presence. *God, this sucks. What the fuck am I supposed to do now when I need a little help now and again?* A thought that pulled him up into a seated upright position.

He sensed or knew something was there. His insides wriggled.

What did I just say that raised the feeling in me that there was something in what I was saying that I need to pay attention to? What was coming out of my mouth when I got that feeling? Jack reviewed his last sentence. *What the fuck am I supposed to do now when I need a little help now and again?*

Jack hated on himself a bit for not being able to see what he knew would be plain as day the second he saw it. He knew something was there, so he quickly gut-checked his truth or current point of view.

"y e s."

Awesome, Jack thought, then ventured further. *The inkling happened when I said, 'What the fuck am I supposed to do now when I need a little help now and again?'* It was time to excavate that sentence. Jack grabbed for his mokee pipe. *Let's stay in curiosity here.* He packed the pipe mostly with weed but just a nip of tobacco for flavor, lit the pipe, and torched the flower to dust. He relaxed back into his chair, sending smoke signals to the beyond. *If I change my perspective, can I find new information about this?* He was curious to know what new bit of information might be presented to him from this new point of view. In a few minutes, he could feel himself getting stoned.

Let's see… the question was…. He tipped in his chair.

"Wow… these ceiling tiles are yellow from dirt." Jack squinted. "That's literally fucking dirt." He mokee-piped and slid toward awe.

"Did the dirt come from the hole next door?" he bemused while the bedevilment of stoned things wandered circularly.

"But there isn't a door next door," Jack prattled, only to realize, "There's a hole." He laughed at its absurdity.

"So, where did the dirt go?" Jack was beginning to tee-hee, knowing the punchline was upon him.

"I'm guessing onto the fucking ceiling!"

Jack burst into laughter and enjoyed his moment with his brain set to weird. It felt so good just to let go for a minute. He sometimes forgot not to be serious Jack. He grabbed more snacks and mokee pipe and walked out into the cold dusky air.

Chapter 20

Unsound

The crispness of the cool summer night met Jack's lungs as he crossed the pedestrian walkway in front of the row of rooms. It was time just to be. No thinking, no working shit out in his mind. He packed the bowl of his mokee pipe and took a vacation from caring.

He hitched his way over to the beat-down fence that corralled the unwanted in place, then stepped over its frame, and its Do Not Enter sign. He looked around. He was actually inside the circle of the unwanted. A grin came across his face. "Why am I happy here?" he noted, sitting against a peel-painted yellow metal pole. He couldn't stop noting how he felt more at home here. He slowed his breathing to search for the thing. *Here. Here in this place? Why does this feel right?* Jack was surprised. He was expecting this place to feel different to him.

Jack looked up to see the stars beginning to shine. "How I wonder what you are," he said smiling. He exhaled while the sense of missing out on simpler things passed over him. *I wonder what it's like to be normal?* Jack teased into himself, opening a new snack. He laughed and let his mind wander where it landed, *What's it's like to be normal. Normal. Not normal... or perhaps....*

"Unique," met his mind.

Yes, thank you... unique. Jack was too stoned to notice the last word was presented into his mind, possibly not by him.

Unique.... Love that. Sounds better than 'not normal,' but.... Jack smiled and piled into himself some more for more of what this place had to offer him, *but...* his mind kept catching, *not normal and unique mean the same thing, right?* He moved to a cross-legged position. *But one has a negative connotation. Why?* Now Jack was curious but slightly annoyed that he couldn't sit with a quiet mind for even two minutes.

When you get right down to the core of Jack, it was the being in curiosity that often fed this restless and relentless brain of his. He puzzled on it for another second. *Ha. Got it. It's the assumed belief that one should be normal.* Jack was all proud of himself for figuring it out, so he stumbled back into the marijuana-driven apparition to see if there was more.

What if we look at the second bounce or layer of the meanings, he stoned. *I just totally made that up.* He snickered at how ridiculous it was. *But maybe it makes sense.* He paused to track his next incoming thought. *The first bounce being what things are on their face, but the next level down is where the assumed things live.* Jack hoped he'd remember this point when he sobered up. *It's on that level that maybe I should pay attention to people's words to understand their beliefs. The latent meanings and assumptions live there. Right?*

His gut check confirmed, "y e s."

He continued in a state of hurrah. *They will tell you what they believe without having to tell you.* Jack always liked to know who/what he was dealing with upfront. He thought this might be a very clarifying exercise. His phone buzzed with a text.

Hey, handsome. I have a work
reception thing and will be here
until at least 1 AM. If you're up
at that hour, text, but otherwise,
I'll be sure to bring you
your ☕ in the morning. Glad
you got the package. Maybe
one day you'll believe that I just
want to help and be with you.
Kiss.

Jack read this and deflated a bit while typing,

Okay. Have a nice time.
Talk soon. xo.

He returned his phone to his hoodie pocket and lit his pipe. The alchemy of its swirl met Jack's raving moment, and the harmony it created gave him brilliant peace. It was the oneness more than anything that Jack longed for, and in this moment, that oneness felt attached to Thad… but also not. *Why am I sad for something I've never had?* There was a truth Jack was discovering about himself. *The lack of oneness…. It's why I mourn.* He sat up. *Wow! That's it, isn't it. It's the lack of oneness.* He twisted with its realization. *But how can I mourn something I've never had?* That part was super stuck in him.

"Maybe you have had it?" came to him — the moment of it divine in its truth, clarity, and brilliance. Jack exhaled deeply as his eye sunk into him, tilting back, warmed with the moment of now. *Damn, I must be stoned,* Jack thought. He reviewed what he had put in his pipe. *No… just the usual, but fuck… I am feeling myself right now.* Jack stood but not without some difficulty. *F U C K…* he let out to the heavens slow and long. The word being pulled out for all its meanings and all the resonance he wanted to give it, if for no other reason than it felt good.

Jack searched himself for what he was wearing. "Bleh… not weird enough." He laughed and stumbled a bit more through the maze of affliction at the Junction of the Mezedian. He sat on what used to be a Merry-Go-Round.

"Wait…." The past moment and its interaction finally caught up to his drugged state. "I mean, maybe I have?" he stone laughed, then laughed more. "Have what again?" he asked the stars. "Oh ya, maybe I have had…." He swatted at something unseen. "Have had oneness." He sat up straight. "Have had oneness? Da fuck I have." Jack laughed more, clearly having a good time. Then he heard it again.

"Maybe you have." It was a soft voice.

Jack's eyes got big as he looked around for the voice source. *Oh…!* Jack thought back, *You're here? I thought you said….*

His thought was interrupted by her again. "Hello, Jack." Hearing this, Jack noted the voice didn't sound all boomy-from-above and like Jesus or some shit but rather soft, warm, feminine, and kinda sexy.

Hello? Jack thought, falling into himself. *Hello?* Then he came face to face with her.

"Hello, beloved." She beamed.

Oh, Jesus…. Oh, fucking fuck… what the HELL! Jack sat up and finally opened his eyes. "No, no, no, no…," he said under his breath, searching for something to reveal the cause of what just happened in him. He stood as he dropped his mokee pipe. Hearing it hit the ground, he turned to retrieve it. "Oh, thank God. Oh, thank Jesus in Detroit looking for a hotel room." He stumbled and fumbled over to the next lump of tatter and decay.

"Maybe this is how it happens?" he asked himself. He was at the level of stoned where it affects your hearing. "I mean…," he turned a few times, searching for a new perch. "It's not like…," he plunked down on some rotten wood that gave way. Jack didn't seem to notice his seat collapsing. "You know… like you gotta be…. Wait?" Jack searched his surroundings. "Am I alone in here? Cause last time…." Jack blew a blustery trumpet noise, "I mean that was fucking cray… crazy!" Jack not so much settled in place as it fell into a new one. "Crazy. Fucking necromancers." His head bobbled as his eyes closed.

"HEY!" Jack heard as he felt the pain in his back and left leg. "Hey, fuckhead." He felt himself being jabbed by something long and pointy. "JACK!" He opened his eyes to see Poppy poking him with a stick.

"Uh, oh, hey. Hi." He righted himself and wiped his face. He had fallen asleep, but it was still dark, but he couldn't quite place the time. "What time is it?" he asked while adjusting his vision to look at her.

"Twelve-thirty," she bubble-gummed while the black and white gleam of the hour shone. "Wanna get outta here?" Jack didn't know what path to take that sentence down, so instead of answering, he panicked.

"Oh… hey…," Jack said, standing and backing away from the weird girl. "Listen…. Isn't it kinda past your…," he suggested as he shuffled in the direction of his room. Poppy's face dropped.

"Dude. What the fuck?" She looked deadpan and kind of pissed. "I'm 27!" She turned and walked off, clearly not pleased. Jack looked at his phone to verify the time.

"Ooh… maybe I can catch Thad after his thingy?"

CHAPTER 21

SUPERVISION

Ring. Jack quickly realized that it was morning. *Ring.* "Uuuhhh…." Jack reached for the phone.

"Monsieur?" A piano concerto blasted in the background.

Jack struggled to get his brain to throttle. "Oui?"

"Monsieur, your card did not clear this morning!" This information rattled Jack. He almost dropped the phone while trying to arrange himself into a more appropriate phone-talking position.

"What?" Jack blinked.

"Your debit card," Mr. Harrow said slowly, "isn't working. Do you have another, or will you be out by noon?" Jack was in full rustling bed covers mode.

Holy shit, he thought, springing to his feet.

"Let me call you right back." Jack hung up, still shaking off Mr. Sandman, who had recently beat him senseless. *For all that is Christ shopping in a mall,* Jack thought to himself, logging onto his computer to check his bank balance. He quickly did the math. How many days have I been here? He honestly didn't know. His phone rang. It was Thad.

"Morning, mate!" Thad perked into the phone, making Jack grumble.

Everyone knows it's a little rude to throw this much perkiness at a person at this hour. Then he thought… *Wait? What time is it?* He checked his phone and then continued the thought, *11:30 AM. HOLY!*

He internally calmed himself to try and come across as nonchalant as possible. "Oh hey…," he sugar-pied. "Nice to hear from you. How was your thing last night?" Jack was doing his best to come across as calm, but he was doing about a dozen things all at once in the background. One of which included packing his bag.

"It was fine, I guess. How was your night?" Hearing this, Jack slowed.

"I dunno." Jack stopped and sat on the edge of the bed.

Silence.

"And this is where you say more about that," Thad jokingly prompted.

"So listen, Thad, I gotta level with you...." Jack paused, putting a fist of regret on his forehead. "I think I'm about to get thrown out of here. Somehow, I lost track of my days. I just thought I'd have it figured out by now."

"Figured out?" Thad asked.

"Ya, just, you know... figure it out. Find a solution." Jack felt weak.

"Well, other than trying to think your way out of the problem, what have you done?"

Jack flushed with embarrassment. "Uhhh...." Jack was frustrated. *I'm such a moron,* he thought, then tried to save face with, "Oh hey! I read most of your book."

Knock, knock, knock. Jack turned to see who was intruding on his last thirty minutes in the seafoam motel madness. "Hey, listen... I gotta call you back. Someone is at the door." They hung up, and Jack reached for the door. It was Mr. Harrow in the midday glare.

"Monsieur."

The short man cleared his throat while Jack sent a flat expression in his direction, indicating a perturbed "What?!"

"Monsieur, here is your card. It is dejected."

Jack chuckled internally at the grammatical error, thinking, *He's probably not wrong. It probably is dejected.* "Merci, Monsieur." Jack flapped for a second, then said, "Can I stay in my car?" He sheepishly tried to come off as trustworthy. Mr. Harrow eyed him up and down, completely unimpressed.

"Hmmmph," Mr. Harrow harrumphed and then turned and walked off. A move that greatly confused Jack.

"Sir?!" he yelled after him. Mr. Harrow didn't budge from his march. "Sir?!!" Jack yelled after him. *Fuck,* he said to himself, returning to his room where he finished packing. It was coming well up onto noon, and he was running out of time — and options. He collected his things and hurried out of sight. He skirted the far back perimeter to avoid being seen, then headed to the back of the garage two lots up.

Finding the lot on the far side of the garage that housed his dead vehicle, he searched for his keys but wasn't sure he got them back from Gren. He snuck into the yard by climbing the fence and then tried the door. It was open. *Oh, thank God*, he thought and fumbled through the interior. Jack eventually found his car keys in the glove box. However, given that it was noon, he was concerned that the car might be too warm to hang out in. He climbed into the back and sprawled on the dusty bed. After opening the back hatch for a maximum breeze, he stripped down to his underwear and t-shirt.

Oh, Jack, he thought as he fell into himself, doing his best not to hate himself in the moment. He turned inward.

A little help, he thought but then cut to a whisper with, *here,* realizing he was on his own. There would be no more help from his guides. They made that quite clear. They were gone, but then who was *she?* The one from.... "Gah. Nevermind." He put his arms over his head as his stupid knucklehead sandwiched while he fought off the webs of self-hate. "Fuck Jack. Fuck. Fuck. Fuck."

"Jack?" breezed through him, too soft to be anything but a faint whisper.

"Hello?" Jack asked, but then she was gone. He puzzled and looked around quickly while also trying to chase after its echoes.

Jack opened his eyes. *What or who was that? There's something there. I keep catching glimpses of her.* Jack rolled onto his side and flipped a pillow to a less dusty side to lay his head-on. The hot car vented musty goodness, and it felt so comforting for Jack to be back in harmony with his old beast. His mind naturally wandered back to Banjo. *Damn, I miss him.* An unstoppable sadness gripped the edge of Jack's mind.

Twinge.

"Of course," Jack cursed the vexing stress of finding new unwanted, internalized movement. He quickly arranged things around him in case this onset got bad. He reached for his phone. Maybe it was time for him and Thad to have *that* talk. His sadness deepened over the fact that this was his life. That he had to have these talks with people to whom he was trying to get close. *Why?* he thought as his spirits deflated.

"Stay in curiosity, Jack.," he heard her say.

Jack's mind was already cracking and starting to slip below the surface. *Mom?* he thought. Jack's confusion was growing over her presence as he hurried to ready himself for the oncoming storm. "Mom?" he questioned into the ethers. Jack grabbed for his phone, but his arms were already powering down, and his fingers were offline, making it impossible to dial. "Fuck," he said, reaching for his meds. He managed his usual chemical defense, which included trying to slow himself with marijuana. He settled himself into a fetal position, blinking back tears. He heard her again.

"I'm here, Jack."

Her warmth enveloped him, as was the normal course of interacting with the divine feminine that sprung from his heart center. Jack wept.

CHAPTER 22

LIAISON

Mom? Jack asked into the universe as he slipped into the beyond beneath the surface of his mind. The rushing winds started.

Jack could feel himself accelerating as he fell. He looked around, trying to bring himself into a slower fall. He shored himself and searched for anything to make sense. *Mom?* Jack repeated, not understanding what he was hearing.

"Beloved." Her voice was all-encompassing, and it warmed Jack's soul. Her touch on this side of his mind took him, his surroundings, and the horizon from the purples of dawn into the truth of warm, bright air. He listened for her. "Stay in curiosity, Jack" met his mind. He slowed himself more.

Hello? Jack sent into himself, noting the evolution of the place, for he had gone from not being able to verbalize or think in the blasting energy to being able to form simple thoughts. He questioned if this was a step toward mastery.

"Do you know who I am, Jack?" Her voice was motherly and tender.

I..., Jack paused. *I'm not sure exactly.* There was a long silence while Jack processed what he knew of her. *I've seen you, I think.* She smiled and sent radiant beams into Jack's world as he had with a new thought. *Are you like my feminine side or something?* He reviewed it further. *I've seen whispers of you in my face.* She embraced him with her formless being, sending Jack emotionally into a deeper sad state.

Why do you make me so sad? He tried to get away from her presence. *Why would my feminine heart make me sad?*

"Beloved...," he heard, her voice pulling at his strings. "I am not your feminine side as much as I am anything because I am everything." Jack noted that this information offered nothing that was clarifying.

105

I'm sorry? He searched for her form.

"Who am I, Jack? What do you know?"

Ah, Jeez. Jack hated this part. The guessing, the veiled intrigue part. Jack's next thought was… *A little help here?* She warmed with a smile at his infancy and pureness.

"You know me," she offered.

Jack tried to stay in curiosity, but his default knee-jerk reaction was, *Da fuck I do, lady.*

She guided his mind. "Come, Jack," she motioned to the shoreline. "Sit next to me."

Jack rustled. *Theta?!* he said in recognition, making her smile.

"Beloved," she radiated. "Expand your mind. Come… sit next to me." This was an exercise Jack knew. He sat at the shoreline and opened himself to what was. "Ah," she said in recognition of them being in this moment. "You recognize the process."

I have had teachers and guides, Jack thought, closing his eyes. *Teachers who were students that are on their way to being Masters.*

"We have met before, Jack," she said. The sound of the lapping shore gave Jack a sense of oneness. "Many times."

Jack bowed his head in recognition of the thing. The handiwork, the design, the all. *Yes,* he said as his mind instantly landed on the first moment they had shared together. That moment played onto his mind.

Jack saw his past…

"HARLOW!" Jack screamed into the phone. "What do I do?" He was a jumble of sobs and screams and terror. "Call 911! Get here!" Jack hung up the phone and then redirected his attention back to Major, who was lying in a pool of his own blood. He ran and picked up his head gently to see if he was alive. "Major." He was shaking but trying to hold still for his friend. "Major!" He tried again to revive the elderly man as his wading into this put blood onto Jack's hands. He started to sob from a place of total overwhelm and did not know what to do. Jack had never held the dying before. "Major."

The old man's eyes fluttered. He wasn't completely gone. "Colton." The rasp of his air flicked droplets of fresh blood. He quietly sputtered and coughed.

"Yes!" Jack's eyes were wide with fear. "I'm here, Major. I'm here." The dying man managed a smile and tried to reach his hand to Jack's face.

"Colton... you are very special to me. Thank you for...," he coughed more, blood trickling from his mouth and ear. "I'm lucky to have had a friend like you." The past tense of the sentence pissed Jack off because he wasn't done, and their friendship wasn't over — and it wasn't going to be. Jack refused the notion.

"Hold on, Major... I got you." The old man closed his eyes. "Help is on the way... just hold on for me." Jack welled and walled, then quietly managed, "Don't leave me."

"I love you, Colt. You get me, and I've always been so grateful for that." His eyes remained closed.

"Yes...," Jack agreed as a smile of a breaking heart crossed his face. The warm recognition of what they had and who they had become to one another. The gratitude that stemmed from that was reason enough for the smile that otherwise might have been seen as misplaced. That was the moment of love's first connection with Jack. She came into the room and held Jack as her blue radiating twin went to meet Major.

The dying man opened his eyes one last time. "Thank you, Colt. Thank you for being like me... for being broken like me." And with that, he was gone.

Jack came back to the shoreline as tears flowed down his face. He fought not to shake.

"You remember," she said.

You were there, Jack realized tenderly, reliving the moment.

"Indeed I was." She glowed, undetectable in form. "The four of us were." This information halted Jack.

Four?

"Did you not know that was the first time you met my soul twin?" This new revelation felt like a burden to Jack as he was already processing so much.

I do not know, he thought to himself, *and I do not know that I want to.*

"But it's already done, beloved," she said clearly, making Jack realize that, as with Reason, words for her didn't need to be fully articulated. "You have already met her." Jack didn't respond. "You held her. You know her, and you have a long-standing relationship with my soul twin, unlike me."

It suddenly came to Jack. *The angel of death.*

"Yes, beloved. I am the other side of her."

You're life then?

Hearing this, she smiled, reflecting his simpleness and purity. "I am what is. And she is what isn't. The stuff between the stuff." She paused, then added, "I am love, but to you, I am your love, your heart — an access point."

My heart, Jack repeated, taking in the exercise. He watched the waves meet the shore and turned into the beingness of the moment. *But why then am I so sad in your presence?*

Her smile now mirrored his inner beauty and unsullied soul, for she saw a presence without a mar. She saw his wholeness even when he couldn't; it was meeting this truth face to face that made Jack weep. "In my eyes, you see a possibility of who you are. A possibility you've never allowed yourself to hold or touch, yet it is always there. It's meeting that truth that ensnares you in human emotion. It's seeing you as I see you that is currently impossible for you to hold without falling apart. Just know that it's always there when you're ready."

The world crashed as Jack heard voices from the beyond. She started to fade as the world turned back to black.

How will I know you? What do I call you? he desperately called out, knowing she was slipping away.

"I am power, the engine that keeps hearts beating, and I am the feminine in you, Jack. You have called me your feminine, your Venus. But there is much more to it than that." She paused to redirect. "The world in which you live is one of the more dense planes in the universe... but you have us. All of us. That is all you need."

Jack started to come back to consciousness, thinking, *All of us?*

CHAPTER 23

DODGE

Jack's eyes opened as his haze lifted, and he was granted access to his body again. The fuzz of it always lingered. He groped and felt for what body parts were available to him. Neck, check. Back, check. Arms, check. Legs, check. He was coming back online.

Searching his surroundings, Jack found things were amiss. He sat up in a panic, "What the...." he scattered through the vehicle. "No." He scattered some more. "No, no, no," he said, taking inventory of what was missing. While unconscious, he had been robbed. His bag, phone, keys... everything. It was all gone. Jack didn't know what to feel or not to feel in the mixture of emotions when everything is lost.

Jack sat in his underwear on the tailgate and boggled. "What... I mean... what...." No thoughts would fully land, then a mini damn broke, and Jack started to laugh. The absolute fucking absurdity of his predicament rained upon him, and there was no more going down, so he could only look up. Jack faced the low-hanging clouds that were now beginning to dapple his face with moisture. He then belly-laughed and loved the moment of being in the rain because fuck it. Nothing mattered in that moment. All was lost, and he figured he might as well give up caring.

Jack eventually collected himself. It felt good to have the release. *But seriously,* he thought to himself. Another laugh escaped. *What now, Jack?* His thoughts trailed off as he flopped back onto the mattress. *Now... what?*

He closed his eyes, yearning for simpler times. Times when things were easier. Funny enough, that time for Jack was when he was Colton. But maybe that's just the lens of youth that he wanted back. Either way, he found himself wanting to be *that* confident in things again. Nowadays, he pretty much was a middle-aged muddle, a bad-tasting mixture of apathy and leave me the fuck alone. The thought of Major and James… of Harlow and the wild exotic nights where he owned the town and was certain in every decision he made. *Where is that guy? Where did he go?* Jack thought, hating how pathetic he was with his aged grossness, the taint of years decaying him before his very eyes.

He sat up and looked at his reflection in the window. *Where did that guy go?* Jack then found a sliver of energy. *Fuck it,* he thought. "I'm still that guy," he said to himself as his reflection told him differently. "Okay… maybe I'm not 22 anymore, but I am so much more because of my experience."

Jack desperately searched for anything to embolden him, then stood and faced his reflection. He stared at it until Colton stared back. "Wanna fuck?" the practiced line of his youth slipped out. At first, Jack laughed but then reviewed it back in his mind. He recalled his reflection doing it. And then did it again, adjusting his stance to a more cocksure position. "Wanna fuck?" Colton said. Jack turned around as if he had just put on a new outfit that he was trying on. He then turned and faced the reflection on the closed garage shop doors and took in his own gaze squarely and very directly, a move he perfected because he loved the power it took from people. He took a step toward his reflection and burst the seams of his old habits' outfit to make room for this proverbial new one. His energy throbbed, and his faculties pulsed with newfound vigor.

Fuck… this feels good. Jack thought, re-embracing this vibrational skin. The rush of him was ecstatic and addicting. He remembered why he was Colton for so long – the feeling was powerful, and it felt good, but then his internal lights dimmed down to low again, and he turned to sit on the tailgate. Jack exhaled. The gentle dapple of rain lent him a sullen mood.

"Damn, I wish I was that guy again." He internally turned with the mull of it. "That confident." He flopped again. "That in control." He looked back in the direction of where he just saw and remembered his former self. The one that was that version and vision of him; he could use a little more of that guy right now. But as per usual, Jack just wanted to cry. He caught himself and asked if this was the right choice for the moment.

"Uh… nope. Now is really not the time for a pity party. I need to figure this shit out now! C'mon, Jack. We ain't got much, but what do we have?"

Jack did his best despite the continuing fog of the dystonic hangover, and he searched and took inventory of what the vandals left behind. He found his cowboy hat, whittling set, a multi-faceted army knife, sleeping bag, his old carpet satchel with old tools, a pot, boots, a bandana, a coat, a radio, lantern, two Henley's, a few t-shirts and some long-johns. Jack was now forcibly keeping back the avalanche of overwhelm.

Maybe I can get some money for this truck? Jack thought desperately, but his mind was so full of the fuck-its that he met his stuckness with rage. So much so that he immediately changed tact.

"Nope. Fuck it. Fuck this place, fuck my life, fuck my situation. I'm plotting a new path forward, and I think I found my driver."

Let's do this, Jack. Let's fuck up our lives and have a little fun, Colton thought, pulling on the long johns and boots. *Imma fucking walking home. Might kill me… might not. Either way, I'm done with this God-forsaken place.* He repeated that last sentence aloud and screamed into the clouds, "I'M DONE WITH THIS GOD-FORSAKEN PLACE!"

When his head returned to the horizon, he saw Poppy sitting on the fence sucking on a lollypop. He couldn't tell if her expression was annoyed or just unimpressed.

"You're super weird," she said, then hopped down and walked back to the motel. Jack watched her go and felt one way, and then he moved over and Colton decided it was time to bring back a few of his better looks because Jack was engorging on having that kind of energy back in his veins. He flicked and pulsed with the surge of it, packing the carpetbag and packing a few sticks so he could convert it to a backpack arrangement when needed. Fully dressed, he grabbed his things to go and then stopped to review his newly rediscovered presence in the world. He fucking loved what stared back at him because it was powerful, determined, virile, and ready to take on any task put before him.

"Come on, Colt," he said with cold steel in his eye. "Let's fuck this shit up." He turned and headed for the highway in boots, long johns, a huntsman's coat, and a carpetbag. *This is how you get shit done,* he thought, getting to the southbound side and sticking his thumb out.

CHAPTER 24

ENGENDER

Jack happily watched Harrow's Motel trail off in the distance. He had no idea what was next, but he saw no other options. At this point, he was going to have to just trust that something would work out. It always does. However, sometimes that also means that how it works out is that you're dead.

After a few truckers raced by blaring and hooting, one finally slowed and stopped. Jack looked up to catch a look at the driver, who scooted into the passenger seat to speak with him.

"Well, what in God's country do we have here?" The driver laughed. "I had to stop if only to hear the story. Lose a bet or something?"

Colton fired on the charm, "So much worse." He twinkled with mystery and laughed as he lured with, "You're going to want to hear this one." The driver laughed and opened the side door.

Once they were moving, the chuckle guy asked, "What's your name, son?" Jack internally discombobulated as the truck thumped them in their seats.

Gah, Jack cursed internally, thinking, *How far do I take this? I mean, I'm not that guy anymore.* But he also knew that if he broke character, he'd burst out laughing at how ridiculous he looked wearing only underwear and boots. *C'mon,* he told himself. *Let's just live a little like we used to. Freedom, no rules, just what feels right.* He then chided himself, *When did you get so old, fearful, and pathetic, Jack?* He took a deep breath and committed himself.

"The name's Colton."

"Ah," the trucker reviewed, "a good Canadian name. I like that." Pause. "Had an uncle back in Saskatchewan who was named Colton, but everyone just called him Colt." Another long pause. "He's dead now."

More miles passed as Jack found himself having a harder and harder time being his previous demeanor.

"So why ain't ya got any pants on?" the guy finally said, addressing the elephant's trunk in the room.

"My car broke down, and then I was robbed. I have nothing but what I have on and what's in my bag."

The trucker thought about this. "Bummer. Where ya heading to?"

"Gambier Island," Colton said. "How far ya going?"

"Well, not down to the Island. Nothing fancy like that. No… I got my orders…." Silence. "Gotta get down to Kitwanga then west, but it sounds like you're not heading back to those coastal parts."

"Nah," Colton said as Jack thought, *Fuck*. He stared out into the rows and rows of trees zipping by. "Prince Rupert, eh?"

The trucker smiled, noting the brotherhood of the town. "You know her?"

Jack shut the hell up as Colton perked back to life. "Ya. Jeez. Had some pretty rowdy nights there, let me tell ya."

The trucker laughed with the register of the thing. "Ya… those down dockside…. You ever get out datta way?"

Colton had this in the bag. "Dude…." He slapped the driver's shoulder, planting his first connection of touch. A master's move in understanding interpersonal energy. Colton had a Ph.D. in that, and Jack welcomed him taking the steering wheel. "Shit! When ya been? My crew… dunno we landed there maybe…. What now?" He adjusted his hat. "Ten years ago." Colton winked a pulse of energy into the driver, letting him know he knew what was down dockside. "Anyhow, we land there, I think it was a Thursday night, and there was this bus just in from the island. A choir group of some shit, right?" He pauses to build suspense for the guy.

And that was the truth about what Colton knew and why his outrageous excuse of an outfit didn't bug him. Ya, sure, it was ridiculous to wear basically only boots, long johns, and a coat, but people love a scandal, especially a palatable one like losing a bet to an old buddy. This was information Colton used to his advantage even when dealing with someone such as this trucker who would never have sex with him. It just wasn't on the table. Neither party was interested, and that was clear… but that didn't mean that there weren't two humans in conversation and that interplay between any two can be orchestrated and played like a maestro.

Colton eyed more scandal into his pawn and smiled, thinking, *Fuck I've missed this.* He then went on to energetically charm the pants off the man with his down-dockside story.

About an hour into their shared ride together, the trucker noted, "They really took your wallet 'n everything?" Colton, still vibing on his everything, took a second before answering. Slower-speaking people are easier to trust. That, he knew, so that he delivered.

"Afraid so." Jack let hang in the air because he knew this would probably come up, and so for the past hour, he had been divining a path for when it did.

"Then how ya going to?" Silence.

"Dunno exactly," Colton said, leading the man down his already well-worn mental path. "Sounds like we're about to part ways, though, what…? Say, half-hour or so?" Colton slowed internally more. The self-assured never rush; the confident linger and set the pace and tone for others who are less present. It's like an energetic trap. Make 'em come to you once, and that's a win. Make 'em come to you twice… and that's training. "If I can send a text, I might be able to get someone to meet me." Colton adjusted himself in his seat to put a foot up on the dash. No, he wasn't asking. He was entry-level taking, the kind that's easier to ignore than make a deal of. It's beginner power-play stuff. "Do you mind?" he said, reaching for the driver's phone.

"Oh. Ya… sure."

Colton nodded, looking earnest, "I really appreciate it. You helping me out like this." He patted the driver's shoulder like a buddy. Touch two from his hands always landed with more welcome. The first had to be a get-in and get-out to break the ice, but after that… well, people generally opened up to Colton's touch. He smiled and drove the two deeper into a best-buds conversation. They shared about being young and dumb. They laughed a bit. "But then where ya off to. I mean, after your drop?"

The driver seemed to sober up a bit from their revelry. "Well, just back home to see the family then. The end of the line, as it were."

"Ah," Colton pulsed. "Sounds nice. Where's home?"

"Uh, Smithers."

"Never been," Colton exhaled, doing some quick math and geography thinking, *Smithers… Smithers….* He still had possession of the driver's phone, so he redirected there where he mapped it and tried to figure out Plan B. He quickly sent a text to Thad.

Hey, it's Jack. This is someone else's phone, so please don't text him back. Just wanted to let you know that I'm fine. However, I'm out of money, so I couldn't stay at the motel. I was staying in my car, but then someone stole all my shit. I'm so sorry to drag you into the disaster that is my life right now. I caught a ride with someone and am heading south. Looks like I'll make it to Kitwanga tonight. Not sure where I'll stay, but I'll figure it out. Again, Thad, I'm so sorry. I'm really embarrassed about the state of my life right now. Just please give me a chance to show you I'm more than that. I'm just kinda in between opportunities right now. I care about you and hope you're still open to getting to know me for me. I'll call you at the first opportunity. Kiss to Joy.

After sending the text, Jack deleted what he sent, then exhaled and sat back. He could feel his personal aging and weakness growing within him, so he stepped aside to bring in the predetermined axioms of Colton. He needed those worn thought patterns now more than ever if he was going to step up and meet his current challenge. Besides, Jack was loving the shit outta regaining his former swagger. *I mean, c'mon… I'm wearing basically tights and boots and a coat. But I guess it's not what I'm wearing but rather how I'm pulling it off, so to speak.*

Jack loved that part about being Colton. The vibe and trigger of him. The rhythm of the sure… because ya, he looked fine other than his busted-in temple — but back when he was Colton, he only saw that as an advantage. A conversation starter and something he could hide when he needed to. Besides, more than anything, Colton knew the truth of the electric messages that pass between people, and the truth in knowing that being attractive has nothing to do with how you look but rather how you energetically feel to others. Everyone has felt the pulse and swagger of someone who's not what most would consider physically attractive, but somehow, they give off the vibe that they'll pull your hair back and fuck you senseless. Sexy ugly as it's been called, and those who own that title fully are in the game to win, and everyone knows those types don't mind putting in the extra work. Glad for it even to prove a point, like Colton. The steely unfettered confidence that's owned and fully self-generated. That's energy.

That vibe and attractiveness is its own skill, and Jack knew how to fully embody it. Not in a cocky way. He simply understood the math and chemistry and used that in his favor.

The trucker couldn't stop picking at the topic, "So… they just took yer everything. Wallet n'all."

"Yep." Colton put his second leg up on the dash as the driver side-eyed the move. "Not sure what I'm gonna do." He let that live in the air. He then let the driver come to his rescue.

"Well, I gotta drop ya before I head in-shore."

"Yes." He grabbed both boots. "I appreciate it. Oh, here's your phone back." There was an exchange of smiles.

About thirty minutes later, they reached Kitwanga. The driver was caught in mid-internal commotion. "So... were you able to find someone to meet you or something?"

He looked down, pretending to be embarrassed. "Ah... nah. Don't worry about it, I'll just, you know...." Colton slapped his carpet bag.

"But you have no pants," the driver said while trying to work it out in his head.

"I got all I need," Colton said as Jack skirmished, thinking that the last line was a tad thick. Internally he eye-rolled; externally, he was golden.

The truck slowed at the intersection. "Well, you need money or something, son?"

"Well, I couldn't take any from ya anyhow," he said, unlocking the door. "I'll figure something out."

"Now wait...." The driver almost grabbed for him. "Listen, I appreciate that you don't want a handout. I appreciate that. Too many people just looking for that and like I said, well, that's a good character there. But, here...." He handed Colton forty bucks. "It ain't much, but it'll get ya dinner and maybe a camping spot."

"Appreciate it!" Colton slammed the door and then waved as he was literally left in the man's dust. He then shored himself up to head over to a nearby gas station.

CHAPTER 25

HAP

Jingle

As Colton walked into the store, the clerk took a double-take to see a guy in underwear and boots. "Can I help you?" he asked hesitantly.

It was at that moment that Jack couldn't hold on being "Colton" anymore. It was starting to feel heavy, like a lie. The sheepish feelings returned as he decided to get real and ask for help.

"Hey…," Jack one-eyed the Hindi gentleman shamefaced. "So, I'm in a bit of a bind. I don't have a phone or a way to leave here." Jack hoped that layering his problem into this man's day might get him to be more productive with a solution. *Damn*, Jack thought. *That's kinda conniving,* a realization internally that felt like a Colton persona hangover. *Maybe I still got some of that in me even if I'm not Colton anymore.* He recognized there were skills there that he could lean into, but also character defects that he needed to keep an eye on.

The cashier just looked at him and said, "Get out of my store."

Jack noted the flat dead expression of the man, thinking, *Ah yes. I, in my infinite wisdom, thought this world was just going to bound me along gently to my destination? Jack, you're a fucking idiot.* He waved to the clerk, indicating "one second" and grabbed canned foods, a lighter, and water. "Thank you," Jack said, finishing paying for his items. He turned with an overwhelming sense of both gratitude and shame as he left the building.

"Where to now, Buckshot?" Jack said, smiling at the memory. He wished he could go back and get his car. He thought about how it wasn't much, but it was home. Something he was missing greatly at the moment. Jack counted his change.

"Ten dollars and eleven cents." Jack reviewed what to do next as the August night started to slip into the ethers. He could feel the world turning from this vantage point, and surprisingly the weight of much was now lifting from him. The wholeness and sense of wealth for being someone who has $10.11 met his mind. He was one who had what most would describe as nothing, and yet in that loose change, he had everything.

This was his choice this evening, the non-attachment to things and the odd sense of freedom that is found there. *Okay, I can probably walk a few more hours but then what? To walk for hours only to find me on the side of the highway? What if I don't find a ride? I'll have to camp alone in the middle of nowhere. Not a safe option.* Jack repositioned his point of view, *Or, I could camp here behind the store. I'd be safer there, but....* He couldn't shake the hours wasted to start camping out now. *Fuck Jack... risk it?* The next thought was hilarious to him, *How about you, Colt? Risk it? What do you say?* He leaned into one of his typical hey-fuckboy stances, and this time he laughed at how completely insane he currently looked. *Ah fuck it,* Jack thought as he headed down the highway with his thumb out. *Safety be damned.*

Jack was surprised at the reaction from passing truckers. This time, as they drove past him, they were silent. The sound of a ship passing him in the night. It made the darkening skies feel odd. *Why aren't they yelling and hooting and carrying on like last time?* Jack kept walking.

Around midnight Jack couldn't walk anymore. His legs were spent, and he was cursing himself for his poor decision. Not to mention that this type of behavior is what brings on a neurological episode. Jack slowed his walk and just stood. The darkness in remote places like this is shockingly absolute in their opaqueness unless, of course, you're granted moonshine, as was Jack's luck this evening. *Half moon,* Jack thought. *Better than new.* Jack was trying to be grateful but finding that internal place difficult to get to considering his current situation. *Fuck!*

There was nothing but a small ditch and the forest all around him. *Survival,* Jack realized. That's what he had to work with. He recognized that he was going to have to get this right to survive the night. Assessing what he had and what was around him, he used the rope and the carpetbag to make a short tight hammock between close trees tied above a bear's reach. At least at this height, he would feel predators before they were on top of him. After tying the contraption together, he got in his sleeping bag but sat up to face and commune with the stars.

"How I wonder what you are," he said, smiling heavenward. Jack loved to just be. He thought back to the picnic table at the old trailer where he'd smoke his pipe and swirl down a beer and simply take in the night. It always just kinda felt like a guy thing to do — a natural and needed resting point for men if the mind has to trudge another day. Men's feelings. The grumble. The thick quiet.

Jack breathed into the background of mountains with the spruce of the night mixing with the crisp of cold. Jack exhaled, and to abandon fear, he practiced being present, and he practiced abandoning the prison of safety. He felt open to the oneness of what he wanted to be. Next, Jack, simply out of curiosity, opened his chest and met the shocking beauty of mother earth at midnight in the Canadian wild.

"Jack," she whispered.

I'm sorry? he questioned what he heard.

"Jack," she repeated. He recognized the voice.

You're here? I mean… don't go. I have questions. Jack saw and seized the opportunity. *Like….* He continued trying to formulate his question out of thin night air. *Why are you here?*

"Where else would I be?" This was a response that greatly confused Jack. He shook it off to finally get his questions out.

So… when I spoke the whole "Mother Earth" thing out into the ethers, was that like me talking to you? Like… I guess I don't fully understand who or what you are. I mean… don't get me wrong. I'm super grateful that you're here. Oh, one more question. Are the other guides coming back? Because that was super helpful and well… things are a bit of a mess right now, and I could use some outside help.

"Beloved. It's you I am here for because I am you. We cannot be separate in the manner in which you indicate. Does that make sense?"

Jack reviewed and noted that the other guides said something similar. *Okay*, he said after not having gained any clarity on the issue. *But, like… you're what? Do I have different guides now or something?*

"How do I put this…?" She arranged herself into a smolder of night air. "The oneness you seek is what I am. Does that make sense? To think of us as guides isn't quite right, for we stem ov you."

Jack swirled with the information, noting that again he was being pulled into riddles, which given his state, he was weary of. *Da fuck does that mean?* He slowed to curiosity. *We stem ov you.* He reviewed. *Okay… so… oh!* Jack depressed with the realization of the truth. *So you're just a voice in my head. Nice. Again, I worry for my sanity.* Jack was tired of this well-worn three-legged race.

A sensation of joy emanated from her. Her delight in Jack's discovery was unmissable. "Jack," she beamed. "Come." He now understood the command, which had nothing to do with moving physically. He centered himself, ready for whatever may come next.

"Look through my eyes, Jack." She inhabited him as he had seen before. Her feminine touch present on his face. She then took his thoughts, and as she pushed his consciousness back, Jack settled into the tree's catch as his body undulated with the universal conversation. She opened their eyes to see the stars' truth.

"Jack," she began. "Stare into the sky, and you stare into my mind. Be with me. Be here, Jack. Be with the sound of my voice. That's right. Look through me, through my lens, and see what's revealed." Jack exhaled, then suddenly, all the stars became known to him. He could feel them, sense them. He remembered the sensation in the hospital room where he was one with something outside of himself, only this time it was so much more vast and overwhelming. He fell into the feeling as the old inhabitance of what was his body slipped off like a tight shoe. Jack left his body.

He swirled and amazed at himself without form. He could finally breathe. He expanded into space beyond himself, and he hummed and radiated throbbing universal energy. The sensation was overwhelming, and he could honestly say he had never been this uncomfortable. Yet it was a new kind of uncomfortable. To Jack's mind, the vastness of this new knowledge was too intense and too big to stand in its presence. As its truth cratered him, he tore into heaves of sobs. The truth of it was too much for his human mind to hold.

She dimmed the vision and returned Jack to the cleat of himself. A hardshell with batter-worn edges. He internally slowed and calmed, adjusting back to Jack. Back to dense. Back to form. The weight of it feeling unbearable. She left him a whimper of himself, and he felt wrung out and changed. He didn't know what that was. He tightened himself in place and slept.

Chapter 26

DISORDERLY

Dawn was finding its way into the sky as Jack stirred. He breathed in the cool morning mountain air as a smile presented itself upon his being. He let it live in him for a while as he came to meet the day.

"Morning," he said to Mother Earth. He then did a quick systems check and wondered why he was in a good mood – a mood that clearly couldn't be trusted. He questioned the mood's lies as he sat up to assess his affixed reality, which could be counted on as tethered to known things. Based on last night's assessment of where he was and where his next destination might be, Jack calculated it was going to take him 18 hours to walk to Smithers, not that he expected to meet up with the old trucker but rather that it was all he had mapped and that was next on the list of worldly things to conquer. He reviewed that he had walked almost seven hours last night… it all seemed overwhelming.

"Just one chunk at a time. One town, one victory, one day." He dismantled his encampment and ate a cold can of Spaghetti-O's for breakfast. Again, he distrusted his newly lifted spirits. "Whatcha got to be so damn happy about? You literally have nothing." A thought boomeranged back with, *And I am unburdened, and I am free.* He packed up to begin his long walk.

The morning was fully broken, and Jack was already starting to tire when he saw signs for Seaton. *A town!* Jack internally rejoiced. *People!* This second thought pulled him up short. *Wait. People. Bleh. But….* The tug of war wasn't lost on him – his prejudice versus new opportunity.

The first building he came to was abandoned and boarded up. Jack walked onto the next warehouse a few more miles down the road. Again, no one. No signs of life. It was becoming clear that this settlement was abandoned, and Jack could feel his tiredness catch. The overwhelm was too much; he just wanted to rest and regain himself. He pulled up to one vacated building and searched for a place to hang out for a bit. *Maybe have something to eat and let the midday sun pass some,* he thought.

Rounding the backside of an old metal building, he noticed a window that had been smashed. Inside the dusty place were some leftover building materials and tarps covering lumps of who-knows-what. Jack cleared the debris from the sill and hopped in.

"Hello?!" Jack checked. "Hello?! Anybody here?" He stood unmoving until the building was silent, long enough for Jack to start making himself at home. It was clearly vacated long ago. He pulled back a few canvas coverings to find old wood, scrap metal, rotted-out feed bags, and lots of mice. "Uh… jeez…." Jack backed away from the swarm. They mostly moved outdoors as he searched the place for something, anything that he might be able to use. After turning the place inside out, he sat on a stack of wooden pallets and assessed his scavenger's find. A short pointy metal spear thing that he thought might have been part of a bird cage or something, some string, a yellow scratch pad of paper, a metal mesh that Jack thought might come in handy if he had to strain water or something, a battered tarp, and some marbles he found in a drawer.

Weird, he thought, collapsing into himself. *Now what? Damn it, Jack.* He hated on himself some more but tired of the exercise and closed his eyes to rest. It was only midday, but he was beat.

Thirty minutes later, Jack awoke to a weird noise. His eyes darted around, searching for a clue. There was nothing but the wind and some old loose building parts, but it made him realize that he wasn't safe and needed to get out of this death spiral of just surviving. He closed his eyes again and regained some of his previous notion of sleep.

"Okay, Jack… whatcha got?" He was still for a second to see what other information might be sent his way. Nothing. "Fuck." Jack thought, *Okay… okay… little help here?* He tried but still nothing, just silence. He recalled that it was the same sensation as when he was in the observation deck of his mind. He sat up.

What? Hold up. He checked for what he knew to be true. *If me, Jack, crazy mother-fucker Jack is now just here... as me....* He stumped with the question, then thought of trying to reverse engineer the thing. *If upstairs big brain Jack,"* he laughed at his joke, *"is there and when I'm him or seeing....* That approach didn't work. *Maybe.... Okay, start at the beginning.* He started to fall asleep again. *When I'm there, I'm there, and only I'm there... but when I'm here as me, it's me, and....*

He started with the realization. *Really?* He blinked as he processed the thing. *So when I'm there....* He recalled how to get "there" and jumped up to it. There was silence. *And when I'm....* He fell back to Jack and thought, *I'm here, and I'm talking to the big guy upstairs, that's me too. That's me having a conversation with my higher self.*

His gut confirmed.

"y e s."

This is awful, Jack thought to himself. *I mean....* He rearranged his face. *So I don't have guides or some guidance from beyond me?* He shifted again. *Just me talking to myself?* The gall of the next thought was gross. *Then how do I know if any of this is true?* He grabbed his forehead. *Maybe it's just all bullshit. Maybe I'm just an idiot.* Jack felt weak and old in the moment. *Maybe I'm just a joke.* He fell into his usual emotional well-worn slippers and decided just to be. *What a joke. I'm a joke. An idiot.*

The list went on, but he soon tired of the exercise and wandered on to something different. *No, really, Jack.* He twirled a marble in his fingers, the sun placing beautiful petals of light on the walls. Jack lost himself through a door named Wonder in the yellow flickering light's reflection. That moment was enough time for an additional thought to side-slip in: *But besides silence, or rather lack of noise, what's up there in the brain attic?* He laughed about the term brain attic. "Hold on..." he switched gears to get there, and when he did, he again found silence. *Meh...,* he thought. *Sure, you can get to this place when you need things to be as they are, without* needing *it to be different, but that's a pretty lame superpower.* He laughed at the notion of lame superpowers. *Oh, look, I'm still funny up here. HA!* Jack forced. *Still hilarious!* But the reverb of silence that met him took most of the fun out of it. Again, he thought, *Meh. Don't see the point.* He tried again. *Hello?!* Silence. *What the fuck is the point of this place?*

He heard himself answer: "To see things as they are."

Jack froze in place, then flipped back down to his point of view. "Oh my hell," he said, pinching his nose between his eyes. "Okay, fine." He went back up and centered into clarity.

Jack paused and thought about the best words to ask his question. *Is there a way for me to materialize some shit to get the fuck outta here?* He recalled what he had just said. *Is that reverent enough?* The twist of the question was on. *Does a universal ask need to be reverent? Nah.... I'm just going to do this my way. Ooh! Again, I'm still funny up here. Awesome!!!* The perk of him now giving him new life. *Ha. Amazing!* He noted that he was in a ridiculously good mood twice now despite having boots and only underwear to his name. He decided not to worry about his sanity this time and just let it be if it felt good to do so for no other reason. He then thought, *Yes. That is the gauge. When things feel good.*

He thought on the question more. *To materialize something out of nothing should be easy.* He paused to regroup. *It's like divining thoughts like Colton does. He "pre-plans" or forward traps... but there's maybe a different approach.* Jack doubled down on it, now curious about the thing. *So....* He fussed his hair deep in thought. *If I need to... what? Just make something happen, like Colton anticipates, I know how to do that.* He knew he was at its tail. *Colton pre-plans or sees how things will most likely happen then plays on that.* His mental gears fired on max. *So to create the future?* But he knew that didn't *feel* quite right. *Pre-plan... or manifest. That was it!* It was like that vision board thingy he and Em did.

Jack's mind wanted to wander back to those memories, but he tried to stay focused on the task, not the emotional tug of the dead relationship. He remembered how they had put pictures of places they wanted to travel to, which then became places they wanted to travel to before his condition meant he wouldn't be able to.

Jack slowed and stopped. His breathing became almost non-existent, and then he sat back up, returning to the moment. He could feel melancholy wanting to overtake him, but he challenged its approach and stood. A moment to take a stand. He headed for the door, armed with more of what he needed. *Okay… let's see if I can apply those rules to this new game. Vision board.* He rolled with it. *It's like an Ouija board. What are the rules of the game?* He strode out to the road, underwear and all. "Let's do this."

Chapter 27

Avow

Jack met the side of the southbound highway exhausted, mentally drained, and physically sore. He felt each of his past years and the resonance of old, which currently accordioned his tired being. He stuck his thumb out and walked.

Mile after mile of silence passed. There were very few trucks in this part of the world, but Jack couldn't focus on the by-passers and on-lookers. He had committed himself to getting home, which he would do. The pang of the reality struck him. *Home. What home?* He dragged the thought through him with unanswered loneliness, then his mind turned to Thad. He considered what he knew of the guy and how he felt in the man's presence.

Thad had a level-headed brain that Jack found comforting and grounding to his otherwise frenetic way. The sureness of Thad was like calm waters that he wanted to be surrounded by. Jack got the sense that in writing his book, Thad had done some serious personal work. The thought made him realize he had lost the signed copy that was given to him, and it stung. He had read most of it but hadn't fully finished it; besides... that copy had personal meaning, and he was saddened that he no longer had it. Reviewing the ideas within its chapters, he found the topic of "Zenith's Peak" curious. Ya, he understood that as a disabled person, he had a serious story to tell, but the lack of serious tone to the subject was unexpected and alluring. Jack trained further on the thought. *That's the part that's so unique and quite frankly sexy about Thad.* He chased the idea further down the rabbit hole. *He's solid in that way,* he ugged at his deficiencies, *in the ways that I'm not. Fuck... I'm so all over the place. Everything is a huge deal or drama.*

His fault-finding mission was then completed with *I'm a mess. Why can't I just be the person with a normal 9 to 5 job, does normal things, settles down with age, has a retirement plan and a nice life with a nice suburban family.* Jack internally muzzled at this idyllic farce as its truth was made clear. *I'm just never going to have that because that would make me insane.* He chuckled with its truth. He knew he wasn't cut out for that level of banality and schedule. *So...,* Jack pondered, *if I know Thad is that....*

He looked at himself from an outside perspective: long johns, boots, carpet bag, and cold leftovers from when he let Colton take the wheel... well, the math didn't add up in his head. *Why would he want to be involved with this?* He doubled down to further skewer himself with his shortcomings. *Especially when this mess has such a short expiration date.* This was Jack's way of giving in when he felt his future wasn't any good. Clubbed. Sidelined. Handicapped. The last word struck a resonance.

But he's handicapped. The thought felt new to him. *But maybe it would be okay? Maybe, the less functioning part of his life that he was about to enter wasn't an ending with Thad. At least not in the way it was with Em. Maybe, it's a leveling — meeting Thad where he is?!"*

This idea gave new life and purpose to what might yet come. Suddenly Jack was awake and rousing on the inspiring possibility. Thinking back on his last moment with Major and the mother of love and her twin, the angel of death, *maybe that's a plus. A way for us to show up for one another that someone who lives on the proper side of okay wouldn't be able to....* The possibilities animated Jack.

Maybe... he could find an eye-to-eye, shoulder-to-shoulder partner in Thad? *Ugh... it feels like too much to hope for and yet, at the same time, a newfound revelation and goal. Holy shit.* The memory of Major's words danced across his new internal vision board. *Broken like me.* But Jack felt dissatisfied with the way that floated in the air. *But not broken — whole maybe?* That landed like a lie. *Whole. Ha.* Jack felt the sting of it. *Jesus in a fucking rowboat, how am I whole?* He slammed the door on that thought to move on and reclaim the broken beliefs about himself.

It was just past 3:00 PM when a driver finally stopped, but it wasn't a trucker. Instead, the driver was a nice old grandmother-type. A fact that Jack found very odd, but at this point, he didn't care. He just needed help. He was tired and was having trouble walking. His legs felt disconnected — but luckily from fatigue and not a more problematic neurological issue. However, he was aware that the former typically entered into the latter. When the woman pulled over, he was almost brought to tears.

"Are you in trouble?" the elderly woman queried. Jack deflated in the truth of it and confirmed her suspicions.

"I dunno," he paused and put his hands on his hips. "Ya," he finally confessed. "I think I kinda am."

She mused with the response, then put the car in park and exited the vehicle. "Let me get a look at ya," she said, rounding the far side of the car, a move that caught Jack off guard.

He quickly reviewed how to be in front of her, but it was happening so fast he didn't have time to access a shapeshift, but it also seemed that that's what the moment was asking for. Ultimately Jack's brain melted and fuzzed with inaction, and he just stood there like a dope — no pretense, and she met him where he was.

"Take off your hat in the presence of a woman, dear."

Jack was instantly embarrassed and armed the cowboy hat off of him quickly, then straightened his stance as if being inspected by an army sergeant. "Sorry, ma'am." He stood at attention as she got the first good look at his deranged face, its catch visible in her reaction.

"Oh," she stopped advancing. "Are you okay?" Her reaction made Jack put his hand to his temple. A habit of shame.

"Uh. Yes. Sorry, ma'am." Jack didn't know why he was apologizing for his disfigurement. She then eyed him more closely.

"What happened to you? Why don't you have proper clothes? Or is this a fashion choice for you?" Her comment made Jack laugh and loosen up.

"Most certainly not, ma'am. I was robbed a few days back and had been trying to make it to...." He wasn't sure how to end that sentence, so he just stopped talking and looked at his feet.

The older woman seemed to be getting a good sense of him, as was her objective. She seemed well worn and no dummy. Jack noticed the bulge of a gun in her dress coat. Seeing his worn condition was genuine and that his trudge was grave and downtrodden, she softened and offered help. "Well, I can give you a lift if you like. I'm heading down valley to Wiley if you care for it."

Jack was overwhelmed at the extension of humanity to his cause, and he had to fight back tears, saying, "I can't pay you money or anything. My wallet and everything is gone." He hung his head.

"Well pitter-patter son." She eye-shot him while also being moved by his weather-battered emotions. "Get in."

Jack did so, acutely aware that he might smell up the enclosed cab. He searched for whiffs of betrayal, but there was nothing he could do about it. He collapsed into the front seat, trying to make himself as small as possible to limit the intrusion. His everything felt apologetic to who he was in the moment.

"The name is Bonnie, but most around here call me Grams." That raised the question in Jack's head as to whether that stood for Gramma or grams as in the measuring device. The car pulled onto the highway.

"Uh, hi Jack," he finally managed. He was a rumple of still and skin, his embarrassment of who he was in that moment palpable, and he was tired beyond imagining.

"What's your story, Jack?" she mused, then followed with, "Are you okay? Did they hurt ya?"

Jack continued to look out the window at the passing trees trying to decipher if *they* hurt him or if he did, as per his typical self-destructive ways. There was fault to be found only on his side. "I'm okay." His gaze didn't budge as he clapped onto the carpet bag in his lap for safety.

Jack noted he was feeling super vulnerable and thought it was okay to allow himself this moment to feel it. He had been working hard to abandon safety, but that didn't mean that safe didn't still feel safe. With closed eyes, he depressed into a state that renders one open: gratitude – a place of trying to be open when his mind seemed closed to its capture. A passenger behind a windscreen, Jack was closed and tight, yet there was beauty just beyond the pane of glass.

"Do you want to put your bag in the backseat maybe?" Her question made him realize how tight he was holding onto it, for it was all he had in the world.

"No, ma'am. Thank you." It was too big of a risk.

"Well, I only have about 90 minutes. Like I said, to Wiley, but maybe you can catch a bus to Prince George or something from there?"

He involuntarily let slip, "I don't have any money."

"Ah, yes…. Well, then, don't you mind." A half mile passed. "Are you hungry?" she smiled. He didn't know but reviewed what he had eaten today. A cold can of spaghetti and then ravioli in the same manner back at the abandoned building.

"Mostly thirsty, ma'am," he said. She pulled over the car and fetched a bottle of sport drink from the trunk.

"Here. Gotta stay hydrated in this heat." She wasn't wrong, and the summers up this way in British Columbia had been taking a beating with the continued onslaught of climate change. It was never supposed to be upward of thirty degrees Celsius in this part of the world, yet now it happened with greater frequency. A thing that struck fear into the hearts of those who were paying attention to the wildfires that grew worse with each passing year.

He drank half the bottle upon opening it, then settled back in his seat, carpet bag still clutched.

Ninety minutes later, Jack was awakened by the old woman opening his door. "Listen, son, I can see you're not in great shape, but I don't have much." She looked around the gas station. "Here are a few dollars to get yourself something, but is there anyone I can call?" The thought of this animated Jack.

"Yes. Can I please use your phone?" When she didn't respond immediately, he offered, "Here. My bag… it's all I have." Jack scrambled out of the car. "You can hold onto it while I use your phone." His eye remained hopeful for a yes.

"Of course. Here." She handed him her old phone. It wasn't anything fancy, so that essentially clinched the deal.

Jack fumbled, trying to dial quickly, then heard the line pick up. "Hello!" Jack practically shouted. His all needed the mooring of something familiar and grounded.

"Oh my God, Jack! Where are you?" Thad questioned.

"I know, I know." Silence. "I'm okay." He checked his surroundings. "I'm in Wiley." He didn't know why he felt shame.

"Jack…," Thad said with care. "Mate…." Silence. "What's going on? For real." Silence.

"Ahhhh… I dunno. I'm such a wreck right now." The bucket of dread he had his head plunged into wouldn't release, and he fought the situation. A fight that was tearing him apart. *Not like this,* he thought, refusing to state more truth. It was too shameful to mess up this badly at the beginning of a relationship when there was no proof to the contrary of what currently was, which was messy.

"Jack. It's okay. Just tell me what's going on."

"Well… it's just like I texted you. I ran out of money then got robbed." Silence. "I…."

"Can I send you some money somehow?" This coming from Thad was all he needed to hate on himself all the more.

How fucking embarrassing. God, I'm pathetic. I'm too old for this shit! Jack cursed internally on repeat.

"Please don't… I mean, I appreciate the offer, but I think I got it figured out." The lie was as putrid as his inability to accept help or be honest. There was a long silence between them.

"Jack?"

"Ya?"

"Let me help you. It would be the kindest thing you could do, to accept it. I want you here."

Internally, Jack was being ripped in two. He looked at the cash he had clutched in his hand from the old woman, and as he said the following, he loathed himself, "Thad, you're so sweet. I'm okay. You know… I got it handled. Listen, I'm on a lady's phone, and I should probably get it back to her."

"Okay." Beat. "But please call or text me when you can. Any idea of when I'll see you? I assume you're still coming here?"

"Oh ya." His ears were red hot. "I mean…," he stammered. "If that's still cool?"

"Oh, Jack… I already said I want you here." He switched gears. "Just get here when you can."

"I will." The sentiment and pull of three little unsaid words hung in the air as the men hung up their phones.

CHAPTER 28

INSTITUTE

Jack thanked the woman with a warm hug. The twenty-five dollars she gave him meant the world. It meant he might be okay for one more day. He would get there one day at a time, and he was right on track so far.

He dipped into the convenience store at the gas station and bought some jerky, canned meals, and water, mostly for the refillable plastic bottles. The pangs of shame were still slipping off him when he sat against the side of the building with the sun in his face. Meeting the day's rays, he put his head back and closed his eye briefly. The good eye burned black red against the dark, the other side blank. Jack tipped his hat back and forth, playing with the rays and seeing what they might offer. He made sun spots and circles appear at points; then, he reached for his clutch of marbles. He held them one by one, admiring the beauty of their flaws. The pecked-out bits and cracks tinkered with the light as it hit those special chips of mar. The light lent beauty to those places. He twirled them between his knuckles like Chinese Baoding balls, where they spiraled bright yellow and gold reflections all around him. Jack laughed at the simple beauty of the thing. He rested back against the building. *Can I make something out of nothing? The Ouija Board thing. The fucking manifesting board thingy....* He tried to remember the terms of the game as presented to him by Em.

"No, stupid." Em was not amused at his lack of proper input on the craft project. "We decided we would put the travel together over here...." She dramatically pointed. "And the relationship goals over here." They both smiled externally and grumbled internally.

"Okay, I have Rome and Norway...."

"Rome and Norway?" Em proffered. "No... like, think more exotic, like Africa or Tahiti." Jack's face was flat and salty.

"But... okay." He consented and then searched for photos of other places from the stack of magazines on the table. Em beamed with victorious delight. He returned to the task. "So what are the rules here exactly?"

"Rules? Like, what do you mean?"

Jack shrugged defensively. "You know... like, how do we do this? What are the rules?"

"God, Jack, you're so weird." Her words greatly confused him.

"So you just stick this shit up on here... and what?"

"It's like that Oprah thing. You know, with the gratitude way of living and stuff."

Since there was a pause in the conversation, Jack said, "Okay... and...."

"You know. Envision it on this board, and it'll come to your life if you're positive and live with gratitude.

Jack's interest flatlined, and he just wanted to drink a beer.

"Ah... a beer." Jack pained back to the present moment with the memory. "Fuck... that would be so awesome." His mind flashed with the pleasure of cold beers and hot summer days. He recounted his change. "Two dollars, fifteen cents." He realized life couldn't afford him the pleasure.

He thought on, eyes closed, back against the gas station wall. *So, no, really... how does that work?* The chase was on. *You just stick the images on the vision board, and what?* Nothing new was coming to him. *Then... just wait until...?* He wasn't getting any further into the equation than that. Hitting a blank wall, he popped into his higher consciousness to analyze the thing. He closed his eyes to train on it.

He slowed himself, *Vision board. Vision. To make something. To generate or create. To create forward or imagine. To create. But create what? To create a wish.* The torrent of visuals that came to Jack's mind with the notion of a wish was what made him land just there and not move off it. *A wish.* There was energy there. *What are the properties of a wish. What is a wish?* He let it float to understand its buoyancy. *A wish, a whisper.* He cleared himself from distraction. *Something lighter than a whisp. A puff of air that carries a message.* He stopped at the word message. *A message to whom?* Jacked stopped there. *A message to whom?* Nothing new was coming. *Like a message in a bottle but energetically.*

He broke down the rules for the vision board game. *One, find the right images. Two, stick them on a board. Three, wait for the magic, I guess? What are the properties of this wish? Delicate. Whisp-like. Like the process of baking something delicate. Like a souffle.* He reviewed the pull of the thing and checked it for lies. *Like baking a souffle, how do we do that? Mix the ingredients, pour it into a pan… I guess this is the sticking it on the board part.*" He was seeing what other associations might manifest. *Wait. Then?* he questioned himself. *What? Wait. Just wait for the dessert, then eat.* Jack knew he didn't have enough steps, but he immediately looked at it differently, *Like a prayer….* He shuddered with the church association with it. *But in both instances, you simply do the "putting things together, putting it on or in something"… then wait.* Jack felt a different weight of the word wait. He stopped. *Wait. What's there?* He paused, checking for more. *Wait. Souffle.* He realized the answer. *It's the waiting part. That's where the chemistry or* magic *is.* He smiled at the realization but knew not to stop there and checked for more. *Wait… what else is there?* Jack listened as a car drove by, then listened to the sound of a prop plane far off in the sky, the smell of the grass, and felt the sun on his face. *Wait. Await. Delay. Expect. Linger. Remain. Trust.* There it was, and he knew it the second he thought it. *It's trust.* He pushed on to search for more. *Trust. Is trust faith?*

His gut immediately confirmed "n o."

Holy shit. Why?

He was on the verge of the thing when a guy gently nudged him with his boot. "Excuse me, mind watching my bike while I use the restroom?" Jack's head still churned from his daydream. "I'll be right back," the man said, entering the store.

Jack came more fully to realize the situation. Someone had just handed him a bike. *What to do? Jack… make a decision quick.* He remained seated. The guy came back in a few minutes and scuttled on. *Fuck*, Jack thought, standing to dust himself off as he headed back to walking, not riding, down the highway.

He sallied on. *Trust. It's trust in the process. What is trust?*

He knew he was at least now getting out of the less populated part of the province. There was some measure of reassurance in that, and the closer he got to Prince George, the better. After that, it would be fairly populated with more opportunities.

Colton sparked to life a bit with the idea of it. "Trust, as in… trust me." Jack laughed, knowing Colton was often the one person in the world he couldn't trust. *But it's the trusting part. Fuck!* He saw the thing. *It's like with frustration. This step is the "not doing," which is the "doing." The yang way of North America might understand it explained this way better. It's in the letting it go and trusting that you've done your part.* Then, *a watched pot never boils* entered his mind. "Exactly," he responded and then questioned where it came from because he could not tolerate yet some other source of information gurgling up to the top in this moment. He chose to ignore it.

Souffle. Chemistry or magic happens behind closed doors and out of sight of our mind. That is the law of the universe. Jack opened to it. *The human mind can, at best, package it up and ship it out, but it's not that which it delivers. The wisher or one making something happen energetically must only be half the equation. Any effort to the contrary will deliver something not in alignment with your intention.* Jack figured that once you put the souffle into the oven, the "No peeking" part made the chemistry work. *Noted,* he thought as he walked on.

The northern summer sun was beginning its slide into the night when Jack felt the attack coming on.

Twinge.

"Fuck." But this was by no means a surprise. Jack had been doing all the wrong things for his condition, and he knew it. He knew he couldn't push himself this hard without serious repercussions. He assessed his options.

Jack figured he couldn't try and hail a ride while in the midst of an attack, leaving him with one option. Set up camp for the night; at least this time, he had a few more supplies, and the tarp he took from the abandoned building gave him some comfort about pitching a make-shift tent. He scooted into the trees just off the road, where he quickly chose two trees to put a rope between and lay the tarp on. He then took the edges and did his best to secure them, essentially making an A-frame.

Twinge. The wriggle of the thing made itself known in his right arm, but Jack didn't fight it. He slowed. Then he slowed more carefully, laying out his carpet bag. Jack grabbed a water bottle to clean himself out to avoid any accidents in his only pair of long johns. He did his best to keep the feelings of being a failure off his mind because there were times, such as now, when having a medical episode was, to his mind, a cosmic failure of his being. He then corrected a thought because, if nothing else, he now *knew* that if it weren't for his neurological storms, he would never have found the other side of him. He took that in with breaths that assured his state. The undulating and writhing of his body began.

"Stand, Jack," he told himself quietly. "Be here."

The thing then animated his spine. It slithered and pulled. It bent him in half, then released. Jack listened for what it might offer. *Come*, Jack thought, a command he understood the meaning of more and more with time. He followed his instructions to sit cross-legged at the shore. He allowed that and then dipped into the other side's being after only a few seconds of the sensation of falling. He took in air and care as his cosmic feelers unfurled to the max.

Ong Namo Guru Dev Namo, Jack said silently on repeat, *I bow to the creative wisdom. I bow to the divine teacher within.* Within minutes Jack had arrested the beast with sleep. The quiet of the night swept over him and his still presence, sweeping him under until the first rays of a new day.

CHAPTER 29

TAKEN ABACK

The following morning was cool but not cold — the ideal outdoor sleeping conditions. Jack awoke feeling so much better after the long night's sleep. He did a quick systems check, but his attack was reasonably mild, and there seemed to be little residue. He noted that he felt oddly optimistic.

Weird, he thought, not trusting what he was being served. He readied for the day, put on a clean t-shirt, ate a can of cold pasta, and repacked his carpet bag while the notion of "simple" tugged at him as joy.

With all systems firing, he was ready to meet the road, and he set the intention of getting to Prince George this day. *How do I do this?* wandered through his mind as he met the roadside and stuck out his thumb. He reviewed the course of action again. *Step one, identify that which is your heart's desire.* He thought, in this case, this step was pretty easy. *Just get me to people and....* The counter thought immediately struck that he wished for people and human interaction. His brain sloshed and fuzzed, balancing out the raging oppositions within him. *Ugh... why is this so?* He couldn't quite get to "imbalanced" as the tug-of-war sacked some clarity he was trying to send out to the ethers.

Fine. He reset to clarify to the trees. *Fine. Ya. People. Bleh, but whatever. Today I'll ask for it and accept help when it arrives.* Jack's internal discomfort was the same, but at least he clarified that which he sought. *Okay... clarity in what we want.* He walked another mile, flipped up to view the thing from a clearer, less noisy angle, and finally arrived at... *A ride. A safe ride to Prince George... and maybe someone can help me out with...* he assessed his current situation, *...food, money, shelter.* He realized how much he currently inhabited in survival mode as he fought back the creep of depression that lowered him back into himself.

Step two, action or do a thing. He clarified to his mind what that meant for him in the moment. *Doing it. Hitchhiking, making an effort to have it known to others my plan and bring them on board.* He mentally checked the box. *Step three is the....* He reviewed his final thoughts on the subject. *The trusting. Trusting.* He plunged in for a deeper look at that word because it was causing something within him, something he thought he should view from a higher place. He flipped up to his brain attic. *Trusting. Verb. To trust.* He remembered the surprising answer from his gut regarding faith versus trust. *The trust of others, noun. I'm trusting in others. Verb.* The auditory chase in his brain caught. *Faith. Noun. The faith I have in others. Singular. Me. My action. My faith... but it....* He couldn't get the thing to roll over into a verb. *I'm faith-ing?* That clearly didn't work. The realization was getting clearer. *So faith has half the power linguistically. It can only be a noun, whereas trust can be a verb or a noun.* He had a small a-ha. He chased on, *So...,* he requestioned the thing, *...is that why trust feels so much more grounded?* He noted how the resonance of it landed in him. *Trust. There's solidity there, whereas faith feels airy, not grounded. Hmmm....*

As the day leaned into heat, Jack stripped off his coat and shoved it in the bag, a move that allowed him enough access to the present to note that more and more cars were on the highway.

So if I have faith, that's just me. Me having faith is a singular one-sided action. He checked himself for lies but found none. *But trust.* He was echoing with the resonance, rolling it around to see how the word *felt* as it was articulated within him. *Trust feels more like a two-way street. I trust you, and you trust me.* Jack noted the subtle difference in energetic exchange.

As Jack was lost in thought, a semi-truck blared its horn from behind him, immediately delivering him back to the moment.

"Jesus jogging in the afterlife!" he burst forth as he tried to calm his rapidly beating heart. "Holy shit...." He bent over and grabbed his knees, hoping to slow his breath. *Good thing I didn't have coffee this morning,* he thought, believing that he would have shit his pants if that had been the case. He turned around to see the beast ten feet behind him. The driver jumped out.

"Are you that guy walking across Canada to raise awareness for MS?" Jack's brain pan-fried and sizzled as nothing in what he just heard made any sense to him.

"I'm sorry?" Jack came back with.

"You know… like on the news. Been a big story about that guy… you know… what's his name?" He searched the clouds for a name, but none came. "That guy…." he snapped his fingers a few times, trying to jog the thing.

"Afraid I haven't been tuning into the news lately… so I'm not sure," Jack said while still hopeful that this person wasn't afraid of him in his current condition.

"Well, ya look just like him." The man was still trying to rouse the name. "You know… the actor…." But then he got a closer look at Jack's face and dropped it. "You need a lift or something?" The 'or something' was doing a lot of heavy lifting in that statement. Jack generally knew what that meant. It usually means, do you need medical help?

"That would be great. I got robbed a few towns back, and my car died." Jack took a chance. "And well… I'm just kinda fucked right now. Spent the past two nights sleeping in the woods." The trucker paused and looked him over. It was easy to tell he wasn't lying. He looked like he had been through exactly what he was claiming.

The trucker approached him. "Do you have a gun on you?" A question that caught Jack off-guard.

"Uh, no." He repositioned his bag. "This is all I have in the world right now." Jack opened the bag for the guy to check it out. It was a rat's nest of discarded junk, the kind of junk that one might find along their way and believe is useful for potential survival skills. The trucker exhaled, clearly in cautious disbelief.

"The name is Pete." He paused and eyed Jack for an energetic read. "You running from the law or something?" A comment that made Jack stifle a chuckle.

"No sir… uh, no Pete… and hi, ya… the name's Jack. Nice to meet you." They stood there for another minute until Jack couldn't take it anymore. "Please. I need help. My story is legit. I don't have a wallet or a phone…." his sentence trailed off with the truthful pang.

"Listen…," Pete said, clearly not in the mood for monkey business. "I don't take on trouble, but I can see you might be in a way." A comment that made Jack hopeful.

"I won't be any trouble. You can put me in the cargo area or anything… I just really need to make it to Prince George today."

"Fine," Pete finally said. "But I'm locking you in the cab then shaking you down for anything stolen before I dump you in town." Jack couldn't help but share his excitement and gratitude for the man's generosity.

Pete unlocked the back section of the cab, flipped the light on, and gave a few cursory directions, then put Jack in and locked the door behind him. Jack made himself comfortable.

"Riding in style," Jack noted as he stretched out.

"Uh… mind getting the fuck off my bed?" the speakers from above boomed. Jack hadn't realized the two cameras that were eyeing his every move. He sat up straight and moved to a small table and chair.

"Sorry, Pete! Wasn't sure…." Jack, at that point, stopped talking. The behemoth vehicle lumbered onto the highway, and in no time, they were heading south. By Jack's calculations, they would be there by noon. He internally woo hoo'd and relaxed into the process, thinking, *Well, that was easy.*

CHAPTER 30

RETICULATE

Sure enough, just as Jack had calculated, they pulled into the Prince George area just after noon. Pete unlocked the cab and let Jack out.

"You going to be okay, Jack?"

He was blinking his eyes to adjust to the outdoors. "Ya, but would it be okay if I borrowed your phone for a second, just to send a quick text?" A question that Pete met with a shrug as he handed Jack his phone making sure to stay very close to his side. Jack typed in Thad's number and sent:

> Made it to Prince George! Hope all is well there. I'm doing fine. Weirdly, kinda enjoying the trek. Very Outward Bound. Lol. Although I may never be able to eat canned pasta ever again. Anyhow, I'd love to chat tonight if you're around. It's noon now, and I think I'll hang out in town and rest until tomorrow, then continue. Big kiss to you and Joy. Xo Jack

He turned to Pete and thanked him for his generosity. Pete fished some loonies from a pocket and said, "Take care of yourself," leaving Jack to calculate that it was roughly a 9-hour drive from where he was to Vancouver, where he could finally catch a ferry to Gambier.

"Let's test the science of the thing," Jack noted, upping his game. He headed over to the center of town, hoping to find a park with a tree to sit under. He needed a minute not to be on the move.

After an hour of wandering around and taking in the sights, Jack found a city park with a fountain and grass. He put his back against a tree and relaxed into the moment. He didn't want to think anymore today, and he was greatly missing his mokee pipe and weed. The late afternoon sun was a perfect match for Jack's spirits, and he enjoyed just being with it and listening to the kids play off in the distance. It was a sound that comforted him, almost as if he had a family by the extension of proximity.

Just past 5:00 PM, Jack decided to see if he could figure out something to eat. He reviewed, "How am I going to survive on so little?" He could then feel the rumble of Colton's past hinting at "the kindness of strangers." He both hated and pumped on that rumble. It's song. It was the most exciting call of all, and it terrified him. "That's one reason why it's easier to be alone." Jack gnarled on. The twist of it was too well known for Jack's taste. Some things are just better left behind in youth. He brushed the thing aside and wandered across town, focusing on not getting into trouble.

Another hour later, Jack was tired of figuring out how and what to eat. A dive bar came into view near the outskirts of town, and he figured he was damn near about out of options. He dipped in the front door and sat in the tempestuous air. The dimly lit red walls offered dank festivity as the Stones 'Light Me Up' accompanied his mood. Jack reviewed the menu and options, wondering how far he could stretch $10.

"Any Happy Hour menu?" Jack asked the bartender.

"Ya… we gots Toonie draughts and dollar wings. Whatcha have?"

Jack remembered he had some other leftover change in his bag from that nice lady, then mentally math-shuffled and asked for five wings and a beer. Minutes later, his order arrived, and he savored the first sip like it was the finest thing he had ever tasted. The coldness hit his tired throat as the swirl and promise of better things to come swam across his being. Jack held the cold glass to his forehead and exhaled everything. He knew in a minute everything would be merrier — something he could use in the middle of a day like today.

"Aren't you the guy who's doing the cross-country, Terry Fox run thing?"

Jack turned to address the questioner, who seemed to be a well-worn version of a pageant queen. At first, the question put Jack on his heels, but then he reregistered the idea from what Pete had told him about the "Terry Fox" guy.

That was the one thing about Jack's design. People always mistook his big presence for being someone famous. It was an immutable energetic thing that Jack had a dual relationship with. On the one hand, he loved it because it would open doors for him. He understood that this was a privilege, but the part he hated about it was in public spaces; he always felt like he had a target on his back, one that advertised, "Come bother me. Yes, please make me tell you that I'm not a special person. Just some rando that everyone thinks is someone else." He sunk into the thought further. "Just some rando." His index finger was running the temple scar track, a habit when he was sometimes deep in thought.

Jack broke from his mental stream. "Ah, hi." He purposely didn't deny or confirm what she was thinking. He needed all the credit he could get in life at this point, and he wasn't dumb. Jack knew how this worked. And how this worked is what Colton made absolute mastery of.

"That's my husband Doug, and I'm Sherrie. We knew you might be around." Jack feigned looking around, joking with a "who me?" expression, but then laughed and gave up the joke. He knew his facial deformity would eventually give him up anyhow.

"The name's Jack. I'm just passing through." He turned to face Sherrie and watched for the catch in her attention when he turned to face her.

"Oh," she said as the registration of Jack's scars took, but then continued unfettered with, "Well, it's nice to meet you." She paused, searching for something in the air. "You look just like that guy… you know the one I mean. He was on that show…."

Jack was all too familiar with this game. The "ooh, let me tell you who I think you look like" game.

"Ah… can't think of it right now. You look just like…."

Doug strode over for a, "Hello, how ya now. Get up this way much?" Jack wasn't sure how he was to be tethered to the geography he was indicating.

"Ya, I get up this way a bit. Trying to get to Gambier, though." Sherrie wandered into his personal space and located herself on the stool next to his. Her barstool position of not-cross-legged was apparent and telling.

"FUCK HER," Colton mentally offered, making Jack internally eye roll. "I bet she has drugs. People like her have drugs… ask her."

"So, what's your story, Jack?" Sherrie's chest brushed him as she reached for the bowl of bar peanuts, her middle-aged styling betraying that she hadn't redone her look in a decade or more. The 90'sness of her sweater was doing its best to be on point. An effort that almost hit its mark in the lurid lighting of the red hall.

"No, really," Colton pushed further down the broken path. "Ask her. See if she's got anything." Jack paused to refocus, but again Colton tried, "You know you want to fuck her."

Jack cut the cord and then replied to her, "Well… I was…." Jack tried to come up with something clever. However, he couldn't find the right story in the moment, so he got honest and took a chance on humanity. "To be honest, I've lost everything. My car broke down back up north, and someone took my stuff." He stared at the ceiling, trying to come up with what to say next, as Doug took the barstool on the other side of him, a move that put Jack on guard. "I had a few bucks, so… well, it's been a long few days, and I just wanted a beer and some hot food."

Doug was seated and staring at Jack's face. "They done did that, man?" A series of similar comments that Jack could never understand. How is it possible that what Doug was staring at was fresh?

Jack never could comprehend how everyone thought that. *It's an old scar!* Jack thought, then said, "Nah. That's old. From when I was a kid. Where are you guys from?"

Doug picked up the line, "Just touring around. You know, summer vacation. Thought we'd drop in on Prince George." Pause. "I went to high school here for a bit. We live in Moncton now."

"Ah… the Merry Maritimes."

Colton winked at Sherrie, who muffled a coo, then turned to face Doug and said, "Gotta love it there. How you out this way now?"

Jack was just fine letting things be, but the alcohol was hitting, which, combined with the turbines of dopamine Colton was measuring into Jack, had sway. Colton then cock-nodded into Doug, testing his self-assuredness. Doug didn't shy.

"Noted," Colton thought.

"Hey, listen," Doug started. "You wanna maybe hit the men's room?"

Colton rumbled with the invitation as Jack did his best to hit pause. "For…?" was the best response the two inside him could formulate. Doug did a side wink as he flicked at his fingers the way one does to a baggie of coke to formulate quantity and quality.

The world slowed, and Jack took the wheel, thinking, *Okay… so what's it going to be? This next decision isn't nothing.* His main concern was that it was unknown how far down a person who had already hit rock bottom could go. Does it matter when the only way left to go is up? What does it matter if he gets messy with this crew? Besides, who knows what "good" might come out of it. Jack knew how to level the playing field of the decision-making process. He flipped up for a clearer perspective.

A little help here, me? He wasn't minding the silliness of his beer lens that he was viewing everything from behind. The next thoughts of clarity then met him. *Jack! Are you fucking stupid?* He laughed and rolled with the thought. He sought further clarity. *Play this forward. How does this end? Are you even attracted to these two, or are you just bored and looking to blow up your life? — Because why not, right?* Jack pulled himself up short for the case being made for sanity. *What do you have to lose? You know… besides, what little you have left in terms of credibility with Thad, your teetering health issues, and your general sense of purpose.* Jack hated this part but also knew it was better to have found this stop-gap now than four days from now after a bender that would cripple him in a thousand new hideous ways. *Fuck,* he thought as he finalized his decision.

"Nah… I mean, I wanna, but I have no place to go, and I'm still trying to make it south in the next few days. Got a hot date waiting for me back home."

"Well…," Sherrie leaned in, "you could come with us." Her tone was leery and making its way to bleary while she gulped on her cheap white wine spritzer.

Gah! Jack punted into himself. *What is it with me and couples?* He turned to her and clarified, "Sounds fun, but I gotta scoot."

Doug then grabbed his hand. "Well, here." Jack felt something in the palm of his hand. "A little something for the road. My cell number's on the card if you care for it." The middle-aged man then fat-winked at Jack, putting an arm around him in a "fatherly" hug while his lounge lizard ways chuckwalla-ed in earnest. Jack fast-peeked at what he had from the guy, and sure enough, a mostly empty bag of drugs and a business card.

Bleh…, Jack internally choked. *Just get me outta here.*

Jack said a quick farewell and departed, notably not returning the baggie. He thought, *Who knows… could come in handy at some point,* Either because of "Fuck it!" – a thought that Colton internally cheered on – or to get something of value in exchange for it.

Leaving the building, Jack rounded the corner and hoovered the entire contents of the baggie without so much as a thought. He leaned against the building as Colton thought, *Oh fuck yes.* Jack then headed across the parking lot toward a lit gas station a few blocks away.

CHAPTER 31

SOUSED

By the time he pulled up to the gas station pay phone, he was high as fuck and wondered what he had just taken. Jack dialed the operator to place a collect call to Thad.

"Hey, handsome. Nice to hear from you. I was hoping we'd have time to connect tonight. Kinda sounds like you got a lot going on," he laughed jokingly, making Jack fluster.

"Ah… ya… it's kind of hard to explain, but I appreciate you letting me handle it my way. Besides, I'm enjoying this."

Thad prompted, "This? As in us getting to know one another long distance or you having your time to trek across B.C. while I'm sitting here wanting you in my arms?"

"Well," Jack flushed and laughed. "Both." He eyed the ground, feeling stuff he couldn't quite put his finger on. "Oh, and full disclosure…." Jack was feeling free of inhibitions. "I'm super fucking high right now." He then started to laugh, which made Thad laugh also.

"Oh! Are ya now, mate?" Thad said with a laugh. "How's that now? What are you up to?" Jack noted that Thad wasn't thrown by this news in the least. He wanted to know more of Thad's story.

The jolly moment was not what Jack was expecting when he made the call, but it was time to start taking down walls if he wanted to make an honest go of a relationship with the man. It was time Thad knew the real him. Jack laughed heavenward, "Well… I had a few bucks and just wanted a beer and a warm meal, right? So I found a place with super cheap happy hour items where this couple from the Maritimes… well actually, he's from here but lives in Moncton now, anyhow, they were legit trying to take me home."

Thad cut in, "See! You gotta watch who you get all that around." He was joking, but it somehow landed a bit annoyingly because of the taint of the 'Father knows best' insecure position it was coming from, but Jack was just pleased that at this point, they were still good.

"Anyhow...," Jack pulled himself back onto the road of the conversation. "They baited me."

"Did what now?" Thad was stumped.

"They baited me... you know... like when they give you a bump." Jack quickly reviewed whether he thought Thad would know what a bump was. "To, you know... kinda get you going, then once you're high, you're easier to pick up."

"Ah yes... that old trick, but never heard it called that." The statement put Jack on his heels. At no time did Thad ask what a bump was, so clearly he knew about drugs, but he was also familiar with this type of behavior of how to bed someone more easily. None of this was lost on Jack, whose head was spinning with abandon while Colton revved in the background.

Jack refocused, "So... have you ever partied? You don't seem like the type." He quickly flapped more at him with, "I mean... you're just so scholarly and appropriate all the time." Thad burst out laughing.

"Oh, mate! Jack! We really are just getting to know one another, ain't we?" Jack was super intrigued. Maybe he could show him a little of his Colton side? "Just remember, my legs might not work at 100%, but the rest of me does. That I promise." This comment motored Colton further into a much higher gear.

"Oh really?" Jack said. His curiosity piquing hard.

"Ya. After my mom died, I kinda... you know, just laid into that part of life some. Like, fuck it. Let's go! Felt like I wanted to *live* because she didn't." Pause. "Dunno, Jack. I think it's part of how I dealt with it by blurring life for a bit."

Jack softened hearing this. "I'm sorry, Thad. That must have been tough." A silence hung in the air for a moment.

"It was, but again… so much of that made this life for me possible. It's what began the journey for me."

"And that's where you got a lot of your material for the book?"

"Well, sure," Thad replied. "It's just that I've had to make adjustments and decisions, even at a young age. They weren't always right, but each of them got me to where I am today, and that's not something I'd be willing to trade."

"Trade." Jack lofted into the conversation to see what might present itself. He was curious if Thad also knew the word to mean 'cheap date' or 'hooker.'

"You're trade," Thad teased back, significantly lifting Jack's spirits.

He fucking knows what "trade" means! he thought to himself. *Amazing!* Not knowing this side of the man, Jack loved that he could joke like this with Thad on this level. Colton stepped up and offered, *Tell him you want to fuck him.* Jack's eye rolled and suppressed the impulse. *Do I tell him now?* Jack questioned himself. He did a quick gut check. *Can Thad handle this conversation?*

"y e s" was offered to him, and he knew that was true, so he waded in….

"So Thad, there's something I've been meaning to tell you." Jack grabbed his forehead.

"Ya Jack? And for the record, there's something I've been meaning to tell you as well." This information coming from Thad was both relieving and concerning. "But go on."

Jack steadied himself and trusted whatever might come next. "I was a sex worker for the better part of my twenties."

"Oh, hot!" Thad said. "Tell me about it."

Out of all the possible responses Thad might have had to this news, this was the one possibility Jack didn't see coming. "Really? You're okay with that?"

"Well…." Now Thad was on the ropes. "I mean, ya. I like you, and I'm getting to know you… and… I'm not here to judge you, Jack."

Jack interjected, "It's just that… well… I've always been brushed off after people find out about me."

"Well, that's stupid," Thad commented flatly. "Kinda like throwing the baby out with the bath water. Besides, I like a guy who's been to fuck school." Jack burst out laughing.

"Oh, honey… then we're going to get along just fine. Now, what was it you wanted to tell me?"

He heard Thad take a breath. "I'm HIV+." Pause. "I hope that's not a problem."

Jack internally dared to hope for what might be something true for them both and then put forward, "Tell you what, Thad. We can be problem-free together. How's that sound?"

Jack could hear Thad's exhale as his potential love confirmed, "Like the best fucking idea ever."

CHAPTER 32

OOMPH

The men spoke on the phone until sun-up. Both were alight with possibility and their hearts' purpose: to love.

"You should see where I am," Jack said, watching the clouds catch the red fire glow of morning. "Wish I had my cell to send you a photo."

"So, Jack…." Pause. "Will you accept my help with full disclosure? My help is very self-serving because I want you here and not there. Would you be willing to do me that favor?"

Jack's tug of war resumed, and with the fading effects of what he snorted last night wearing off, well, he just felt tired, and the thought of being in a warm bed after a long shower wasn't something he could say no to any longer. "Okay," he said softly.

"Really!?" You won't be mad to shortcut the walkabout thing you're doing?" Thad was expectant.

Jack chose his following words carefully. "I'm just used to being able to take care of myself… and… well… I just feel so pathetic right now. I'm embarrassed, Thad. I'm embarrassed that I need help." Pause. "But I do. What do you suggest?"

"Awesome. Hold on." Jack could hear whooshes and pings of e-messaging and texts in the background as Thad drummed on his keyboard, sending hope into the ethers. "Actually… is there a phone number listed on the pay phone where you are? Can I call you back?" Jack was a bit confused, and the discomfort of his body and situation were waking up with the day. Jack searched for the phone's number and then read it to Thad. They hung up, and Jack, standing at the pay phone, felt the part of an expectant morning drug deal. He knew how this looked to strangers.

Finally, the phone rang, and Jack lunged at the ring of opportunity. Maybe there was hope? "Ahoy!" Jack sang into the phone. Maybe he was still a tad high, but more than anything, he noted that he was happy. Probably another thing not to trust, but Jack was ready to be wrong about this.

"Hey, mate. Listen, my buddy Frank who arranged most of my book tour there, has a brother Mike in Prince George. He'll meet you at the Western Union where I've transferred some money. He'll then take you to the airport to get you set up with a car. The address to meet him is 807 N Front Street. It's downtown. Can you get there? Do you need directions? I can look up walking directions if you need."

Jack could feel his internal silence growing. The familiar place he'd inhabit when he felt less-than.

As if Thad could sense this was where Jack was headed, he stopped his flurry of information. "Jack? Jack? You got it mate?" Pause.

Jack hated this part. "Ya... and thank you. I'm just so tired and overwhelmed. But, God... to just be able to sleep in a car...."

"Well, you'll do no such thing. Are you okay to drive today?"

Jack assessed himself. He still had some reverb of energy, and he knew he wouldn't be able to sleep for a bit with the drugs still in his system, but he was tired. "I guess."

"Can you drive for five hours to Cache Creek?"

Jack thought this felt right. Five hours he could do even in his beleaguered state. "Ya, I think that's doable."

Jack heard Thad's fingers flying around his keyboard again. "Great. I'm making you a reservation for a hotel there. I'll text you more info once you meet up with Mike downtown. And yes, he is bringing you a phone so we can keep in touch." Silence. "Jack?" Pause. "I feel like I'm losing you, Jack. You okay?"

Finally, the overwhelm of goodness broke Jack's cemented toughness, and he could feel himself getting teary. He was simply exhausted and wrung out.

"Ya...," Jack finally managed, trying not to let on that he was crying. Thad then swept in calmly with care in his voice.

"It's going to be okay, Jack. I just want you here."

"Ya. Me too."

The men spoke for a bit more until it was time for Jack to leave to meet Mike downtown. They said goodbye for the moment, and then Jack, adrift in emotions and discomfort, trudged in the morning light to the downtown meeting point.

In just under an hour, Mike had him in a clean vehicle with a thousand dollars cash and a cheap cell phone in his hand.

Jack thanked him repeatedly and couldn't help but apologize for his appearance and stench. He knew he reeked from the wear of the travel, but he was finally good and relieved that maybe he could eventually leave his survival mode. It had cost him a lot, but he couldn't help but feel that he had also gained a lot from the experience.

He started the rental car and pointed it toward the freeway.

He was ready to be home.

Chapter 33

Flux

The drive south was the perfect escape for Jack. He could feel himself softening. That's the thing about survival mode; it requires an incredible amount of life force to just be in the world. The constant sense of danger and being unsafe because feeling unsafe is real, unlike the veil of safety, which is not.

Jack kept getting stuck on that last part. How can safety or the illusion of safety be bad? He flipped up for clarity. *Safety? Why do I know that I have to abandon that? Why is it an illusion? But more importantly, why is it a dangerous illusion? Gah.* Jack thought about this further as the exit for Hixon passed his windows. The clarity finally arrived.

The illusion of safety is what people defend against — an illusion of something that isn't a thing. It's an imagined danger, and one cannot imagine danger while trusting in the universe. Those two are at odds. So which is it? Do you trust the universe, or will you build yourself into a prison that only serves the illusion of safety? Jack knew what this was. It was one of those moments that are heftier and weightier than an a-ha. Jack called them a "universal download," a concept that, when brought to mind, completely changes the entire landscape of one's understanding. "F u c k . . . , " Jack sat with his mind blown.

"That's it, isn't it?" he asked himself. "That's why the illusion has been bugging me. It's a cloud we put over ourselves when we should be standing tall and living fearlessly." Jack instantly saw the chasm between living stupidly versus living fearlessly. He was still awonder with the thing as it opened new options and possibilities before him. He then met himself with a new question while also wondering if he was still high. Certainly, he was on the verge of something for not having slept. Jack didn't care. He was living his life in his perfect style: long johns, boots, carpet bag, stink, and all. Passing Quesnel, he laughed; a laugh that he noted sounded a tad maniacal and that he was probably going to have a massive neurological episode when he sobered up.

Mile after mile passed, the process dizzying and trance-inducing in Jack's sleep-deprived, slightly chemically-lit state. His mind wandered and landed on the fact that he felt like he was short-cutting the journey leading him home. Jack hated this lingering feeling that he hadn't fully completed what he set out to do. The final part of that thought was that Jack felt like he had lost an opportunity to test his Ouija board/future determining game. He felt like he had teed up the perfect punt into the future by making something off-grid happen, but then he let himself be rescued. Jack was getting honest about this with himself. *Damn.* Jack pushed into himself. *Okay… let's just readjust to a new punt. No problem… just find step one again… identify your wish. Cool.* Jack thought about what might be next for him. *Okay… whatcha got, Jack. Just whatever comes to mind.* His brain hummed with the blankness of narcotics. *Okay… no one's home.*

Jack repositioned because, sure, higher consciousness might not be available in Jack's current state, but that didn't mean that his state wasn't going to serve a helpful purpose if that was his intention. *Jack… c'mon… whatcha got? First thing you think of?* His buoyant mind bobbled, free-floating, searching for new ideas. He eventually landed on *a family*. The thought surprised Jack, but maybe it was his current feral state. He longed for normalcy and routine. *Bleh,* Jack thought both to and of himself. *Okay… family, maybe… whatever,* Jack deflected. *But seriously… what am I going to do? I have no job, no income, no car, no address.* The next thought landed annoyingly. *Looking for your next object to punt into reality? Well, there's a pretty damn good place to start.* Jack chuckled while thinking it, then admitted that it wasn't precisely unclear why he was currently single. He looked in the rearview mirror, saying, "You some next level batshit crazy. You know that?" Jack refocused and pushed on.

Okay… so ya, I have a fairly clean slate to work from to make something happen. Cool. So what do I want? He remembered that the last time he asked himself this question, the answer was to be whole and not broken. *Well, fine… that was… whatever. I know I'm not less than. I get that. I know my supposed physical brokenness was the arrival of many amazing things in my life. I get that… so maybe I can answer that question differently this time.* He puzzled on the thing. *I choose groundedness. I choose….* He dug deeper. The equation was on, and Jack would test and push its limits. *C'mon, Jack, you high-as-fuck, batshit crazy mother-fucker… whatcha got?* Then it came to him.

I want to change the world. The instant he thought this, he came back to the present only to hear and see the road. "Fuck," he said under his breath while slamming walls into place. The thing that was just called was too big. "Fuck."

Jack wanted to unvex himself from the thought, but the resonance hung in his cocaine-mixed chemical airwaves, its echoes terrifying to Jack.

CHAPTER 34

TROUBLED WATERS

Jack was getting himself settled in the room when he felt an attack coming on. *Totally not surprising,* he thought, given that he had done everything imaginable not just to bring on a storm but to make it so much worse than normal. Over-exercise and pushing himself, being tired, drugs or alcohol, and stress were all major contributing factors to how bad a situation could get for him. He knew he was staring down the barrel of a crippling vortex. He could feel it, but strangely enough, Jack was able to hold onto his less anxiety-riddled mindset, and he was curious if he could tackle a category five storm.

Jack quickly dialed Thad. No answer. Then again, no response.

Fuck it, he thought, *let me see if I can handle this big of a beast.* The seriousness of the situation, however, wasn't lost on him. If it was going to be bad, which all indications confirmed, he could die if someone wasn't watching him. *But who?*

Jack remembered the app he and Em would use on occasion when she was at work. He opened it and sent his personal meeting link, which would allow anyone with it to access his camera directly. He hated that he didn't have time to explain in person. Still, it was this option or live stream his episode to social media with a note declaring, "Please don't freak out… this is totally normal for me, and ya, I might look like I'm dying, but I'm totally fine unless I'm choking on my own vomit or some such thing." There was no way to language it that wouldn't seem awful, attention-grabbing, and terrifying to all who witnessed it.

Damn, Jack thought. Either this or burden a friend who would probably be fairly upset at Jack's past 24 hours. Besides, maybe it was time Thad saw this part of his dumpster fire life. *I mean, we've come this far, and the man hasn't thrown me to the curb.* Jack sank internally and tried to call Thad one last time. No answer.

"Fuck."

Jack ran to the bathroom to do his best and get himself cleaned out and make it back to the bed. He finally cratered onto the bed with his long johns mostly still on. Jack finished a text, and upon hitting send, his innards doubled him in half with a crack that he didn't so much hear as was reverberated throughout his network of bones. He struggled to right himself, but the wriggle of him was vexing and searing. Every move slung his clothes off further as the air flow within him crept to a halt.

"Aaargh...," Jack wailed as it contorted him backward, mouth and eyes flown wide open and hissing as his ribs compressed and squeezed the air from him. His spine started its dance as the song of the beyond met his mind. He was slipping. His body writhed and fractured from one grotesque shape into another. His last thought was to arrange the phone on the nightstand so Thad could see him if he clicked the link he sent. He leaned it against the lamp facing him, then carefully brought his shaking arm back to his side. With that, he was gone.

It was like Alice in Wonderland slipping through the surface of this world into another. Jack was falling through emotional plane after plane.

He flailed with the sensation and then slowed, commanding the sensation to bow to his will. However, this storm was blowing from a new direction, and was still hailing torrents of man-made chemicals that queered the berzerk and shattered what Jack previously knew of the potential hellscape. He fell. Then sped up and fell faster. He tried to gain some control over anything, but nothing would tether to his mind. It was too frantic and frenzied, and there were no stop gaps to regain a toehold of form or thought. The winds picked up and changed course. Jack saw the hellfire coming. An inferno of neurological disorder whipped into a violent fiery hurricane.

Jack slammed into the first layer of the place and then fell into the next plane. "Aaargh. NO!" Jack screamed into the hotel room with his head craning back, almost touching his naked backside. It then found a new path they had never been down before. It was a back alley of searing pain that made it feel like his chemically-steeped brain had found holy fire and found sick humor in dousing it with gasoline.

The place ruptured and fell from the abstract, and the whipping winds of the place denied things that were supposed to make sense. Then it finally met him. He felt a click from the center of the two spheres of his brain, then slowly, everything began to melt as he detached from form to find the place of absolute nothingness. He free-floated in this place, understanding that this is where the mad live. He chose to meet it as peace, and experienced the white-out of existence without resistance. He let go as he saw himself sitting in the abandoned playground back at the Junction of the Meziadin. The playground of devils was now his new surroundings. He floated with its presence and then *understood* what was ov that place, was ov him. A connection had been made despite the information not yet making sense.

Hours later, when Jack began his ascent back to earth, his first conscious thought was, *that's why it felt right.*

CHAPTER 35

DOUBLED

Knock. Knock. Knock.

"Hello?" The hotel manager asked politely, opening the door. "Hello?" he asked again into the dark room. He turned the light on to see Jack's lifeless, half-naked body thrown across the bed. "Oh," the man said as Jack was just beginning to come out of his episode.

Jack realized what had happened and forced himself to whisper, "I'm fine. Just fell asleep." The manager apologized repeatedly and excused himself from the space.

"Jack. Are you okay? Talk to me," Thad implored him through the linked phone's speaker.

Jack curled his position a bit while trying to get himself right. "Uhhhh…," Jack moaned, trying to form thoughts and words. As he came back to the world, he was eternally grateful for the warm timber and presence of Thad's voice.

"Jack, mate. Are you okay? Can you talk to me?" Thad said softly.

"I'm okay." Jack deep-breathed for a bit, willing himself to recover, then eventually pulled the phone off the nightstand where it had been propped up so the camera could be trained on him during his episode.

"Jack." Thad's tone held the measure of direct honesty. Jack could hear fear on the line.

"Yes…?" he tried, still shaking away entanglements, knowing something was up.

"Do you know what just happened to you?"

Jack's mind was struggling. "What?"

Thad stepped in with a fatherly tone and repeated slowly and with care, "Do you know what just happened?"

"What, with my storm?"

"Yes."

Jack grabbed the phone off his chest to replay the video transmission sent during his attack.

Realizing what Jack was doing, Thad asked, "You can play back what I just witnessed?"

"Ya. Just hit the 'play from beginning.' Like this...." The transmission started where the first thing they heard was Thad screaming.

"Jack!" Thad's voice was anxious. "Jack! Can you hear me, Jack?" Pause. "Jack!" Again, no response. As Jack continued to watch, his eyes trained on his exposed flesh as he witnessed himself become inhabited by demons. He heard screams of "No!" as he bent and piled into a hundred different horrific shapes, each more contorted and disturbing than the last. At times he could hear the hiss from the air being compressed out of his ribcage and the crack of bones while being strangled from within. It was monstrous and horrifying. Jack saw himself practically get lifted off the bed and slammed down with incredible force.

"AAAArrrgghhhh...," Jack screamed.

Again it was Thad's voice yelling, "Oh my God. Jack!"

The poor transmission of the cheap phone and remote cell service reminded him of something from *The Blair Witch Project*. It was something that even he couldn't get his mind around. Again, he was thrown about as if something unseen had him.

Jack had never before seen what he looked like during his storms. This was brand new information. He didn't know... and felt shame in seeing himself like this — a gothic horror show, an inhuman expression of silent screams and vexed wails. It was not something that could be understood because it did not seem to be of this earth. It was dark magic, and it stopped both Jack and Thad cold.

Then Jack heard his love say something in the transmission that he couldn't understand. "That was supposed to be just theory."

However, Jack was too ashamed to ask Thad what that meant. He stopped the replay, and silence returned to the room.

"Jack?" Thad urged.

Silence.

"It's okay… mate? Jack?"

The silence that crested within Jack made tears silently fall out of his eyes and onto his chest. He didn't want to talk about it. He didn't want to even know about it. He simply wanted to disappear and not exist.

Thad slowly brought Jack around so they could at least say a few words. However, Jack's melancholy mainly offered silence.

The men stayed on the phone for two hours before the sun started to set. The new nightfall offered a closeness to the moment as their bending and melting hearts grew in attachment to what they were to one another.

Thad had some food delivered to Jack's room, and they ate together in relative silence. Jack had never had a relationship with someone where they could be in each other's presence without feeling the need to talk and yet somehow still be in constant communion. The sweep of it shored up Jack's depleted reserves, then Thad tucked in Jack's remaining jagged bits and quietly whispered, "Good night, my love," as Jack fell into a deep sleep.

CHAPTER 36

ALIGHT

The following morning Jack awoke to a text from Thad.

> Morning, mate. Here's your coffee.
> ☕ I hope you slept okay. Call me
> when you're up. I'm headed to the
> office this morning.

Jack rolled in bed for a second as the last remaining morsels of sleep evaporated from him. The sun was up, and Jack noted how much he had needed that sleep. Jack recalled that sleeping done in an actual bed does wonders for a person, even if the last tendrils of thunder could still be heard in the distance from Jack's last neurological storm. His brain hurt.

"Damn." He flexed himself awake, verifying that everything was back on board. After taking a shower, Jack heard a knock at the door. It was the manager from last night.

"We were asked to deliver this to your room, sir. Sorry again for the intrusion."

After taking the plastic bag from the man, Jack fumbled to do what he could for a tip but remembering he had no wallet or cash, there was little he could offer him other than, "Not a problem, sir. Thank you so much." Pause. "You have a very nice demeanor with guests." Hearing it leave his lips, Jack hated his position in life. But he had to give what he had, and a compliment was the last scrape of that barrel.

"Uh." He closed the door behind the man, internally face-palming. "I promise I will not be poor forever."

Jack returned to the bathroom mirror, where he dropped the plastic bag on the counter, saying, "You are a crazy mother-fucker." He was brought back to the realization that he had in the abandoned building on the side of the road. The one where he found the marbles. The one where he felt the truest sting of disappointment over what he thought he might be gaining but instead had been kidding himself about. The moment when he realized he didn't have guides and that it was just him talking to him.

God, I'm such a bullshitter. His thoughts continued. *I mean*, he churned. *If it's just me talking to myself, how can I believe anything I say? It's just made up. It's just… whatever… like nothing.* Jack searched the ceiling for clarity, then flipped up for a quieter inspection of the thing.

Why is this, which is happening here, not bullshit? Jack thought that was an interesting twist on it. *How can I trust this knowing, inkling, or voice?*

Silence, then Jack's truth replied, "Because you *know* truth when you hear it. You *know* the essence of a thing when you hear it." He paused, searching further for more honesty, adding, *How do I know anything is true if I'm involved in my answers? Am I just making it up?* Jack grabbed his eyes in the reflection. *How do I know that it's real? How do I know anything?*

Jack stopped, realizing he had just landed on the heart of the matter. He repeated to himself, "How do I know anything?" He answered the question. "I know something because I do. It's that simple. How do I know my name?" Again, Jack searched his answer for lies and then declared to himself, "Because I do. I know when something is true. I can feel it. I know it, and there is no need to make things more complicated than that."

Jack retired from his upper conscious thinking. "Oh. Cool… I guess. I mean… if it's just going to, you know, go with the simplest, most explainable answer… sure." He tilted his head in the mirror. "We can do that."

Jack reached for the bag, curious about what had just arrived. It was a pair of sweats, socks, underwear, and a "3 Valley Gap!" t-shirt. Jack hadn't yet realized he had nothing fresh to put on after his shower… but luckily, Thad had. Jack blushed with the waterfall of emotions he was feeling. He couldn't believe someone would do that for him. Jack was speechless, but more than that, he was confused and stunned. Attention and care were being focused on him in an uncomfortable way. Jack questioned whether he should go to Gambier Island to meet up with Thad. His stomach twisted with the thought of being or feeling "caught," wondering if he should run. But then he realized how hard he was breathing and the near panic state of his being. He was spinning a web of safety.

Jack flipped up to his higher consciousness to end the hallucination, and the world returned to quiet. He dressed and got ready for another long day on the road. Leaving the room, he looked at himself in the mirror one last time and confirmed to his own eyes that he could do this – he could allow himself to be loved.

CHAPTER 37

CONVEY

Jack was on the road for about an hour when his mind wandered back to a topic he had marked "Do Not Enter." Jack mentally picked up a stick and poked at the thing while also wanting just to be and not think. The dual frustration picked at him.

Can I have a fucking minute? he pleaded to his innards. Jack longed for an off switch, but the niggle was on, and Jack couldn't help but try to put his finger on it. His upper sense hinted that clarity and madness are close cousins.

"I want to change the world" flashed the memory of his own words.

No! God. That's insane. Jack refocused on the road. *I mean....*

He looked out the window. *I literally have nothing. I'm a joke. A washed-up, used-up basket case, which, at best, is probably going to be a fucking cripple in a few years. That's who I am.*

Jack angled for something different while the sting of that awfulness buried under his flesh. *I have no money. No job or career. No fucking clothes. I'm pathetic, and no one will take me seriously as a broken handicapped piece of human garbage.* The ring of the cut against the handicapped refused to quiet even after he did. It stayed in Jack's ears with a newfound feeling, for it now wasn't just him he was maligning but his beloved.

God Damn it, Jack! The internal feelings mixed, and the churn was so deep it made him vow that he wouldn't do that again. He promised himself, *My disorder is not a handicap, and I will not use anyone's disability as a cudgel. Not against myself or anyone else.*

But he did need to get honest with himself about one more thing. He took a peek at it again from as far as possible.

I want to change the world. The absurdity of it left Jack speechless.

"Me?" He looked at himself in the rearview mirror. It just didn't make any sense, which of course, for Jack meant that he would try and make it make sense.

"I mean…," he paused mid-stump, then caught his gaze again for a quick second. "Like…." He moved in his seat, trying to get comfortable. "How would…." He wasn't sure how to phrase the next thought. *Like, how would that even work?*

The town of Lillooet was passing by in his windows. Realizing he had several hours left of driving, Jack figured it might be amusing to puzzle on the thing.

Okay… but seriously? Jack shifted his gaze to the horizon. *I mean… how could one person do that? How could one person make such an impact? Besides*, he rattled with the thing. *Let's say my life depended on it. What would I want to change about the world, and how could it be achieved?*

Jack percolated with step one: "Make a wish."

Fine. He reviewed what he'd like to see changed in the world. The first answer was evident to his mind the moment he posed the question. *End institutional bigotry, most notably in religious arenas. End the torture of queer people. Help chart a world where we can at least hold hands on the street without fear from a world that punishes that. We are not born a sin or a crime. Have people return to empathy and kindness. Create understanding.* He repeated that last part — *create understanding* — while a vision of young queer kids entered his mind. *To free them. To let them exist in the world without punishment for something they cannot control.* Jack noted for a quick second that his first wish was for him alone to not be broken, but that this wish was much bigger than that. This wish was for all people like him, but from where he sat, it felt too big of an ask, especially coming from him, a man who had nothing.

He reconfirmed the evidence stacked against him in the mirror. *Fuck,* Jack thought. *It was simply impossible.* He refocused on the drive.

Ring.

Ah, shit! Jack thought, realizing he had been lost in thought and had forgotten to call Thad as he had asked. *Ugh… get your head outta the fucking clouds, Jack! C'mon.* The sense of disappointment and angst grew as he answered the call.

"Hi, Babe! Just hitting the road." His voice was too urgent and flappy to be a simple truth.

"Morning, handsome. How'd you sleep? Did you get the clothes I sent to your room?" The swirl of this action on Thad's part made Jack collapse further into his embarrassment over his current life situation.

"Oh my gosh, yes. And…," Jack was still overwhelmed. "Thank you." Pause. "It's just that…."

"It's just nothing," Thad leaned in. "And you're welcome."

"I…," Jack tried but then was cut short.

"Jack?" Silence.

"Ya?"

"I like taking care of people. It's what I do, and being able to do things for you brings me a lot of personal satisfaction. Can you give me that? I want you to be okay with that. Let me be in my purpose, which is that of care."

This information made Jack want to drive off the road into the ocean, never to be seen again. *Gah*, he punctured internally. Jack's brain fought the intention of Thad's ask. He knew he'd be more comfortable with someone who just cohabitated with him, preferably if a partner also simply ignored him. That was Jack's preference. That was comfort. But this? What Thad was asking, to find joy in doing things for him, was madness because it felt like it called out his failings — all the things Jack couldn't manage for himself.

"I mean…," Jack shook with the idea, fighting what was being presented to him. It was simply too new to him, and it made him feel shackled and owned.

Thad waited an appropriate amount of time for a response, then prompted with, "And…?"

Jack managed an "Okay" but the internal battle was on. He was formulating walls to manage the current crisis that sought to undermine his sense of personal space, freedom, and safety. Jack realized what he was doing and cut the cord of bullshit.

Jack redirected the current of the conversation, "Looks like I'll be at the Horseshoe Bay Terminal in four hours. Hoping to catch a ferry to Gambier by 1:00."

"Yes!" Thad let fly. "I can't believe you'll be here today!" The excitement in his words spoke volumes.

They stayed on the call for another thirty minutes making plans of things they wanted to do when they were together. After hanging up, Jack drove on, trying to resolve the fractures in his emotional landscape. *Just breathe…* he told himself. He then thought, *It's the allowing that is ov love.* His next thought was, *Fuck, I'm weird. Why do I have to be so 'Deep Thoughts with Stuart Smalley!' Ugh!* Jack lowered the brim of his hat to put a measure of something between him and his pitiless noise.

But is it my brain? A new puzzle formed. *Or is it from beyond my brain?* Jack caught himself in the new web and wanted to scream. "Stop. Just fucking stop!" He forced his attention on the road and did his best to untune himself from the constant stream of figures.

Jack pulled into the ferry terminal and paid the fare. The ship eventually moaned its way onto its course, and Jack departed his vehicle, remembering his last voyage of this kind. He headed to the upper deck to view where he had been versus where he was going.

God, I'm such a fucking disaster. Jack looked back. Then with the memory of the "Be here" lady, he walked across the ship to see where he was headed. The bug of the thought still burrowed deep in him: *I want to change the world.* It's fester not finding relief.

Jack breathed into it and fought the fight in him. "Be here," met his mind. "It's no more difficult than that." He searched the horizon in the midday glare. "Okay," he finally came to as he could feel the agreement within him being met. "I can do this. I can allow love." He then inhaled the sea air as he watched and allowed a new world as it came into view.

CHAPTER 38

INDUCED

The ferry landed with a heave and a lurch as its inhabitants braced against solid objects; their sway a greeting from the sea.

Jack checked his GPS and drove off the boat in extreme frustration. He couldn't understand why the people in front of him weren't in his hurry.

"C'mon, fucknuts… let's go!" He was failing at containing his excitement. He was now on the same shore as Thad. *Finally,* he thought, exiting.

Twenty minutes later, Jack pulled up to Thad's driveway. "Holy…," Jack said under his breath, unnerved by how nice the house was. He noted seeing this that his innards kicked up his nerves a notch because 'nice' was a concept Jack didn't see himself aligning with. He grabbed his carpet bag, which at this point contained long johns that needed to be burned and useless scraps and survival tools. He thought twice about bringing his garbage into Thad's beautiful home. "Gah," Jack pained. "It's too.…" With that, he mentally tried to get his not-nice-personhood to somehow fit into Thad's world of beautiful things. It confused him as to how this might work when on the surface, it was mismatched.

As Jack got out of the car and headed to the front door, Thad appeared at the window and then, a moment later, greeted him by pushing the electronic door opener.

There they were. It was the briefest of seconds, but the men had to switch gears from what they had been and knew of one another to the clear present. They stood once again in each other's presence and were forced to resolve the emotional electronic depths they'd been to against the physical strangers they were to each other. After all, they had only been in each other's presence four times before this moment, and each of those initial encounters was brief and awkward.

"Hello!" Thad beamed at Jack, shuffling his legs toward him.

Jack had forgotten how Thad walked and wasn't sure if he needed help or what he was supposed to do. They had a quick kiss on the mouth to break the ice and hoped they could reconnect to all they had talked about. The addition of physical presence was going to be an adjustment.

"Come...," Thad ushered. "There's someone who wants to meet you." Jack followed, noting Thad did pretty good between his legs and the crutches, and he seemed to have a hitching gait that worked for him, although it was inelegant.

They walked into the kitchen, where Joy's tummy was on full display.

"Jack, this is Joy." Jack's heart was a squish of melting emotion. He couldn't help but scoot under her for a tummy rub and some cuddles. However, her response was less thankful than he had hoped for, as clearly, her priorities were elsewhere, including being left to snore in peace.

"She's amazing." Jack laughed, his heart full of delight.

Thad gave Jack a quick tour and showcased a few things he had done to make their next few days pleasant. However, Jack found it odd that Thad didn't show him the basement or attic. There were stairs, and Jack wondered how he managed them.

Finally, sitting outside in the August air, Thad looked at Jack. "How do you feel? Are you tired?"

They were still adjusting to the fact that as strangers, they had been writing notes on each other's hearts. Jack checked in with himself and then clarified, "Ya... sure." He stopped hoping to do or say something to clarify the flaming disaster he was to this world. "I'm just glad to be here finally." The warm air found its way around the big pine trees, giving the constant call in this part of the world. The sound was always a song that allowed Jack's heart to dock to a newfound place. He exhaled gratitude, knowing he was safe.

"Well, it's nice to have you here finally."

A tiny spark of fear prompted Jack, "I don't know how long I can stay." Thad seemed to know this dance.

"Okay, handsome. We'll cross that bridge when we get to it. Just be here with me today." The comment lifted Jack from his falling sense of "what next?"

The day passed as the ice between them melted into something not quite yet comfortable but at least a step toward the familiar and intimate. Thad had dinner made at the house and introduced him to Nancy, the woman who came by once a day to cook and assist with things he couldn't manage solo.

They ate dinner on Thad's deck overlooking a wooded glen. The food was incredible, and the wine even more so. As hoped, they became more familiar with one another, and the social soothing of nerves found in that bottle of wine did the trick. By the end of dinner, they touched each other more, and the sensation tightened their bonds and allowed for deeper meaning.

"Can I be honest with you, Jack?" Thad poured them both a glass from the second bottle. "Oh, and I assume wine is okay for dessert?" They laughed as Jack toasted to dessert.

"Perfectly acceptable."

"I really like you." The stars he gazed in Jack's eyes were mid-summer's night clear.

"I like you too. I'm glad we met even if we did get off to a rocky start." Jack twinkled teasingly.

"You're something else," Thad said mid-melt.

The men openly flirted and touched and soaked in the moment that they were finally sharing. It had been three months since they first met, yet, as with many couples, they felt like it had been longer than that.

Jack stood to clear the dishes.

"So how is it you've been hitting the gym while not even having so much as a wallet or a phone?"

From across the open span of the outdoor dining area, Jack laughed, dropped off the dishes in the kitchen, and then returned. He drunk-winked as he sat and said, "My little secret."

Thad piqued. "Oh. What other little secrets do you have?" A comment Jack didn't love as there was the faintest tone of distrust present, but he brushed it off. A bolder statement met Jack with a smack. "I don't do secrets, Jack." There was too much energy there to be nothing, and now it needed to be addressed. Jack repositioned himself next to Thad so he could take his beautiful bearded face in his hands.

"Good." Pause. "Neither do I." There was a slight weirdness now in the air. Jack could see the red of this flag. It was a deal for Thad.

"Tell me why, though," he added, still holding Thad's face.

Thad freed himself from Jack's hold and backed up.

"Dunno. It's been a problem in my life."

"What do you mean?" Jack was curious.

"It's just that everyone I've been with has cheated on me in some form, and it makes me crazy."

Jack wanted to lead with an "I can see that" but even offered as a joking comment wouldn't land appropriately in the moment. He finally said aloud, "Okay." A brief silence passed between them, then Jack added, "So how about we agree up front to commit to honesty? No veils or boundaries."

Both men were very aware of a concept that was a pivotal point to Thad's thesis of *Zenith's Peak*. The highest heights of the truth of oneself.

"What if we are just completely open and honest with each other... but there's, I think, going to be an uncomfortable catch."

Thad adjusted his seat to see Jack more head-on, then replied, "You wonderfully weird creature. I like your style. What's the catch? And why is it uncomfortable?"

Jack laughed into the cooling evening's Canadian air, wondering how to say the next bit.

"I guess." He looked away from Thad. "I guess that would also require us to be absolutely honest with ourselves. Like in your book. I dunno." He faced Thad again, his tawny-red hair not something Jack had seen on a man before. "Does that seem difficult to you?

Because if I'm honest… ha ha," Jack laughed with discomfort, "I'd say it can sometimes be difficult for me."

"I guess I can see some of what you're saying." Thad mulled on it a second, then asked, "Like, how honest are you willing to get with yourself about how you see yourself dying?"

Jack's eyes went wide. "YES!" He was chair dancing, realizing that Thad was catching his meaning. "Right?! Like there's just some shit that you gotta wonder whether you can go there." They started laughing and collapsing into each other. They couldn't help themselves, and it felt so good.

It was getting late, and they were starting to get sleepy. Thad asked, "What are you comfortable with in sleeping arrangements? Of course, I would love to spend the night with you."

Jack reached over and put his arm around Thad expectantly. "Tell me honestly. May I pick you up and carry you to bed?" Jack then nodded respectfully to Thad and said, "If I'm being honest… I don't think I have the patience right now for you to walk."

Thad burst out laughing and said, "Sure. I normally would never in a million fucking years let someone pick."

Jack grabbed Thad behind his back and under his knees. He stood and practically jogged to the bedroom with them both screaming and laughing the entire way.

The first time for the men was emotionally high, but if they were honest, it was also clunky. There were a lot of new factors between the two of them that were going to take time. The same is true for anyone who picks up an instrument for the very first time. The mastery of orchestrations is made over time and with great attention.

As they were falling asleep, Thad asked Jack, "Are you serious about the honesty thing? Is that something you'd be willing to do with me?"

Jack rolled over to face him, so they were both lying on their sides. "It's a bit of a shame that it needs to be verbalized. Of course. I wouldn't want it any other way."

Thad perked at this response. "Really?" He was curious if this could be a thing between people. "You'd tell me anything?"

"Sure. Why wouldn't I?"

"Well, that's just the thing. Everybody says they're going to be honest but then...."

Jack took Thad's face and smirked, "Ask me anything." It was a dare. The catch of it alighted in Thad's eyes. They were snickering, recognizing how foolish they looked. Thad then grabbed Jack's head in turn, holding each other's faces close.

"AwAwAwAwAw....!!!!!" Jack yelled to punctuate the weirdness of them.

"AwAwAwAwAw....!!!!!" Thad yelled back, keeping eye to eye with Jack's crazy. They laughed so hard they had to separate for air for a second. They regrouped and retook each other's faces.

"Okay, okay...." Jack laughed. "No, really. Ask me anything. I'm an open book." They had already talked through much of the big stuff, so Jack felt comfortable committing to this.

"Okay...," Thad devised, "what do you *not* want me to know?" A comment that made Jack roll onto his back and whistle.

"Whoa, dude." Jack was a ramble of fuckery. "Thad! Whoa...." They were both still lightly laughing, but the question wasn't nothing, and it hung in the air waiting to be addressed. Jack internally searched himself for what moves he might make next. He made a quick pit stop to review with his higher mind. "Just be honest."

Jack returned to the moment, thinking that response wasn't feeling quite right. He thought about perhaps using charm and half answering the question, probably a Colton move. *Blah*, he thought. *That isn't right either.* His gut was offering him nothing in his current drunken state, but he recognized why he wasn't finding resolve. This wasn't a question to be answered with sex, the mind, charm or logic... or even insight. This was a question that needed to be addressed from his feminine heart. She drifted across Jack's face in her usual way and told Thad what "she" was ov.

"Okay." Pause. "Here's what I don't want you to know." Jack refocused on Thad's handsome face. "I don't want you to know that it's work for me to be here even though there's no other place I'd rather be. I don't want you to know how confusing that is to me." Jack thought, then continued to speak from his heart consciousness.

"I don't want you to know that I'm scared. That I feel strongly for you… and… the future is such a shit-storm for me, and I don't know where I'm heading or how I'll get there, but I also know that I'm done playing small. I'm done missing out because I haven't bothered to level up to my expectations from this planet because they seem to think I have more to give than I do. I'm done fighting who I am." Jack was crying now. "And I know I sound completely insane, and I honestly don't know how sane I am sometimes." Both men had eyes filled with tears, and breathed heavier with the pulse of the conversation, "But I think I'm finally ready to grow up and play ball." Jack wiped back a tear. "And I don't want you to know how scared I am that if we become a couple, I'll be a burden to you. I can't handle that." Jack started to cry openly, and Thad grabbed onto him and just let him have the moment. There was no judgment, just quiet, loving presence, as was Thad's way.

"You crazy little bizarre bastard," Thad said quietly to himself. "I got you." He turned his head to express himself more openly to the heavens. "As long as you'll let me, I got you."

Chapter 39

TREAD

Thad and Jack spent the next week growing close while plotting Jack's next career move and general place in the world. There were many surprises along the way, such as the afternoon when Jack finally asked, "So what's in the basement?" The question had arrested Thad in his tracks, a reaction that made Jack all the more curious.

A silence hung in the air. Then, finally, Jack pushed, "Thad?"

Thad turned from the counter where he stood to greet Jack with a gaze that asked, *Can I level with you?*

"Ah," Thad finally managed. "Some of my studies and work… and other areas of interest."

Jack seized onto the thing that was just said. The second bounce and meaning of what was said, or what wasn't said in this case, was brown paper plain, and Jack sought to unwrap it.

"Other areas of interest?" Jack asked, then searched energetically for possibilities. The following came to mind: *1) Cult. 2) Deep Sex stuff. 3) More cult shit 4) Murderer.* Jack then retreated from his formulations to realize that none of these were true. Knowing Thad, it was probably more like dinosaur bones, old church relics (which could also be the cult murder thing?), or a weird ceramics collection.

Jack rationalized the thing to death, then landed on, *Probably the world's largest ceramic penis collection. That's it!* Jack smirked at his stupidness and decided the best path forward was to stay open. It was probably nothing.

"So, we're doing the honesty thing, right?" Thad asked, making Jack stand and walk over to Thad, slightly wide-eyed.

"Ya?" The air was rife with expectation and mystery.

"Let me back up a second." Thad put his crutches down and sat in a nearby chair. Jack followed suit. "What's your greatest sexual fantasy or scenario that gets you off?"

Hearing this, Jack was destabilized yet also incredibly intrigued. "Do you know any questions that aren't this difficult?" They laughed.

Thad prompted, "Tell me."

Jack couldn't quite get to the point of the question and how it related to what's happening in the basement, but okay. Jack steadied himself and told the truth.

"To be tied up or handcuffed and raped." Jack then bottom-lined it. "Being used."

Thad's eyes went wide in a silent scream. "That's your *thing*?!" he shouted. His mouth was open in surprise as he processed the information.

Jack fought the impulse to shrink from his truth. "Ya. That's what gets me off."

"H o l y f u c k . . .," Thad said, dragging on the words. The comment offered Jack no insight as to whether this was a good or bad thing in Thad's mind.

"Hold on...." Thad left the room, then yelled back, "Stay there. I'll be right back."

Jack sat alone in his squirm of awkwardness. It felt like Thad was gone a very long time. He returned with a devilish grin that Jack hadn't seen on his face before. He took Jack's hand to help him stand, then put it around his waist so they could walk this journey together.

"Come."

They crossed the room and rounded the corner on the backside of the kitchen, where a small corridor housed a storage room, mechanics, and the like, but there was also an elevator door tucked around the far corner that one couldn't see from the hall. Thad pushed the button, and the doors slid apart. Thad didn't comment but entered the space where a nervous yet excited Jack followed.

"I thought you said you didn't do secrets?" Jack eyed Thad while pinning him against the wall for a kiss.

"I don't. I do areas of study that I elect to share only with those who have gained my trust."

Jack felt the skew and arc of something big. The doors opened to the basement, which had two main areas and an extensive set of double doors. On one side was a typical home gym, on the other a collection of what seemed to be witchy art, vessels, orbs, and goblets.

Jack walked over to the artifacts, dumbfounded. He sheepishly dared to ask, "Is this the ancient relic stuff you study?"

"Kinda," Thad said as Jack noted a new presence to Thad. He seemed to be leveled up, bolder, darker, and wickedly sexier in this space.

What the fuck is going on here? Jack thought to himself, then asked, "And what's there?" He cautiously pointed to the big double doors.

Thad had a twinkle to his air. He went over to the door to hit the big silver button that Jack had come to know as the way to open doors automatically in this house. "Come." He outstretched his hand, which Jack moved to him to take. The doors opened while Thad answered Jack's question.

"Fuck school."

Now Jack was well versed in the ways of the world, and pretty much nothing surprised or shocked him. However, as the big doors groaned on their hinges, Jack's mouth dropped open. Thad wasn't kidding. In the room, there was a bathroom and a shower, a bed, a fuck bench, a sling hanging on chains in front of a mirror, cabinets full of sex toys, dildos, and some items that Jack had no idea what they did… but he also couldn't wait to find out. Mirrors were everywhere, and there was a giant X thing against one wall and an open floor area that looked like a wrestling ring.

Jack ran around the room, eyeing everything in amazement. He finally turned to Thad and screamed, "Are you fucking kidding me?!" making Thad laugh.

"I wasn't joking when I said I like a guy who knows what he's doing." Thad then wobbled over to a stool on casters and sat. He put his feet into a small box at the base of the thing and started to wheel himself around the room with surprising speed and accuracy. He stopped at a workbench with what looked like a huge tool kit, opened it, and took out black gloves, his look giddy and slightly maniacal as he slipped them on and asked, "Ready for your first lesson?"

Colton revved and threw off his clothes, and then the two men tore into each other with a force Jack knew and yet couldn't believe was being met toe to toe by this devilishly handsome handicapped man.

Thad grabbed Jack by the back of the neck and flung him to the floor so they'd share the same level of purchase and mobility. Jack was in awe of Thad's upper body strength as they rolled into the wrestling area. Thad manhandled Jack's body with accuracy and deftly moved him to his liking. There was a power in the new scent of Thad that Jack wanted more of. Thad picked up on that and showed Jack what he could do. He forced Jack's head back, then ate at his neck and pits, diving into the scent, and powerfully took control of Colton's will, a will Jack loved giving up.

At one point, Thad removed his entire mouth from Jack's face, looked him deep in the eye, and said, "Why didn't you tell me sooner fuckboy?" Jack thought he would explode from the raw emotion building in him. Thad knew all the right buttons, including calling him fuckboy or slut.

In seconds they were again exploding with force, power, and sweat. The space they shared was ripe with male human odor, musky and raw. They drove each other deeper into the throb of it. They clamored to get closer to the point where they couldn't get close enough. They buried themselves in the depths of one another as the instinct to unite and become one overtook their senses.

They crashed together through wave after wave of raw emotion. They flexed their strength into one another and allowed themselves to slide into the tender and crying and then back to the physical exertion of men doing battle. It was athletic, sensual, and morphed from one human expression into another.

Thad pulled himself back up onto his wheeled mechanic's stool, threw his wheels back in the direction of one wall where he grabbed long black ropes with metal clips on the ends, and in one second had wheeled himself back to Jack, where he purposely landed on top of him with extreme force. He then pinned Jack under him and, with shocking expertise, roped him like a calf. Colton's mind was exploding at being handled and controlled in this manner.

"Oh ya?" Jack wasn't new at this and set his rugged visceral power to the max. After that, it was game on, and the more they wrestled, flexed, spit at each other, and kissed deeply, the more they won.

They spent hour after hour in this intimate space, sharing and exploring each other and themselves. The abandonment Jack was experiencing with Thad was unlike anything he'd ever known. It was as if Thad's scars met Jack's and vice versa. They were in a sacred space of being united. A space where there was nothing outside of "them." They were one, and they pulsed and resonated their deepest desires and set each other free. No rules.

Around dinner time, they found themselves on the bed in the room, panting mid-tangle. They couldn't get over the sense that they just wanted to be one and that, on the physical, they couldn't get close enough to share the same space or breathe the same air. Thus began their physical journey that had nothing to do with the physical world.

Over time they freed one another from bonds they didn't even know they had.

Chapter 40

Palpitate

Jack had been in the comfort of Thad for about three weeks when he decided his next move was to go to forestry school. It had become a lot to live with Thad while he footed the bills and took care of Jack even though it was becoming clear to them both that, as a couple, they were both all-in.

Around noon on a mid-September day, Jack leaned into a seated Thad and asked how they might make this happen for him.

"So… UBC has a forestry program that I think I'd like to enroll in. I can do the first half online and then the field training in November and December in the Yukon."

Thad looked up from what he was reading on his laptop and said, "Fine, but I'd like to see the ranger's outfits before deciding." Thad winked, making it clear he was teasing and flirting.

"Oh really?" Jack responded in delight, nuzzling in for a chomp on his beard, which always made Thad laugh. "Nom, nom, nom." Thad man-squealed and then laughed.

When Thad regained himself, he had a hesitation in his presence, which Jack had sensed over the past few days. Finally, he decided it was time to unearth the matter.

"It seems like you have something on your mind? Am I right?"

"Ya…." Both men arrived at full attention, then Thad put his hand on Jack's shoulder. "You know I love you, right?" Jack sat back with the register of it, then his eyes melted into puddles. It was the first time he was hearing those three little words.

"Thad!?" Jack practically yelled. "Awww…." Jack kissed Thad, then squared with him, eye to eye. "You are a lunatic… and I love you too."

A minute later, they pulled themselves apart and Thad straightened himself up, a move that Jack noted as different than what he would have expected in the moment.

"And there's something else...."

Jack's walls immediately slammed into the up position while thinking, *Oh fuck. Here it comes. I knew I should have had a safety backup plan. Fuck me and my trusting stupidity. I am a God damned moron for trusting this.* Jack fumed. *I knew it... I fucking knew it.* Then Jack slowed himself as he did on the other side to e-motion and navigate the place. *Hold up,* he finally managed. His next thought was, *I need a better perspective.* He flipped up and cut the cord to his mind's past. It was instantly quiet and peaceful. He saw the beauty in Thad's face. He smelled the food cooking in the kitchen. He felt the sofa's material they sat on, and he exhaled, telling himself, *I am ready to know what Thad has to say to me, and I will not bring baggage or garbage to this conversation.* He opened his eyes and asked Thad to go on.

"Ya?" Jack asked. "Everything okay?"

Thad was fidgeting a bit. "More than okay." He turned from Jack to speak more openly into the air. "You know I am all in on this relationship." Jack's response was to immediately stop breathing. "And I want to share something with you." Jack was now literally on the edge of his seat.

"Ya?" Jack begged.

"So...." Twist. "Your episodes."

Hearing this, Jack wanted to cry. He knew his damaged brain was going to be a deal breaker. *Nobody wants this junk.* Jack internally cursed at himself for being... *What was the word? Oh ya, Defective.* He could feel tears wanting to form, a feeling he fought in the moment, waiting to hear more but not sure if he could.

Thad continued, "I didn't realize they were so bad." Jack's only focus was a speck on the floor. "Are you... you know... like getting medical help? Cause Jack... I mean, I can help or arrange something if you need."

Jack didn't know why his response to hearing this was to apologize for who he was. "I'm sorry."

"Sorry?" Thad grabbed Jack's shoulders, shoring him up to face *his* truth. "Jack. Mate...." He gave Jack a little shake. "Look at me." Jack did. "You are perfection. Yes, we need to deal with your disorder, but we will. Together." He pulled up closer to Jack's face. "I got you, mate. We're bloody in this together. You got me?" Jack was a bobblehead sob. "Cause I got you." They both cried into one another for a while, allowing themselves to sit in what was and be with it together.

This was the moment they knew they'd be together for the rest of their lives.

CHAPTER 41

MISSIONARY

The following day, Jack finished his forestry application, excited about the new opportunity. There was just no way he would live with Thad and be "kept." That went against everything he stood for, and in a way, Jack kind of resented the fact that Thad was doing well financially. There was the tiniest sting that Thad being successful called out his shortcomings, but he also knew that was a lie he was telling himself. On a good day or when he thought clearly, Jack even knew his worth wasn't to be calculated in dollars.

"Looks like we're all set. If I get approved, I can start the course next week." They both held a mixed bag of emotions about it, particularly because it meant Jack would be away for long periods.

"That's awesome, babe. I'm proud of you." Jack beamed awesomeness as his reply.

"AaAaAaAaAa…" Jack howled stupidly. It was pretty clear he was excited.

"You are a lunatic." Thad laughed.

"Tell me something I don't know." The men regained themselves, then Thad grabbed Jack's attention.

"So listen…." Jack noted the mood was changing. Thad continued, "There's more to our conversation yesterday." Jack stopped laughing to refocus.

"Ah…." Jack offered.

"I mean, well…." Jack was having deja-vu as Thad grabbed control of the situation. "You know all that old stuff downstairs, and we've just brushed it under the 'work-stuff' umbrella." Jack had no idea where this was going but stayed open to what might happen. "It's more than that."

Jack internally holy-fucked then said, "Ya…?!"

"Actually... I think it might be easier to show you." He took Jack's hand and grabbed his crutches, heading in the direction of the elevator. "Come."

Jack once again had a nerve-wracking elevator ride into the basement, unsure of what would come next.

"Is this...," Jack swirled his finger in the air, "you know... this whole situation where you, the guy who said he didn't do 'secrets,' rock my fucking world? Because I'm not sure I can take it." They both laughed.

"Relax," Thad assured him. He then turned to face him. "You fascinate me, Jack... and... it's not just... you know... sex and...." Thad cut his stammer and then stated clearly, "As I told you before, there are things that I study that I can only share with someone when there's a certain level of trust between us. Does that make sense?"

Jack shimmied, perusing responses. "I mean... ya... I guess it depends on how sensitive the topic is. But you were pretty upfront about your HIV status, so...." Jack was toying with a weird conclusion that he needed to clarify as not an option. "Is it something worse than that?"

Thad laughed, "Worse?" He laughed more and then clarified, "You are unbelievable. But your responses also align with what I want to show you and talk to you about." The elevator door slid open. "Come." He hobbled to the first black cabinet in the display section of the room. He unlocked it and released its doors, which opened with an audible air exchange indicating that the contents had to be air controlled by some means. Jack was a blank of expectations. His eyes were alert and ready for whatever wanted to come next.

The doors opened, showing that it housed black materials and leather adornments, its walls wafting of shou sugi ban treated planks, which fascinated Jack. The charred blackness of wood held both life and death simultaneously. He watched Thad extend out a rod and what appeared to be a jacket. He moved it to a rolling cart and then added a few boxes to the cart's shelf.

"Pull this around," Thad said, walking over to the area between the sizeable air-compressed storage units. Jack hadn't noted the spaces in-between them, but where Thad stopped was set up like an alteration booth for fixing clothes and such. The little box to stand on in front of the mirror and all. Thad indicated with a point that Jack should stand on the box and face him and the mirror. Jack did.

"What do you see, Jack?"

Jack laughed from self-consciousness. "Thad. God… you and your questions." Jack turned directly to face Thad, saying, " I thought I had too much going on in my brain." After that, it was Thad's turn to be self-conscious.

"I know. I know… I just want to do all the big stuff right."

Jack bolted up-right. "Big stuff? You fucking mean there's more?" Jack was laughing at the fun absurdity of it.

"Take off your clothes," Thad told Jack, who immediately lost his path from laughter. Jack went from mid-chuckle to Colton in half a heartbeat. He straightened on the box and cleared his throat.

"What?" Jack said flatly.

"Take your clothes off," a statement that made Jack gulp again as his voice was cut-off and silenced. Colton stripped as the mood in the room dissipated and then hummed with a newly rung tone.

Thad continued. "What do you see?" Jack had no response as he stood there naked, formulating an answer. "Because I think I see something that maybe you don't." A queer silence then met them and changed the air in the room. "I saw it on the video of your episode."

This wasn't a comment Jack expected, and he crumbled with unsure-footedness. "What?" he asked, confused. Thad continued his march across the front of the mirror, unyielding in his direct focus. Jack was becoming uneasy.

"What is it that you think I study exactly?"

Jack was shrinking in place a bit and didn't know how to utter a response, so as was his way, he was simply silent.

Thad moved around Jack in his usual manner, eyeing the catch, his scholarly air punching the walls. He asked it again slowly, forcing clarity to his matter. "What is it that you think I study exactly?"

After a long silence between them, Thad continued, "I study spirits." He then made his way to Jack's naked body, and standing in front of him, he continued. "The human spirit, as indicated by my books," he said, taking a little bow, cutting the tension in the room a little. Jack felt Thad's calculations of power. Thad's intentionality was apparent to them both.

Jack fell inward and internalized, *A little help here? I don't want to mess this up.* Colton threw Jack to their mind's floor. *Seriously! God, you're fucking pathetic.* Colton took the wheel, leveled himself to the horizon, and said, *I got this.*

Thad continued his walking monologue, "And 'other' spirits… because what I think I see *or saw*… as the case may be is, I think, what has fascinated me about you from the start."

Colton revved in his starting blocks and stayed silent in typical fuckboy form, showing he *only* speaks when spoken to. Jack watched as Colton doubled down on his vision, staring straight ahead, and pump-flexed again.

At Jack's side, Thad pulled the black fabric off the dressing cart and handed it to Jack, whose eyes went wide.

What kinda cos-play adventure is this going to be?! Jack thought, grabbing at the dress to put it on.

Jack stood upright, confused. He turned to Thad, who didn't flinch. Thad seemed to have anticipated this, so he stepped in and firmly commanded, "Put." Pause. "It on."

Jack had mixed emotions about where this was going as he put on the ceremonial robe. It was masonic, slung down the front to barely cover Jack's hardening dick; he shapeshifted as Colton and then stood not the least bit self-conscious. There was a steeliness to Jack when he inhabited this mindset. Thad then added additional adornment and a king's crown of obsidian metal.

Next, Thad pulled down a small wooden case from the cart and then stood in front of Jack. "Bow." Jack moved his head to be lower where Thad could reach it. Thad opened the box. It was black and charred on the inside.

Thad continued.

"Truth." Thad smudged his thumb in the box, and soon it was covered in black soot and dirt. "Is sometimes more than perspective." He then reached up and smeared Jack's cheekbones, eyes, and a simple cross on his forehead. He crossed his own forehead, their matching smoke residue signaling a divine presence somewhere.

"Look," Thad prompted.

The reflection that looked back at Jack was one he didn't recognize or know. For the first time in his life, Jack felt like the outside matched the inside. His facial deformity named the denomination of the deal and added the punch that conveyed to the external who he was on the internal.

Jack opened his chest and his mind to greet it, taking in as much new information as he could gather. His senses swept into their heightened 25 positions while they hummed into the room's walls, which reverberated dark in resonance. Jack met himself anew, who met his divine feminine heart, who met his higher consciousness, which was one with his gut. It was all the parts of him meeting and becoming one. Jack watched in the mirror what was happening, pride beaming off his lover's face.

Standing exposed this way, Jack's eyes welled, watching himself transform, the process integral, combining and morphing. What Jack was witnessing was not of worldly stuff but ov the stuff behind the stuff, and Jack welcomed it into his truth with gladness. He had taken a huge step in becoming whole. He had realized his very first wish. Tears streamed down his face, reaching heavenward as he repeated it from memory.

"I want to be whole." He felt it. He *knew* it. His mother fucking *knew* it.

"This is what I felt in the motel!" Jack was a raging swirl, "This is who I saw in the mirror!" Jack turned with the thing. "This is why the playground of the abandoned felt like home despite being of the dark!" Jack realized he finally had spoken the truth, *his* truth that he *knew* to be true.

Jack snapped to attention, then trained on Thad, "How did you know?"

Thad laughed. "Like I said, beloved, I study spirits." He took a sure-footed step toward Jack, who was watching Thad also level up. "I needed a certain level of trust between us before I could say what I'm about to tell you."

Jack's being was pulsing with previously unknown solid form energy, his image skewing and shifting with the sacred radiance of the moment. "I love you, Jack, so what I tell you is not to hurt you but to enlighten you."

"Jack." The back of Jack's head then flung backward, hitting the top of his spine, his blown open presence taking in Thad's direction. It was as if the news of Thad's words met Jack as a torrent of truth delivered in a vortex of channeled energy, and these were words he knew from lifetimes before. When he heard his truth, he stood in it. A thing had finally been named as Thad changed Jack's life with his next words.

"Beloved." Thad was transfixed by the transmutation occurring before him. "You are ov the dark."

CHAPTER 42

QUIETUDE

That evening in bed, Jack had his head on Thad's chest as he lost himself in thought with new insights.

Thad finally broke the silence. "You okay, mate?" Jack nodded. "Was…?" Thad stopped and redirected. "How was that for you? You've been quiet, which I get. It's a lot to process, but…."

"I'm okay. And ya, it's a lot to process." Jack settled into Thad for comfort. "It's just one more thing I guess that I get to try and not be sad about." A comment that brought Thad to life fully.

"Whoa… hold up." He eyed Jack's face with awe and amusement. "Where are you?" Thad palmed Jack's forehead and hair while he looked out the window. "Jack. Mate… love. You can't…." Thad then shored up his presence to do the same for his love. He pulled Jack's chin, so their eyes met. "What you are is beautiful and good." Jack's sad state showed he wasn't convinced.

"It's just my whole life…." Jack hated himself for feeling emotional. "Why can't I just be fucking normal?" Thad chuckled a bit hearing this.

"Normal to whom? What does normal even mean? And why can't what you are be your version of normal because being what you are… this big beautiful hunk of a man is your perfect design despite its color." Jack caught the register of the word *design*.

"What did you just say?" They both were now adjusting their laze to engage with one another anew.

"What?" Thad added.

"Design. Why did you say it that way?" Jack then flashed back to when Thad completely tore down who he thought he was for an exchange of what he *knew* he was. "And…." Jack stammered with the tail of the thing. "And ov. You said ov." Jack sat upright while further opening for new meanings to meet him. "Why did you say that? Why did you say it that way — that I am ov the dark." He mystified further. "How do I know that?" Thad sexy chuckled and touched Jack softly.

"Oh, dear heart… so much to learn. Come." Thad indicated a direction back to his chest. They refolded themselves, breathing back to the moment. "I got you. We'll figure it out."

"I'm not sure I want to know." Jack was overwhelmed by how vulnerable he felt in the moment. He was tired of the game, the chase, the knowing, the unknowing, the shifting worlds, and the constant kiltering altar of change. "It's too much."

Thad nuzzled the top of Jack's head. "I know." He chose his next words carefully. "Just trust. Trust that what you are discovering about yourself isn't good or bad."

Jack didn't believe him. His badness didn't need to be explained to him. He knew it, chapter and verse.

"Trust me, if you can't trust in the process." He took Jack's face. "Can we agree on that?" Jack couldn't verbalize a yes, but he nodded and then left it at that.

The following day Joy was demanding attention, and Thad happily took her out and then brought Jack coffee in bed with a "Morning, my Prince." Jack stirred with a smile.

"Morning, my Princess," Jack teased, making Thad crow and laugh as he continued getting ready for work.

"I have to head into the office today. My publisher is meeting me to talk about my next book."

Jack took a sip of his coffee and asked, "How is that coming, by the way? I'm not slowing your process, am I?" Thad stood and crossed the room.

"Slowing my process?" He turned to face Jack, "You *are* my process. Everything is as it should be." Thad headed into the bathroom to shower, saying over his shoulder, "Get your books and things together to start your classes. Take the car if you need."

Jack refocused to get ready for his courses, jumped out of bed, then helped Thad shower as had become customary. It was one thing

Jack could do to help make his partner's day more pleasant and more effortless.

Jack met the steam of the tiled enclosure and breathed it in. He then snugged behind Thad and held him upright. The soapiness awakened him, his muscles meeting the day. Holding onto Thad's body to steady him while he washed, Jack concluded an equation that had often stumped him. The question about his "design," the word now actively back in Jack's brain. The question about why he was given extreme human strength.

In that moment, Jack got it. He finally understood. "This." Jack let the realization flood over him, filling every corner of his understanding. "This is why." He steadied himself and Thad as his lover finished cleaning himself. He then gave his partner's body a little hike up to regrip on his frame, ensuring that he was safe and secure in his arms designed for extra human strength. "Thank you." He sent heavenward, awash in the realization of the thing. The realization that once again, his design was both perfect and complete for the assignment the universe had devised for him.

CHAPTER 43

SLIT

With Thad gone for the day, Jack took care of a few tasks, including getting ready to begin his forestry education.

He opened his mail, which contained a replacement debit card, credit card, and a new driver's license. Next, Jack checked his bank account, noting no more payments had arrived from Workman's Compensation and that he had to stretch Dennis's $500 the length of an entire month. Something that's simply not possible when using Canadian Dollars. He ordered what he needed online and added the owed amount to his increasing debt pile. A mountain he hoped wouldn't avalanche and arrest his current forward movement of a promising new career. The math wasn't great, but Jack willed himself to table that worry until new opportunities presented themselves that made his current financial problems moot and inconsequential. Jack *knew* his current financial crisis was a timing thing and not a financial thing.

Money. Jack chaffed at the concept. *Like, how is that even a thing?* The chase was on. *When it's not even a thing.* Jack shifted in his seat to look out the desk window to see a chickadee bandit eyeing his every move. "Bleh," he exhaled in its direction, scaring the thing off.

Now what? Jack asked himself, noting his to-do list was complete. His mind wandered… bugging him to formulate what money was ov.

Jack crossed the room to connect to his favorite spot in the house on the backside facing the woods. He saw another, or perhaps the same chickadee, flit into view. "Can I borrow a couple of bucks?" Jack asked the feathered scoundrel. "Meh…," he internally turned with the banality of the topic. *Money. What is it ov?* Then, Jack did a

ninety-degree pivotal thought jog down a new rabbit hole of 'ov.'
He chased it.

How did Thad know my word? Jack was stumble-stumped. He just
couldn't make it make sense. *And what the fuck was that?* Jack finally
allowed himself to breach the topic with himself. *Ov the dark. I mean.*
Jack looked out the window while feeling a terrible case of the "go-
fuck-yourselves" come on. *Ov the dark. C'mon. Ya… Okay, there was
the sense that….* Jack was unsure how to name what he felt. *It kinda
was….* Jack reached for the word and landed on, "right." *But why?*

Another mental path opened, and Jack quick-turned into it.
Ya… Yes. Okay…. Jack searched for lies and truths, sorting them as
they hit his mind as fast as possible. *Yes.* He flipped up to a quieter
perspective for access to clarity as to what he knew to be true.

Yes, he repeated to himself, but this time as an admission. *It felt
right. What Thad said.* Jack didn't like that this information was living
in him as truth. *Fuck.* Jack hated himself for a bit. *Dark.* Jack was
appalled at the notion. *Dark? How?* He reviewed his core being. He
knew he was ov love. Jack knew he wasn't evil and that he felt
deeply for others. Too deeply. That was Jack. Not dark or evil. It
made no sense. *Why is this so frustrating?* Jack yelled in his mind. *Why
can't I just be fucking normal? Why do I have to be in this position all the
time? Why am I always the uncomfortable one? Why?* The mental stretch
of it was too much for the moment, so he stopped there to rest. He
shifted to look out the window again, noting he was breathing
heavier.

"Okay." He collected himself with a breath. "No fear. Let's face
the thing." Jack said as he cleared his mind to a vacated void of
bright white air. *What do I know?*

Jack listened and waited. His mind wandered on its path.

I know. The ethers tethered to posts. *I know that I am a loving man.
I know I am of love and empathy. I am not of the dark. LIE.* Jack stopped.
I am not of the dark. He was immediately met with the sense that was
untrue. Jack backed from the mull of it and stopped. When his mind
began to meander again, he tried, *I am not evil.* The silence he held in
his mind was proof that this *felt* true. He repeated the exercise. *I am*

not evil. That felt true. *I am not of the dark. LIE.* Jack slowed to a float. *That was a lie.* "That was a lie?" He paused again, then put forward, *I am of the dark.* The purity of the ethers didn't ring of a lie. It still felt true. Jack sat up. *What the? Awww… C'MON!* He stood and walked into the bedroom closet where he packed his carpet bag, which he had decided to keep as a souvenir, with binoculars, a writing pad, pencils, and drawing charcoals. He hoped an afternoon walk would help him find his next whittling adventure, but more than anything, he wanted to get out of the house and level his head. There was a buzzing in his hands that he knew a physical task would quell.

Mid-path, Jack rumble-fucked back to the topic of his finances. "Stop, Jack." Then the word "trust" met him, and he stopped walking. Looking around, he saw a reasonably flat log and thought he should at least try what he set out to be "better" at. *Fine,* Jack thought while sitting and opening his journal to write his third entry. Turning to the other pages, he was embarrassed for his lack of effort. "I'm trying…." Jack self-soothed. He was feeling the pressure, but pressure from what? "Perfection. Being the best."

Jack came flying back to the moment. *Perfection. Nope, we are not even so much as thinking about that! Nope. No time for anything else until we fucking finish up what we started. Focus.* During moments like this, Jack had a lot of clarity as to how he would cease to exist on this planet. It was constant. It was the song of wanting his mind that played in the background on repeat to stop at any price. He ignored the call and refocused and retrained.

"Okay, Jack." He began a simple doodle. "What do we know about money. What is it ov?" He accessed his higher mind.

"Money is ov nothing. Money isn't a thing. When countries need more money, do they print something anymore? No. They send a bunch of energy zeros and ones into the internet, and that's that. The paper notes once represented this energy, but we've even given up that illusion now. It's simply energy. It's directed in the same manner as other energy."

Jack felt its truth. *And what do I know about directing energy?* Jack dove further with complete blankness.

"It is as we discussed when reviewing making wishes come true. As I already have done once. I wished to be whole."

Jack reviewed himself and his newly adopted state.

"I am now whole. I made a wish, and now it is true."

Jack searched the thing for lies or falsehoods. There were none.

Jack was still doodling, free-flowing, unattached. *I am whole.* He pushed. *But why?* He knew he had an answer if he'd just look for it. He searched on for more truths.

"I am whole because I am integrated." Jack came back to Jack's mind.

"Integrated? What the…?"

He threw the question to his higher access, hoping to catch the wind of something new.

"To be the core of integration… like blending into a unified whole of my parts."

Jack felt he was both doodling and running in circles. *Parts?*

"As in aspects, perspectives, or attributes. As in all my perspectives and places from which consciousness lives within me."

He squinted into it. *To be whole. But what does that mean?*

"That all aspects are one. Not fragmented."

Jack went wide as the next thought met him.

"To not be broken."

Jack stopped drawing and put his pencil down. "Holy shit." He looked to the horizon, then put the following into his upper conscience: *I am not broken.* The silence verified the truth, and as was Jack's way, the notion struck a tender chord.

But how did I do that? Jack was filled with internal satisfaction that he had done something – really done something – for himself. He fixed a thing. Just like he had done with frustration, he figured it out. *But how?* He was internally possessed with the vex of it. Jack doodled on with a twisting churn.

"I made a wish. Step one. Got that, check."

He doodled faster.

"I -blank- -blank- -blank- did a thing."

There were blanks in the *knowing* that he'd revisit, but first to get as much of the macro framework of the thing as possible.

"That's step two. Then step three, it comes true."

Jack sat back and continued to search.

"Make a wish, do a thing, and it comes true.

The sensation was both queer and plain. *Huh,* Jack pondered. *What's the 'do a thing' bit?* He accessed his higher self for answers from outside himself.

"It's the trust bit. It's the yang bit."

Jack had hit something.

"But those two things are in opposition. Yang, doing, telling, saying, writing… versus yin of allowing and trusting."

Jack knew he was onto something.

So it's actually four steps? Jack reviewed.

"Make a wish, do a thing, allow a thing, then it comes true."

He doubled down on his focus, drilling into the core of it.

"Yang of it. Do tell, work. Talk about it, get others involved, do do do… then, don't do."

Jack's mouth slightly opened with the realization.

"Step three of four is the most important and the most misunderstood."

Jack *knew* that felt true. It had to be both.

Just then, Jack's phone rang. It was Thad.

"Where are you?"

Jack came present and looked at the time.

"Holy shit, Thad." He was dying inside. "I'm so sorry. I lost track of time." Jack couldn't believe it was getting dark. How had he not noticed? He looked down and saw pages and pages and pages of random doodling. Circles and branches and houses and weird cryptic numbers and symbols and words. Realizing what he had done, he threw his stuff in his bag and ran for the house.

Uhhh…! Jack injected into himself. *I'm such an idiot.* He had overlooked the physical world and its demands. He was late for life, lost in the clouds.

CHAPTER 44

OPIA

The next afternoon, despite the drizzle, Jack headed back to the same flat log to sit and stare and puzzle, hoping he could pick up where he left off. It felt like there was more if Jack went after the "source" ov… stuff.

He sat, crossed his legs, and went inward chasing tails of consciousness and whispers of things yet known.

Ov the dark, money, wish, time, future… allow, happen… met Jack's mind as he began doodling again. He repeated, *Ov the dark, money, wish, time, future… allow, happen.* He wasn't getting a live vibe from anything, so he put the matter into his higher being, then paused and began to write.

Money… which is ov nothing… well, not nothing… energy, I guess.

Jack slow floated on, open-wide nets cast searching.

If something is of nothing physical but is merely of energy, it can be directed. It can be created.

Jack refocused yet again. *So….* His drawings were getting faster. He flipped the page. *If it's just energy, which can be directed, can it be created, foretold, forecasted, or caused?* Jack stopped drawing. "Caused?" This was one word he wasn't expecting. He questioned its truth. "Caused?" He left it hanging in the air to see what it resonated with. There was no twist of the thing. It didn't wriggle in protest by being named. "And so it is." Jack got sunny in the midday gloom. *And so it is? Really?* He came back into himself. "Caused." The jokey hoax of the thing stuck in Jack's craw. He sent himself back in for further clarification while resuming his work.

Next, he settled and listened for any inkling of untruth.

This felt like a lowball warm-up shot. "C'mon, Jack… whatcha got? We're not in the beginner's class. We can do better than that." He shook his hands and then resumed drawing shaded circles one after another. He settled in for an inspection, flipping lenses as he dove in deeper to examine it.

He quieted for more and tried, *I can…*. He chose his next word carefully: *Cause.* He didn't so much as dare to breathe while listening with all his might. No weirdness appeared. He took a beat, then tried it again. *I can cause.* Again, silence. Jack stopped drawing and trained to the horizon.

"I can mother fucking cause shit to happen." Again… silence. Just the hum of what was. No untruths rang.

Jack looked around for the hidden cameras and readied himself to be let in on the joke. For a moment, that felt like clarity. He figured his read of the thing was off. He had made a simple mistake. Clearly, clearly, clearly, it had to be a mistake.

Okay… easy enough to fact check. Jack switched lenses. He asked himself slowly, *Can I affect future outcomes?* His gut confirmed.

"y e s."

Huh. Jack tripped on. *Really?* He searched his surroundings. *But wouldn't it also then stand to reason that I could only affect the future if I knew it? Otherwise, how would I know that I wasn't just possibly again…,* he laughed, *bullshitting myself?*

Jack stopped, realizing he was hitting a dead end and a dead horse that no longer needed to be flogged. He took to review what exactly he was being led to draw. It felt the same connection as his whittling. *But why?* Jack sought.

Once again, time had flown, and it was rounding suppertime when he started walking back to the house, fulfilled that he had done his work for the day. Most people probably wouldn't see what he was doing as *work*, but that's only because it wasn't human-time work. It was his life's work, much of which was done off-grid and showed up to this earth-plane merely as forgetful daydreams. He entered the back patio sliding doors to a house filled with baking sourdough bread and fall stew scents.

Seeing Jack, Thad smiled from his core, "Ah, you're home!"

Jack ran over to pick up Thad with a kiss. "Yes… and you are too." He set him down.

"I had Nancy prep a few items for the BBQ tonight. How's that sound?"

"It's a date," Jack said, speeding off to put his stuff away and get ready for dinner. "Get wine…." There was some "stuff" Jack wanted to speak to Thad about. He'd had some time to process what they had discovered together, and he had questions that Thad might be able to provide insight to. A bottle of wine, or two, might open new paths of latent potential because, in Jack's experience, the hidden often peek through while engaged with the stuff in-between.

Thad's voice entered the closet while he unpacked. "I got you something." Jack fast folded his bag to return to the kitchen quickly.

"Golden slippers!?" he said, eyes wide.

"You want golden slippers?" Thad said, clearly confused. He was still hanging with the unreason of the ask and trying to figure it out.

"No. Of course not." Jack sly-smiled then puppy-eyed his way, teasing Thad. He thought about it further. "Well… they would be fabulous." Jack then said mysteriously, "Especially for dancing." His wink of mischief made Thad laugh.

"Oh ya?" Thad managed as Jack picked him up, relieving him of his metal braces.

"Yes!" Jack then hit three buttons on his phone, making music start throughout the home, then held Thad just slightly off the ground and gently adjusted his partner's feet onto his. "Like this."

As the plucky perk of the music began, Jack danced Thad alongside the kitchen counter so his mate could grab it if needed, but the footwork they found required no such assistance and no such guardrails. Soon they were in mid-floor flight while the house slipped away, and only they were there holding onto one another. Thad laugh-protested, then let himself go to be held and danced across the room. Between them, a fit, a mastery of form, where one mate picked up where the other left off; a meld of their physical and a blessing from off-plane places. A place where things lived better than the jagged dystonic plane of the disabled and physical.

Jack put Thad down and returned him to his crutches. The room was alight in delight, and its beam set the tone for their supper. "I'll grab us jackets. It's getting cold out." Jack set out to make merry their outdoor dining, lighting the fire pit and heaters for additional warmth. The nestle and nudge of their shared space were perfect for what Jack wanted to pursue.

"Ready!" Jack yelled back into the house.

They ate and enjoyed their meal that evening, reviewing their day and its yang.

"How'd the meetings go today?" Jack asked while Thad poured them a drink.

"Good." Thad glinted his eyes. Pause.

"And this is where you say more about that," Jack teased, referencing their early conversations when Jack was a shut of words and a close of trust. Thad's eyes were a giggle as he came in for an intense stare with his eyes appled delight.

"You ever get the sense that...," Thad waved an arm toward the woods, "this... us... being together is...."

He didn't finish his thought, so Jack tried, "Written." The word confused Jack as it came out of his mouth. *Written?* Jack asked himself internally. *Gah, Jack. So dumb.*

Thad was saying something, but Jack was still lost in the embarrassing affliction of his stupidity. *Written. Like, who seriously talks like that?*

"Jack!" Jack came back to the present to look at Thad, who was searching him for presence.

"Oh. Ya... sorry. What were you saying?"

"You didn't answer my question." Thad waited for a response.

Again he apologized for checking out from their dinner, "Sorry. Can you repeat it?"

"Why did you say written?" They both stopped all else to fixate.

"Uh, I'm not sure exactly." Thad's paused energy leveled, waiting to see what might come next. Jack reviewed himself but again came up with nothing.

Thad took the reins. "I think we both know there's more to talk about." The topic didn't need to be named. Jack settled himself, knowing this was true, but at the same time, he questioned whether he was ready. "Your past." Thad was speaking low and soft. "The violence." He slowed for new words. "Your sexual desires… and what gets you off." Thad turned to look Jack more directly in the cool night air. "Do we need to take care there, mate? Do we need to walk cautiously through that stuff?" He paused as if forming a question. "Because we need to clarify that we're working with clean desires and not beating you senseless out of your self-hate."

It was said, and it hung in the air. Jack checked the thing for untruths and fabrications, but the stuff he was sharing and enjoying and engaging within the sex realm with Thad was clean. There was no taint to what he sought from it. There was no self-hate that he was bringing Thad into. Jack knew this was true, which was a new realization for Jack.

"That's amazingly sensitive, Thad." Jack expressed gratitude into the night that he had a partner who'd check for this type of thing. "I get what you're saying… and ya, maybe the origins of what I like *was* rooted in ick and issues like that." Jack checked his next words before saying, "But it doesn't live in me like that anymore. I think I've *healed* my stuff around that." Jack shrugged, "Dunno… I like what I like, and it gets me off, so in a way… I guess… I've given my past trauma…." Pause. "Purpose."

Jack bolted upright. "OH WOW!" The realization of assigning a purpose to past trauma clarified why it had shown up for Jack in that way. *I'm free of its ick,* Jack thought, then refocused to Thad.

"I think…." He searched for the right way to say it, "I think… somehow… we cleaned it up. But how?"

Thad laughed. "Good. I thought that was the case as we worked through our shared bondage work, but you hadn't yet verbalized it, and…."

Jack jumped on Thad and pushed him into a lying position on the bench. Thad was a roar of laughter as Jack continued his thought, "Was this part of it? I mean… did you, or were you consciously trying to help me work through that stuff?"

"Well, no… pretty much I was just having fun and since… well," he chuckled, "since you like what I like doing to you and vice versa, I wasn't going to get into the weeds on it, but the other part of my brain and what I know from studying spirits… well, I thought it might provide new ground for you to see, work with, and ultimately free yourself. But it was always going to be up to you. I merely showed you the arena."

"Holy shit, Thad. Really? So you knew there might be an upside or healing to tying me up and fucking me senseless?" Thad again laughed full belly, the best sound in the world to Jack's ear.

They were lying down on the cold cement built-in bench, too much of which wasn't covered by a cushion. "I was just trying to help," a coy comment of stupid that sent Jack into belly laughs in return.

"Helping me?" Jack flashed glitter of contentment into his partner. "Or helping yourself!" They laughed at the real of it. It was one of those moments where the world was right, and two disabled men realized they could move mountains.

The tone between them got serious, and Jack saw tears form in Thad's eyes. A sight that significantly moved and slowed Jack because Thad never cried.

"I just want to make sure you're good. That none of what we're doing, exploring, and learning about one another is too much or triggering or damaging for you." There was silence in the night as Jack watched a tear roll down Thad's cheek and disappear into his beard. "I don't want to do *this* without you Jack." They both knew that *this*, in this context, meant life. Thad rolled onto his back and exhaled into the night. "You have me completely undone, Jack." They both laughed. "So this brings me to my next question."

"Oh shit!" Jack laughed. "Here we go…." the mood returned to crows of charms as Jack tried not to laugh into Thad's face directly.

"What?" Jack prompted. "And don't make it so fucking hard this time! God...." Jack flashed with the memory. "You have a knack for asking bloody impossible questions."

"Well, then you sure ain't going to love this one, mate." They were both a river of childhood flowing in and out of one another. "It's more a follow-up to what YOU started."

"Oh, and what was that?" Jack asked. His laugh leveled to slow.

"You had said there were some things that we don't always want to get too honest about."

"Ya?" Jack confirmed with a question.

"Then what I said was, like, how honest do you want to get about what you know about your death?"

A curious quiet returned between them. "Ya?" Jack said again, then followed it with, "And...."

"And you fucking vexed me with that question," Thad said into spaces behind places. "Why did you put that in my brain?"

Jack laughed. "Oh, you know... I'm just casual like that," Jack said while he stupid-grinned.

They both laughed.

"Casual?!" Thad questioned through an, "Oh my God." Jack twinkled while Thad wondered. "Casual. You're a fucking lunatic, mate."

Jack loved it when he called him mate because he could hear what sang beyond slang. It was the "life-mate" tone that Thad's deep tenor lent it that shored up Jack's soul. Connection. That's what feels good. That's what feels right. Jack was a gentle beam of it.

They settled back to lying beside one another in the cooling Canadian evening air. Thad then got serious. "But can I ask your answer to *that* question?" A comment that made Jack shift a bit. Not shapeshift, but shift to a land away from wild moving parts.

"Really?" Jack asked. He then leveled to serious. "You want me to tell you what I know of my death?"

"Ya," Thad confirmed, not letting the men move past the point.

"I'm not sure I want to go there in my mind," was Jack's best reply.

Thad pulled Jack into his face. "Fuck it. Fuck them. Fuck the world. Let's go there."

Jack leveled to steel and said, "I'm in."

CHAPTER 45

FIXING

Jack stared into Thad's being, searching for answers. "Tell me about losing your mother."

Thad stirred but didn't shy away from his turn to be asked a tough question. "What I remember most was when my mind began to feel the horror of the situation." Thad paused to refocus. "It was like I had been numb for an entire week, then one morning, I started to feel what was really happening. It was like the morphine my body had lent me was wearing off, and I could feel terror." Pause. "And sadness. I recognized I was truly alone in the world. I had no one at that point."

Jack remained silent, letting Thad relive that moment.

"I remember a social worker rushing me down a busy street in downtown Liverpool." His gaze left his eyes. "Knowing she was late, she kept trying to get me to walk faster, which, as you recognize, only trips me up." He was lost with the memory. "I remember her yelling at me, 'We don't have all damn bloody day, boy.'" Thad mocked. "I tried, but given the lateness of our appointment and the woman's frustration, she left me there."

"Left you there?" Jack said in disbelief.

Thad turned with the thought. "Well, not for good, but yes. She said she'd take care of it and that I was to stay put."

"You didn't stay put."

Thad laughed. "In fact, I did not." Jack joined in the laughter as his mate journeyed on. "I remember looking around trying to figure out where I was, but I wasn't experienced in these worldly matters, and it was all very confusing. I remember stepping away from the wall where I stood. And I was like Holy Shite… it was a Cathedral. Realizing this fact, I, of course, popped in to check it out."

"Of course." Jack laughed. "Is this when your obsession with old church relics and stuff started?"

Thad grinned like the redheaded devil he was. "It was the most dark and glorious thing I had ever witnessed. But there was more to it. It wasn't solely how the place looked with its stained-glass depictions but also how different it felt. It steadied my soul, and I felt drawn to it." Thad refocused to the ceiling. "I remember hobbling forward down a long aisle. When I got to the end, I stopped and looked up. There were spires of clouds painted on the ceilings with naked bodies frolicking! It made me feel the pulse of the place, and I leaned into its breath to find new life at a moment when I felt like I had none. It was the moment many people of faith describe – dense and dark and real. And I loved it." Thad became more animated in the telling of it. "The multitudes of dead and dying on crucifixions highlighted in beams of light. The death of Christ hanging on the wall, gasping for air and dying. The pain of his experience inescapable. His torture real, depicted on his battered face." Thad looked at Jack. "I felt the dark corners, the secrets, the power over the child, and the crippling weapon found in the concept of teaching ov their guilt and ov their sin. It was the first time my spirit hit max." Thad turned to address Jack directly. "Know what I mean?"

Jack nodded as Thad went on as if telling a ghost story at summer camp. "I witnessed them coming one by one in after-life drone form to receive the highest gifts and 'Drink of his blood and eat of his flesh.' I witnessed that all firsthand on my first day of church… and I got it. I understood what it was ov, for I could see with my own eyes what was steeped in myth, cloaked in blood, and uplifted story after story of slavery, cutting off hands, torture, and dashing the newly born against rocks."

"Wow…." Jack trailed off once again, seeing this side of his love. A side that equally frightened him and turned him on.

"But this is the part that fucking woke me up." Jack sat upright to hear more. "I walked to the side of the open space where a lone statue stood of a young woman whose fate had been sealed." Thad now became more animated. "I was immediately drawn to her, so I scuttled my little butt to where I could look into her face. She stood there gleaming for some unknown reason. It was transformative, her gaze upon me. So I stood there staring for a few moments, but then I began to recognize her as my mother."

"Holy shit," Jack interjected.

"She slowly stepped toward me, and I froze in place." The silence was intense. "I remember her saying, 'Don't be sad, my child. I am here.' She looked around and started speaking again. 'I have to show you that I am with you and where to find me.' Which I didn't fully understand at the time. Next, she took my head and pressed her cheek into mine." Jack was slack-jawed in disbelief.

Thad continued. "I remember her singing in a beautiful clear tone. 'Match me,' she said, so I did. Next, she sang a new note. A higher tone. A sparklier tone. And again, I sang and matched it. In the lone dark corner of the stone cathedral we were in, the exercise continued with me matching her note after note." Thad seemed to drift off with the memory. "Next, she moved from musical notes to vibrations, where I found the hardest part of this exercise was discovering where to begin and that the rest was merely an allowing. It felt like an access point."

"Love that," Jack confirmed.

Thad thought about this more. "I found that striking the vibration correctly for the first half a second was the trickiest part because that's where I narrowed in on it… then discovered it was not a note or a sound but a sensation. From that moment on, I would forever know what the other side felt like and what lever to pull to get there."

Jack exhaled, his mind blown all over the place. He was trying to square the place that Thad had gone to – and apparently knew how to visit often!

Chapter 46

Cynosure

Thad tacked back to their earlier conversation. "So tell me about your death."

Jack backed up energetically. "You're serious?"

Thad, with more intensity, confirmed. "Ya. Yes... I wanna go there. I want to find the edges of the human experience. I want to live fully. No rules. Absolute truth."

"That's going to have to be a completely ego-free environment, my friend." Jack laughed. "And you have trust and jealousy issues." Thad was caught.

"You noticed."

"Oh yes, sir, I did, and that is the bridge between what you're asking for and how far I'm willing to go." Jack shoulder-shoved him, stating, "And please... let's not act like you're good at hiding that character defect." Thad burst out laughing even harder, mostly from humor, but there was also a dash of embarrassment in it.

"You are a bloody lunatic." Jack joined in the laugh. "But wow, you are perceptive." Thad gained an embodied air, saying into Jack, "That sensitivity... and while it's hell on earth, it is the portal many seek." He held Jack tighter. "Direct. Ov Source. A fountain." He eyed Jack closely. "That's what I see." He kissed Jack. "Some can glean from the gifted." He paused, choosing his words correctly. "They are sorcerers. But you? You, I think, are the level above that. That's what I see. A sourcer. Direct. Tied to. The ones who channel."

"You're a lunatic," Jack said aloud. The mire of what Thad said was too foreign for either ear.

"AaAaAaAaAaAa...," Thad yelled, breaking the tension. He knew how far one could be stretched in a day.

"AaAaAaAaAaAa…," Jack tried, but mostly failed because he was laughing too hard. They let their souls swim in the moment together, naked and without pretense, for the restorative measures it lent.

Jack regained his composure and finally said it. "So ya." Thad slowed himself to hear what seemed to be important. "I'm in." Thad's eyes became wide as he swooped in for further verification.

"For real?" He scooped up Jack's face. "All the way?"

Jack laughed. "I'll meet you shoulder to shoulder. How's that?"

They were a hum of emotions and the moment felt reverent – the quiet of them writing testament to this fact.

"So can I ask you what I wanted to earlier?" Thad said softly.

Jack smiled, already hating some of this new *truth* process but also very open to being new with someone. "Sure."

Thad focused on looking at Jack from a soft distance. The distance of middle age to get better focused on things.

"What do you know about your death?"

Jack knew that was coming back like a boomerang but was still only partly prepared. Because how does someone properly *prepare* for that conversation? He readied himself.

"Honestly? I have always assumed I would take my own life." He let that hang in the air. "That I'd shoot myself in the head. That's how I would go." Jack let himself feel how that sounded now that it was out of his mouth. He felt perturbed by its nag. He turned to face Thad. "Why do you want to know that, and why are you making me say it out loud?" Jack's stare into Thad was intense in its mix.

The corner of Thad's mouth found a smile. "Because I get you. I get where your heart and wounds are." He stroked a thumb to Jack's deformed cheek. "It's written all over your face." Jack once again found himself taken aback by Thad's directness and clarity.

Jack turned. "That's not fair, Thad." Thad took his face.

"Tell me, what part of that is untrue?"

Jack was getting more irritated at the rightness of his partner. He scanned the thing for untruth and found none. *Fuck,* Jack thought as he internally squirreled, searching for places to hide the other ugly bits of himself that were yet to be found. The gig was up, and Jack was in a panic.

"None… but gah," Jack exasperated more for humor. "Rude." They both laughed then Thad continued.

"I see pain in you, Jack, and you've been told that's bad." Jack internally what-the-fucked, and the conversation halted for them to feel the resonance of what had just been said. Thad continued. "And I'm sorry for that, but I'm hoping once we explore the edges of what's possible, we can find a purpose or meaning for that truth and experience it in a new light." He kissed Jack's forehead. "And I want that for us. No rules. Just what feels right and good." Thad paused on the verge of naming a big thing. "I have *finally* found a partner I could even pose the question to." Thad moved into Jack's face saying quietly, "Because of you, I have found my Zenith Peak. I knew it did exist, and now…," Thad smiled, "I have finally found it." Jack could sense his explosion of gratitude.

Jack populated with the new concept and then arrived at his words. "I want that too… but Jesus, you just fucking *go there*. Like, do we have to be that fucking tricky and gut punching all the time?" They laughed.

"Good." Thad laughed. "I know it's going to be a challenge for us both. And I know I'll fuck up, but I promise I just want to see what level of existence we can achieve. It's the reason I asked you to confirm what I already knew about you. Your type often has a hard-on for suicide." Jack laughed at the annoying truth of it. "So it was one of the first things I wanted to address with you because I only ask one thing."

Jack stopped. "What's that?"

"That you don't do it without me."

Jack sat upright. "Thad! What are you saying?!"

"I'm saying I'm smart enough to tell you that you CAN kill yourself, but that only if you do it with me."

Jack didn't know what to say or think.

Thad chuckled and then said, "Kinda takes all the fun out of it, doesn't it?" He winked his devilish grin. "Promise me." Silence. "Total honesty."

"Gah!" Jack let fly. "Fine. Deal."

CHAPTER 47

WATERLOGGED

After the first week of school, Jack had tried his best to fall into a routine of working out, classes, lunch, homework, tree time, dinner, stoned TV time, and bed. It was a day that worked for him. "From yang time to hang time," as he saw on some assholes bumper-sticker. However, his episodes continued to show up randomly and now at all times of the day. Jack lied to himself that he was okay and that things were getting better.

When he could manage it, one of the best parts of Jack's day, was his outdoor tree-time, the wear of the day meeting the stillness of the woods. The internal massaging of it loosened the unwanted and sloughed the unintentional. The weather was well into autumn, and the chill of the season was on everyone's breath. Jack found its crispiness gave him new homes and places to check for life's secrets. He opened his journal, noting he was on the next to last page.

"How?" He rummaged his book for answers. "But...?" Jack flipped the pages again   an activity that only confirmed what he knew. He had scribbled on every single page. He internally searched himself because that reality was not making sense. But it wasn't the how that was his ask. It was the why. He searched his bag for another notepad and found one.

Jack measured himself, noting where he was on this day, and then put a fresh charcoal to the pad. He began. The stroke was deliberate. "Don't think...." He shook it all off. The charcoal started to loop, and Jack focused there. There, to its living second of life as its hunk gives way to a message. Jack trained on that second alone. There was no one else. There was nothing else. His breath. His movement. His spark of life that existed all in the one millisecond of his mind. He settled. Moving. He danced the thing deftly into being, seeking anything that might present to his blank mind. The one he knew from beyond the 'click.' His nets hit open as thoughts were caught alive, ready for Jack's devour.

And then he found it — the access point located at the intersection of a blanked mind and the absolute present. Before him, he found a new new. A new possibility. It was like the fourth dimension of color but tied to time — a place where they all arrive as one. The past, the present, and the future were the loop of the eternal. Jack held it only for the briefest of seconds, but to know this access point to the plane of time felt *big*.

Jack returned the world's vision to himself and then opened his eye — the one that lived in his mind, the one that watched the blank screen. "I want to change the world."

His vision getting clear, he worked that day for hours on the chase of the thing, and when darkness tinted the sky, he stopped and breathed, knowing he had done great work. He then walked in silence back to the house, hoping they had another bank of blank pages ready for tomorrow's hit, and he smiled, knowing that he was just warming up.

CHAPTER 48

SEXTANS

Thad and Jack had gotten into a routine that they loved but were also aware of the clock as October came to be. It was the last month of them for a few, not that either of them cared to think on it much. It was just a fact.

The first weekend of the month, they decided to see fall in all its glory with a trip up the Canadian west coast. Jack's neurological issues had been slowly worsening, and they thought getting away might help settle the matter.

After a particularly bad morning, Jack was motionless and powered off. His mind failed to meet any moment. Thad held him as he always did, locking into his breath so Jack could feel and hear his presence. In this sacred place between them, Thad had Jack and met him right where he needed him, never annoyed, or off, or anything less than perfect. It awed Jack how this man could hold him for hours without complaint. How he could clean him with dignity and not so much a sliver of wanting to be anywhere else existed.

Thad knew all the dances by heart. He, in lockstep, would move right along with Jack. It was a dance of affliction, callous to those it touched, but even in that, they held on and laughed and lived.

Jack finally started to come back to the room, but he struggled to focus or find English for the remainder of the day. At dinner, Jack was a flop of flannel housecoat and bones where everything felt disconnected and detached. They sat for their meal.

"Babe," Thad said, sitting after helping cut Jack's food. "We need to get you help. I know how you feel about that, but this isn't good… and if you want to make it for field training next month, well… to be honest, I don't know if that can still be on the table." This annoyed Jack in two ways. One, that Thad should "fuck-off" for making him feel bad. And two… for it being true. Jack's sadness was back. His last remaining whip-worn pole of hope tattered and now breaking.

One of Jack's greatest fears was that his mind work and tree-time were causing the deterioration. Was he breaking his own mind? He didn't know, and quite frankly, he didn't want to know because he knew even mental deterioration wouldn't stop his life's work, for that was who he was. A thing one can't arrest even if one wants to, for one cannot contain one's nature. What is, is.

Jack ate in silence, trying his best to navigate the treacheries of hidden paths, internally shorting his nerves' communications. He eyed the daily tasks and hoped for working parts such as how to use a fork while bites fell into his lap, few finding his lips. His brain was too fragile yet mushy to work on anything past surviving the stimuli of the room. Each flash of it blinding and painful to Jack's brain.

The next morning over breakfast, Thad tried again, "Babe…." He moved to sit next to him. Jack slapped at brain-fogged words but recognized few.

"Okay," Jack acquiesced to accepting help and then returned to his silence.

After breakfast, Thad made some calls, and set the appointment for the 15th. The day before the appointment, they decided they should talk.

Thad began. His concern was legit and annoying to Jack. "So, what do you want to do about heading up to the Yukon?"

Jack was ready to answer the question and hoped they could make it work. "I want you to come with me. Is that at all an option?" He pushed on the matter further, unwilling to just give up. "Please, Thad… I need something in my life. Something to work toward. Something to give my days purpose." The prefix "remaining" hung in the air unsaid.

Thad thought about it, reworking a few appointments in his mind. "Ya… I mean…." He looked at his phone, scrolling. "Ya… well…." He reshuffled his phone's contents and said, "Except the weekend of November 18th."

"Well, maybe we can work something out." Jack was pleased enough with this arrangement. "Besides…," he winked like an asshole, "maybe they'll cure me at my appointment." Thad laughed and pushed him.

"Lunatic."

Jack had another question on his mind that now felt like an okay time to ask. "So, how is it you always seem to be a step ahead of me? Like you almost know what I want or need before I do?" Thad adopted an amused expression.

"Oh, dear heart." He kissed Jack. "I've just been around a while, and I've had an opportunity to do more work than you."

"Like how did you somehow just *know* about… to ask… you know, about the suicide thing," Jack hammered home the point. "Like, how?" He looked up, devoid of humor. "How do you know shit like that about me? I swear it's just some magic voodoo shit." They laughed. "But seriously. How did you guess I was kinda weirdly wired like that?"

Thad took Jack in his vision. "Like I said, I've been around a long time and where we are isn't exactly new." This was news to Jack. "I know what color you are, mate. I know that sounds odd, but you are of a deep purple. You are of the dark, and I know what I see. And I know what I know about purple people." Thad winked.

Jack collapsed, annoyed. "Purple people?" His tone flat, then he laughed despite himself. "Are you insane? Purple people. I swear, Thad. You make *me* look normal." They both laughed, knowing the truth of what was just said.

Thad interjected. "But the truth is… I just kinda know some things… but it's also because I've pursued a lot and learned a lot."

"Like what? What do you know, Mr. Old and Wise?"

"I know that you're a special being, and I know you are more than you even know you are." Thad's pride shone into Jack. "I know you only need to be as the creator intended. I know you will find the strength in the dark because those of that realm are the fiercest. After all, it's they who fly closest to the night terrors – the furthest out to the farthest reaches. So far, no one can see your loving care, only your inequity when grounded, because that's not where you belong. You are not ov the earth and its people... so that's why they do not feel ov you. You are ov the night. You are ov source. As I am a helper, you are a sourcer, and your wounded heart is your greatest strength because that much sensitivity and humanness found in one person is the only thing that keeps back the malevolent. It is why you are both so entwined. It is the gales you soar on wing to wing — Dark and Evil. They are soul twins, two sides of the same sword." Thad paused. "I know you want to do more with your life but can't see how yet." He took Jack's face. "I can help you. I know how to do this next part." He leveled then named the unsaid. "The handicapped part." A tear streamed down his face. "I got you, babe."

Jack sat unmoving, silently crying.

CHAPTER 49

INJECTION

Jack sat on the doctor's examining table as they awkwardly waited longer than they had hoped. Finally, the neurologist and a colleague entered the room, and introductions were exchanged.

The doctors reviewed Jack's charts, confirmed their awesomeness to one another, and finally turned to ask Thad a few questions.

"Has he been sleeping on a regular schedule?" the head doctor asked.

Jack piped up, "Ummm… the he of whom you speak is right here." They ha-ha'd and redirected to Jack while feeling under his armpit for some unknown reason. No explanation was given.

The appointment led to further appointments and tests, and the chase was again on for what rattled Jack's brain.

After the appointment, they got into the elevator. *It doesn't matter.* Jack mentally signed off as he watched the doors slide closed.

Thad turned to Jack. "What was *that?*" Jack laughed and was reminded again why he loved this man so much. He just always had Jack's back.

Laughing relief and life back into himself, Jack agreed, "I know? It's so confusing to me. Like… I'm in the room. Hello?!" They laughed to the bottom parking level to get the car. It was a weird dynamic for Jack to drive Thad to Jack's doctor's appointments. The fluidity required to deftly navigate those relational waters was awesome.

The men agreed to talk about "what next" over dinner, but for now, they had responsibilities to address. Jack dropped Thad off at his appointment and then hurried home. He gave Nancy a quick kiss and then took Joy out on his afternoon stroll for tree-time. He unpacked his bag and set out a place for Joy. She loved these moments and was happy to have been invited. Jack hummed to blank and began his work in a newfound journal. He scrolled and disjoined to find perfection through radical detachment. He opened to higher places and sent thanks into the wind. The moment and Jack were one, both fleeting and alive.

He sat and focused until he hummed of birds, Joy noting the newfound smile as Jack dove deeper into clarity. Pausing for new, believing what was.

He asked himself a question. "What do I know about this?" The *this* clear in his mind as to how to move forward with his concerning medical issue. Clarity. He focused on the clarity that he needed from the matter, the antimatter, and all the stuff in-between. Next, he leaned into a master's trick. He sent gratitude into the ethers for the answer that had yet to arrive. A trick, of course, that confuses the beyond because you're thanking them for something that hasn't yet happened… so they make right what they think they've skipped over. It's a trick. It's magic. It's science he didn't understand. Yet.

Jack was silent throughout, then flashed to the fringes of his feelers, searching for whispers. His offering was a void in the universe; by nature's law the universe would fill that void again. But fill it with what? Jack would often wonder, but what he knew to be true was that it was something new and not ov him. The following message met him.

"The problem *is* the portal." Jack didn't respond or acknowledge the enormity of its truth. Instead, he simply stood, collected his dog, and walked home.

That was enough for today.

CHAPTER 50

INTERNING

"So, how do you want to handle your health moving forward?" Thad finally asked at dinner.

Jack searched for the perfect words. "I think I want to give up on medicine and get serious about other ideas and options. I just don't feel comfortable taking all those medicines without first addressing the root cause of what's making me dystonic. What is it? No one can even tell me that. They just don't know… and I'm tired of the chase to nowhere. Can we please…." Jack was emotional, as was his way. "Can we please just stop before we start? I know how this goes, and once you get on the treadmill, it's so fucking hard to get off." Jack's volume was increasing. "It's like a well-worn path you get led down. A path that only requires passive consent, not even a verbal yes… and trust me, 'no' isn't even an option in some cases. And as North American's we have no fucking access or ability to say no. It's like you're a problem when you say no, or that you're not serious, or that you don't know what's best for you. I'm tired of being talked about and not to." Jack wiped his tears. It was clear this was old stuff that he needed to purge.

Thad rubbed his back and remained present without judgment. Jack found his voice again, which cragged, "Because you don't know who you are… or if you can live without the medications, and you don't know what's you and what's the drugs." Jack thought about it hard. "And you don't know who you are if you get well. You don't know if you can even do life like a normal person anymore." He looked up at Thad. "Please don't turn me into a sick person. I'm not. I, ya… might have some weird ways I move or disconnect to and from the world. Maybe that's my normal? No one EVER said this thing would kill me." But he also knew the bound and unable to move part, which was the path he was on, and if you had asked Jack about that final part, the crippled like Steven Hawking part… well….

He stopped the thought as was customary with those thoughts and searched for clarity. "So why do I care? Why do I care if one hour of my day… okay, sometimes more, but it's not my entire day. It's not my entire life." The "yet" part hung in the air unsaid. Jack was searching Thad's eyes for connection. "If we ever feel like I'm in more danger, we can reassess. I mean, so long as someone is there to watch me, I'm okay. I can still hang." Thad seemed swayed.

"Okay, mate." Thad's tone wasn't joyful. "We can, but if anything starts to go off the rails, I get to say so."

Jack smiled. "I can live with that." He lifted his glass of vino. "To stopping before we begin." Jack laughed. "Oh my God, that sounds awful. Ha." They both laughed. "To trusting our ability to know what's right for us."

Thad clinked Jack's glass. "I can work with that."

The next afternoon, Jack headed for tree-time, still gnawing on a kernel from last night. The "passive-consent" part and our inability to access "no" as a complete sentence. Jack was getting better at pinging truth when it met him as vibration. They were like little snacks he'd pocket for further inspection later in his day.

Jack arrived at his usual spot, took out and put on his obsidian crown, and then sat on his usual wood throne while assuming the tone that connected him to universal truth. Jack shored up his tendrils of feelings lying scattered about, just waiting to get stepped on. Not an advanced trick, but a required one for anyone who wants to move past the density of pain inflicted by others then wounding ourselves with a reaction. Jack didn't have time for those messy distracting bits and knew when he was now inhabiting a solid container impervious to casual hurt. Today he was on a mission. He folded his everything into a tightly packed him to begin.

Leveling to zero presence and finding the perfect connection to the now, Jack threw himself into the unknown, searching for morsels he knew were just there for the taking. He could smell it.

He could smell it last night at dinner when it first entered the room. Jack focused with a drill down onto a singular vibration that flashed to him the moment it had been said.

"Passive consent."

The universal bell rang with its resonance. He blanked and waited for more.

Nothing. He rang its gong again with even more clarity and focus.

"Passive consent. Why does that feel dangerous to me?" The resonance hummed while the wind shifted, and Jack zeroed in, remaining curious about what might be found. His mind drifted to a conversation he had with his mother when he knew he was queer but hadn't come out. It was couched as a conversation about bigotry in their church against a lesbian friend.

"But how is that okay? That we belong to a religious institution that discriminates? I thought we as Christians were better than that?" He fumed in her direction over all the things waiting to be said.

"Well, we as good Christians follow the church."

"But the Church is wrong." Jack turned sharply, "Not to mention so fucking vicious and mean!" Mid-exasperation, his mother had enough and left the room. That's what tools Jack had to work with to navigate a world of problems. A move known as cut n' run.

Jack returned to the present. *That's passive consent,* he thought to himself. *That's how people can tell themselves they're good people while belonging to and funding institutionalized bigotry.* The realization was clear. *That's where it lives. Bigotry lives in passive consent. The unsaid. The silent majority. It lived on in the control of those who have made us afraid to say no.* The twist is apparent. Access to No. *Why is that weird to me? Why does 'Yes' feel better than No? What is that? Why are they not the same?* He recognized the exercise from the "unique" versus "not-normal conversation." The latent judgment of the "not" that's found in the thing. Jack recognized the wriggle of it. It just felt different. In his gut, he knew more discovery awaited.

NO! Jack yelled into himself. It resonated powerfully. *Oh fuck ya!* He pulsed with the resonance. *Me, likey.* But then he got honest that the throb of the thing might not be for everyone. He checked again, searching for its power and echo. *NO!* he yelled. Again, Colton pump-throttled. "Niiiiice!" Jack was having fun seeing things from different perspectives within himself. *This is powerful stuff, this "no."* He checked in more. *I can see why people would be afraid of this. Afraid of this power. This power of no. No. A complete sentence.* Jack rambled, enjoying the rev of it.

NO! He felt it again for truth. It had a rumble of thunder to it. Seeking a different perspective, he tried the word from Colton's perspective. *NO!* then, *Fuck ya.* Jack internally face-palmed at Colton's one-track mind. *So dumb.* He flipped up for clarity, vacating the voices and presence of the busy hive-mind. He could think again in this space, and there was always a sense of relief when he returned. *Why don't I get up here more often?!* was always the first thought when he met this place inside him.

His mind was silent. He sent gratitude to the universe for the answer, although he hadn't received it yet. *Let me punt it into the future. Let me tinker with outcomes; let what I know appear. Thank you for clarity around why we don't have the same access to a no as a yes. Thank you for clarifying the underlying stub of it and making clear to my mind what's tripping me up.* He doubled down on the ask while the universe set into motion conspiring acts and then corrected their mistake, which met him with, *The feminine no. The no delivered from a mother to a child, the "no" that is a thousand percent love is a very powerful tool for empathetic people willing to meet it where it lived.* It met Jack, and he knew he knew this bit. He knew the thundering resonance of the feminine no. He recalled his favorite saying: *And then love said no!* His feminine heart smiled and stepped into that resonance of a fierce warrior, its presence humming of a silver white she-wolf. She gained in presence and then offered her night vision and her insight. Jack hummed with something new, reviewing her resonance and message.

"The scream of a 'NO!' from a mother lifting a car off her child will move time and bend space. THAT is what you are missing. That is the part you do not yet know or inhabit as a global consciousness.

Search no more until that is emboldened, empowered, and laser-focused. End bigotry. End hatred. End selfishness through love's clarity. She is the fierce energy needed. The time is now, Jack. We cannot wait any longer. You must chase this thing and this thing alone."

Jack recognized the absurdity of the imbalance in life. The traps. As instructed and taught, being forced into a passive yes denies us access to a no, even when the no is the better and more loving choice.

Jack had a new thought because he perceived this white wolf's presence from past lives. Her virility and unmatched power. How she inhabited him as a warrior. The vision of the white wolf unapologetic in her protection and fierceness. Her resonance in him, which throbbed and pulsed authoritatively without ego or ick. The bold threat of love that contained no resistance to what is.

She sent to his vision. "It is better to be a warrior in a garden than a gardener in a war." She steadied on with her clarity, leaving Jack with a clear understanding that he'd pay the price for this later with a storm that would shackle back that which dared to universally untether. He was too deep this time. However, Jack knew that it would be a debt he would gladly pay for this new landscape of understanding.

"It is why men subjugate women," floated into his mind. "They fear her power. It is why politicians divide women as skillfully as they do and why women cannot coalesce around a subject as a major voting block. They're pit against each other, and that's planned. Women are a threat to men. Men instinctively know this. The double edges of that sword being lust-laden eyes and desires of the flesh versus the fear women strike in men's fearful hearts."

Jack reviewed more of the message that was coming to him. "That's why men dominate, indoctrinate, and control women. It's about the fear of the mighty divine finding her voice in an absolute NO! Not on my watch!" The message scrolling on… "We can harness, direct, and even exploit that power once it is collectively owned."

Jack found the access point to time. An access point located at the intersection of the precise present moment and his blank mind. He stepped behind the causal plane's curtain and peered into the dark, blinking-light-filled room. He floated to clarity to search openly, feelers set to the max where Jack felt the intersections he wanted to affect and twisted something into it anew. He then returned to himself, sitting on a log, and said skyward, "How I wonder what you are."

Closing his book that day, Jack thanked future time for receiving his tinker and walked back to the house with his heart full of joy.

Chapter 51

Hold On

That evening at supper, Jack decided to find out what Thad might know about the things he had been thinking about earlier.

"I'm getting a weird vibe from two things." Jack mused about how to word the next bit. "When I said the phrase 'passive consent' and again regarding my issue in saying no to medical help, why is that weird? I can't quite place why yes is easier to say than no." He chased it further. "It's like giving away your power is easier than not adopting the wish or will of others."

Thad smiled wide, seeing what Jack was tripping on. "That's the vex of it." He smiled into his love. "It's because we live in a world that believes in two polar options as the best solutions. There's no color to that sort of thinking. It's very black and white and not enough grey."

Jack smirked and said, "Or purple." Thad laughed.

"Yes. Or purple," Thad confirmed. "But you get what I'm saying. It's so much the thesis of my book. Why do we live in a colorless world with no options? Why is frigid better than slutty or any shade in-between? Why is monogamous better than open relationships or polyamorous ones? And better to whom?" Thad rolled into Jack's direct view. "That's why it was so important to me to be with someone like you. Someone willing to break some boundaries." He did a quick aside, "By some, I mean all," then returned to his main thought. "I need to know and see what life feels and tastes for me without adopting the thought prisons of our culture."

Jack laughed, "We're like the weird leading the weirder." Thad soft punched him upon hearing this.

"No, mate. No… no." Thad jokingly brought the room to attention. "How about the curious leading the curiouser."

Jack thought about it. "We're super weird." Thad laughed until he almost cried.

"That we are, my friend. That we are."

Jack cleared the dishes and poured them another glass of wine. He loved their odd and snuggly ways and conversations that were endlessly fucked up, mind-blowing, and hilarious. They shared curiosity and, in ways, pushed each other to ask more challenging questions and seek more profound truths.

The night was still when Jack leaned into Thad's chest, enjoying the chilled air, toying with a burr. "And then love said no." They let it hang in the air for a second, taking in its resonance. He repeated it, the moment feeling right. "And love said no."

There was gravity there, and an ask. A quick side push Thad redirected with, "Yes…." The silence chirped its night song. "It's the complexity of its resonance. The full spectrum of vibrations. It's the solution because of how it…." He thought about it and started to laugh with his mental description. "How it kinda neuters the yang of it."

Jack burst out laughing. "Oh my God… ha ha…." They were a tidal roll of stupid and gasping for air. "You are a ridiculous person!" They laughed more like little boys telling nighttime stories.

"No. No." Thad was trying to draw the room to attention again, but neither party was falling into good form. "Okay… ha…." He cleared his throat and swatted Jack, "Okay, shut up," making them both laugh more and scattering the hopes of a restrained conversation.

Calming themselves, Thad continued, "I mean… but it's kinda true, right? The power found in 'no' is about 100% yang. Right? It's like super masculine… so…." He paused on a snag. "The feminine no. The 100% yin… when telling them to back up, and no, not ever on my watch will you lead with bigotry and hate." Thad was amused with his latest imagining.

"Whoa, dude," Jack said in a slight straight-guy tease. "Like, the weapons of war but… glitter bombs! Hooray!" Jack clapped, being stupid but then leaned in and finished his newfound point. "Knives that heal and bombs that end hate. To…." Jack had a flash of something he once told himself: "I once wished something." He thought about it, wanting to get it right, "To end institutional bigotry, most notably in religious arenas." He chased on, "To end the torture of queer people. Help chart a world where we gays can at least hold hands on the street without fear from a world that punishes that. We are not born a sin or a crime. Have people return to empathy and kindness. Create understanding." He paused. "That was my wish."

Thad smiled, as he loved this part of Jack. His attitude of, "go-fuck yourselves, you fucking raging homophobes!" to anyone who dared say their relationship was anything less than it was. They both knew that what they had was special and unique. Their love was vast and changed not only them but those in their circle for having seen what they modeled in the world.

Thad the gentle rocking of a steady boat, Jack the fierce wind.

"That's a perfect wish." Thad looked out into the night. "You should tell people about it."

Jack side-stepped the ping of it, and it wasn't missed by either of them that Jack was saying no to taking chances in exchange for a safer future. "Cool," Jack said, settling in for comfort. "I'll post it on Facebook tomorrow." The aroma of its truth was small and stale.

"What do you want, Jack?" Thad let casually greet the night.

He twisted with the charge. "I just told you."

"What if you wrote a book?" The sound of it slapped Jack awake.

"Thad?" Jack was not conveying pleasure. "C'mon. Be serious." He moved in his seat, trying to regroup. "That's your thing. I…." Jack was arrested, seeing the hole in his life where formal education was supposed to go. It just didn't make sense. "Thad, you know I don't have, like, your education. Besides, what would I say?"

"I can help you, and you're going to say what you just said when I stopped you."

"What? My wish?"

"Yes. Your wish."

"That's going to be a pretty fucking short book, my friend." Jack did some math in his head. "What like fifty words?" Jack laughed, shaking the matter for anything other than the absurd. But then he continued, "Like, what else would I say?" Pause. "Like, could I say that I've never seen any kindness or empathy from religious circles and that I am fucking exhausted from faith communities continually demanding that I feel some kind of way about their beliefs that have vilified queers since the dawn of time?"

Thad started to laugh. "Feisty bugger." A comment that made Jack mad as his life partner was clearly, and too much, enjoying the show. A show of his outrage was no laughing matter.

"Or should... No!" Jack was alight. "Maybe, I can say how I want to find a way to 'weaponize' empathy and love... but, obviously weaponize is the wrong word." He took a second, then it came to him. "Oh fuck." Jack went wide-eyed. His thought brought back to him: *I want to change the world.* Jack churned contrary to the thought. *Gah. Fuck. Stop.* He was swatting at ethos. Thad intervened, laughing.

"You okay, mate?"

Jack came back to himself, embarrassed that he had so lost himself in the idea's emotions. It was like a vast vortex of thoughts that just took him down rabbit holes, and he had gone chasing after wonderful fleeting ideas. "Ya... sorry. Just...." They let it go, but Jack noticed that Thad had a new curious pry he wanted to try.

"So what would you write about?" Thad shimmered a wink. It was clear he knew the barnburner he was stoking. "Maybe, religion?" KABOOM.

Jack sat upright. "Okay, now I know what you're doing, dear sir, and I suggest you stop. Besides, writing is your thing."

"Yes!" He zoomed in on the point. "And ideas are yours. You get so much further out into the ethers of new information with this stuff. The ideas that come to you...." Thad slapped his forehead.

"God. It's just not fucking fair." Jack was on a spin cycle with the news. He laughed.

"What..?" Jack continued, "God. What? Why are you mad? What do you mean?" Jack didn't understand.

Thad paused as if searching for words. "So… we each have our process and way. Right?" A quick rumble of agreements went around. "And we see what we 'get,' as an a-ha, new concept, idea to roll around with." Then Thad stopped. "But Jack, you're outside even that circle, and I know you haven't even told me everything you're seeing yet."

Jack could feel his walls wanting to rise. He was getting caught on the verge of a half-truth, not a full disclosure. *How does this man fucking know this?* Jack grumbled while pinpointing a redirect.

"Fine," Jack said as Thad smiled. "We can talk about it next week once we get into Whitehorse. I gotta sit with that. It's very… not me."

Thad soft clapped and loud-whispered a "YAY!" while Jack laughed.

Chapter 52

MACROCOSM

On the first day of field training, Jack was excited to be on his new path. The topic of forestry had always fascinated him, and the online work was enjoyable. Besides, trees always spoke to him, so it felt right. Day one was classroom introductions and scheduling. As had been arranged, Jack would be in the morning classes as was his best chance of attending, given that he was still okay more mornings than not.

That afternoon back at the hotel, Jack was trying to take care of some paperwork, but his brain was leveling to zero, so Thad had to help him fill them out. Once they had logged off the computer, it was time for Jack to rest. Thad pulled up next to him calmly. However, a touch of bedevilment in his eye put Jack on his proverbial heels.

"What's up? What's with the mystery and excitement?" The cheerfulness annoying yet funny to Jack. He started to laugh, "What?" Jack side-eyed him further, awaiting a response. "Weirdo."

Thad pulled up close, doing a happy dance. "I've waited to bring it up, and here it is…." The sing-song of it again, annoying yet funny. Jack knew Thad had been on this in the back of his mind. Jack couldn't figure out why his lover wanted this for him.

"So…," Thad magic-eyebrowed. "What do you think? It can be just like that. Just like your homework we completed together. I can help you with the writing. You just chart the course to that dark little imagination of yours." Jack's response was to relax further into his pillow, and without opening his eyes, he swatted in Thad's direction.

"Can I just ask you why?" Jack finally one-eyed Thad. "Why can't you just leave me alone?"

Thad laughed. "Nope, mate." He poked at Jack. "Not this lifetime."

"Fine… but answer my question," Jack said without tone.

Thad considered his answer. "Because I want for you what I got out of the process." Not a response Jack was expecting, but he took it in as Thad's response somehow changed the idea of him writing a book because from behind Thad's perspective, it no longer was a task… but possibly a journey. This was entirely new for Jack, and he could feel it take to his soul.

"I guess I could write about.…"

Thad cut him off, wrestling him, "The limitlessness of happiness?"

Jack pushed back. "Ha. Ya. Sure." He was laughing through his words. "Ask the sad dark-purple suicidal guy to write a book about the limits of happiness." Jack was deliberately flat-lining his tone. They both laughed. Jack continued. "I think I want to teach people how to.…" He sought clarity for his following words. "Fight back. Take the world back. Restore common sense and goodness. It's just gotten so crazy and fake and weird and.…" He wasn't sure how to say it. "Inhumane. And I know we're both tired of it but also feel stuck without a clear path forward. I want to find that. I want to.…" Jack reached into his chest to speak from his feminine heart and said the thing most delicately written on it. "I want to be able to sleep at night knowing that sensitive boys around the world are safe. That's all. I don't want my experience to be that of others, especially from their church." Jack was mainlining his truth. "It is such a betrayal. How they just stopped being able to see my humanity. That I was a person. That I was their son and brother." He paused, allowing the following words to simply fall out of him. "They fucking vilified me."

Thad practically picked Jack up off the bed and held him in his big arms. "I know, babe."

Jack continued. "It would be one thing if it were just me… but it's not." He then snot-nosed his way into Thad's shoulder, seeking dark comfort. "I mean, can you even name a single queer person who isn't significantly and irreparably damaged from what they were taught in church or by religion? How is this still going on? Why, when I bring it up, is it me THAT'S THE FUCKING PROBLEM?" Thad knew Jack needed to get this stuff out. "WHY?!" Jack went on spilling his guts. "Why am I the problem? Why isn't the fucking institutionalized bigotry the problem? Why isn't the fact that my parents were taught to hate me at church not the problem? Why?!"

Jack allowed himself to be held, feeling exhausted from a lifetime of it. His level of done with the bigoted, excoriating the status quo. It had to change.

The next day of class, Jack had a chance to meet more of the students, noting most of them were at least fifteen, if not twenty years his junior. He saw how shiny and new they were, how fresh their skin, and carefree their brows. He caught a glimpse of himself in the classroom window. Weathered, tired, battered, and scarred. The difference was stark.

Jack had done well in the online work despite having to rework a few things due to his health issues, but he was excited to get started working in a national forest for their winter training. Summer training will be done in six months south toward the U.S. Border.

"The situations we'll be experiencing here will be extreme," the teacher began after directing everyone to a page in their workbook. "That's on purpose." She walked across the front of the class drill-sergeant style. "For the next two months, we will be in the field at least six hours a day." Her instructions were pointedly clear. "You will learn survival skills. You will learn search and rescue. And you will be responsible for one another's success. We don't leave anyone behind and are accountable to one another at all times." She paused to cross to the center of the room. "This brings me to our next point of business." She trained on Jack. "Mr. Daw here has medical issues and is subject to sudden attacks that render him unconscious. The more able-bodied students need to keep an extra eye for him, but he is also being assigned a service dog who will serve as his first line of defense should there be any issues." Her militant air controlled, pausing for the class to fully absorb the information. "There are four dogs who will be in training along with us. Jack will be assigned and work with Maheegan, our full-time on-site response dog, and there's a sign-up sheet on the board for anyone who wants to work with the dog trainees. However...." That last bit yelled and silenced the chatter. "This will make your life difficult and most likely make your grades suffer. So be wise about what you can handle and clear-eyed about what you need out of the next two months. I'll post who'll be on the team by the end of the week. Jack." She redirected to him. "You start today right after afternoon classes. 5 PM. Don't be late."

Jack was internally collapsing a bit as he felt the reality of a schedule he knew he couldn't manage. He wasn't sure if he could make it to 5:00 despite having a few hours in the afternoon to rest. "Uuuuhhh...," he said to himself, noting his guts were an angst sandwich. He hoped for a good day with a functioning brain.

At the end of orientation, Jack met Thad back in the room, where he informed him of his schedule. Thad assured him to take his time and that he was finding new inspiration in his work and, quite frankly, a new time to write now that Jack was in class. Jack rested and slept some in the afternoon and took his meds to hold back troubles for the next part. The late afternoon part. The part of the day that always held no guarantees.

Back at the training building, Jack met the field sergeant, who drove him to the kennel. It was pitch black at 5 PM, the sun this time of year down by four o'clock.

Jack looked into the stars, his constellation companion, "Space. Time." The figures in the heavens were like music to Jack, and he knew their wrinkle by their twinkle, their messages not yet known. Their elegance by night and intelligence by day begging to be unearthed. A night ray of sunshine that seems to shimmer with information, the knowing in the warming from somewhere off-earth. Jack had a weird thought.

"Is time a place or a distance?" He reviewed his latest trek to tinker on its causal plane. The place one goes to affect future outcomes. He meddled with it more. "Infinity." He held it in his mind as the black night sky continued to roll on its path. "Is that linear?" He flipped into a higher vision for a paused, quiet look. "Infinity and time. They are an occurrence. A continuum. A loop."

Jack dropped into his mind to formulate, "It has to be. The only unending thing in the universe is a loop or a sphere." Jack folded a mental note into his reticulated activator to ping him for examples when they appeared in his life. "Causal. Causation. Tinker." He was getting a message of future understanding around this. "You will see how it works and understand it," were the words he picked up from the dark Canadian heavens. "To think otherwise is to see the world as flat." Jack returned to the moment as they arrived at the dog building.

"Welcome. Glad you can be on the team. We've never had a handicapped person make it this far in the program." The greeter said. "So... nice work."

Jack let that live where it did and detached from its message immediately. "Ah. Thanks."

"My name is McCullough, and you'll be working with me to bring you up to speed on the basics. We'll then be the lead and example for trainees, so you got one week to learn the course."

Jack was pleased to meet the director who, even though much higher in the ranks of the place, was still significantly younger than him. A fact that pointed and laughed at his middle-agedness. Jack did his best to rediscover his lost perk of a twenty-something, but that sheen was well dead and indeed reincarnated by now.

"The dog run course?" Jack was confused by the notion that he had a week to learn "the course."

"No moron, the course. The entire educational course. What we'll be teaching over the next two months." He redirected and reached to pull the dog out of the truck. "This here is Maheegan. She's our station dog. Full time." Jack had never seen such a beast. He froze, trying to take the thing in.

"Wow…." Jack stammered. "She a husky or Giant Pyrenees… or…?"

McCullough laughed at him. "What were you expecting? A Clumber Spaniel? Her name is Maheegan, that's Algonquin for Wolf. Do the fucking math."

The white wolf dog walked toward Jack to meet him. She checked his presence for danger while he did the same in return. They realized they were fine and then leveled to being open to one another.

"Here." McCullough threw ropes and a harness at Jack. "Saddle up." Jack was a flit of indecision. Even the bitch dog called out how fucking queer he was in the moment.

"Aaah…." Jack tried. His rainbow feathers were ruffled. "I'm sorry…." Jack didn't know how to "saddle up" as directed. He hated how he stood before the commanding officer a purse of ill-habit, practical to none.

McCullough sent a noise of frustration to Jesus, then grab-handled it back to show the fucked-up old new guy step one. "There!" He slapped it back at Jack. "C'mon, it's going to take us an hour just to get there."

Jack was willing not to be a racket of undone and to make it through at least the first day, but he was already exhausted, and the frigid air was wicking his abilities. His slip gave way to less clear thoughts while the world went weird.

Suddenly they took off, and Jack did his best to follow McCullough's lead.

"Here!" He set the tone. "Grab here!" He showed on the fly as the world began to spin faster. A long looping tether the only saving grace between Jack and hope. On they sped, Jack clamored to hold anything that wasn't a flail in the night. The night air stingingly painful as his eyelids froze together, rendering him temporarily blind as he bumped over the snow and ice.

CHAPTER 53

PARTICLES

By the time Jack returned to the room, Thad was asleep. He quietly let himself in the room, showered, and snuck next to his partner. Jack was exhausted and hoped he would grow accustomed to the whip of his current schedule. He wasn't sure.

Falling asleep, Jack noted, "One down, fifty-nine days left." He was going to will himself through this even if it meant bringing him to the farthest reaches of himself.

The next morning Thad brought Jack coffee in bed and took Joy out for a pee break. Jack found his way to the cold dark of a northern morning with a groan noting how sore he was from the previous day's work.

"Babe," Thad said, returning to the bedroom. "C'mon, you're going to be late."

"It's pitch black out," Jack complained. "My people aren't good at this sort of thing."

Thad's response contained no pity. "C'mon. This...."

"I know, I know...." Jack got himself dressed and then sat to have a bite of breakfast before the tilt of the whirl began.

Thad finally voiced his concern. "So the dog training is on top of your other course and field work?" Jack knew this was coming. "And it's mandatory for the guy we've been working with to cut down to a bare schedule?"

"Looks like it." The air was silent yet was calling out a thing.

"You feel solid about this?" Thad pressed on.

Jack searched for his best answer. "Dunno," he said mid-deflate. Over the next several minutes, the silence in the room continued to say more than their words. Jack finally got up and collected his things to head out for the day.

Thad stopped him. "You know, Jack…." He kissed him goodbye for the day. "If it's ever too much… I mean, they know what's going on."

"I just want to do this." Jack exhaled. "I have to at least try."

"I know, babe… and we will, but we have to do it as we can. You're not Superman." Thad kissed him again. "I just don't want…."

Jack cut him off. "I'll be careful. I'll see you tonight." With that, he headed out for day two of field training.

The week's balance was hell, and Jack willed himself to fire on max. It exhausted him to his core, but he found reserves of try he hadn't unpacked in years. By Friday, he was a carload of aches and complaints, but he had managed to get through somehow.

The dog trainee team was posted, and they all met with McCullough and Jack at 5 PM Friday as a formal introduction of the dog trainees.

McCullough took the reins as was commonplace for him.

"Okay, team," the leader said, introducing the students who made the cut. "This is field agents, Hendricks, Johnson, Castor, and Yang. Trainees… meet Field agent Daw and I'm McCullough. Hendricks, you'll be working with Lupe. Johnson, you're with Artemis. Castor, Odin… and Yang, you're with Scott."

Yang perked up, "Scott?"

"Yes, fucknuts, Scott. I don't name 'em, just train 'em." He said, handing the young Asian man the dog's leash.

Yang then did an aside and turned to the other trainees. "Scott? My damn dog is named Scott?" He didn't seem to be able to get past it. "Why'd you all get dogs with cool names?!" McCullough brought the dogs around, making them sit as their new handlers approached. Each was more excited than the last to meet their new canine work partner.

"Take your pup for a walk, get to know one another. You have one hour, then that'll be it for your meet-n-greet today. Singer will meet you back here to collect the dogs from you in 60 minutes.

Daw, Meheegan, and I are back on the grid until 10 PM. We will see you Monday."

With that, McCullough pushed Jack into the one-man sled and strapped himself behind him. By this point, Jack at least knew how the skim of the thing worked as he focused on the trail ahead.

Thankfully, the following morning was Saturday, as Jack was a riddle of inflammation and sore muscles. He groaned, this simple act even seeming sore. Thad turned over, realizing Jack was awake. Much to Jack's displeasure, Thad was all mischiefy and bubbly in his energy. "Ugh," Jack managed, hoping to put a curse of the deep-purple tragic people onto his bubblegum-pink partner's aura.

"So…," Thad wagged with excitement, "How do you feel?" He flew in for a closer inspection of Jack's face. "You made it through your first week and only had to miss one day." The celebration was set for one. Jack was still stumbling and tripping over his current antediluvian state. He had never felt so old.

"Kill me," Jack blacked in response.

"Ha!" Thad was a tickle of the day's possibility, and Jack was getting clear he'd need to commit murder to make it cease. "How about I get you coffee?"

Jack's response was steely-eyed. "That's an excellent idea." His smirk was the damn holding back a figurative murder of drama despite being glad his partner was there for him. He rolled to life, watching Thad exit the bedroom while checking his systems for connection. Everything was firing as it should, but he couldn't get over how damn sore he was.

"Even the muscles in my feet are sore," Jack complained.

Thad smiled while returning to the room and handed Jack some coffee. Then, with a morning kiss, he said, "I bet. That was some crazy schedule. Are you handling it okay? What's the status of that?" Thad waited expectantly, his nerves visible.

"I know…." Jack started feeling defensive. They both knew this schedule just wouldn't be sustainable and that Jack could, in a way, suppress his tics and episodes but that it would be epic and dangerous when it did finally erupt. This is the recipe for a return trip to the nearest hospital. They both had been down this path enough to know where it led. Jack continued, "Ya… I'm pushing myself super hard right now, but so far, I'm handling it." He grasped at straws. "Next week should be a little easier… you know, given that I'll be in better shape and… and, the dog trainees will be involved so… maybe now everything with Meheegan and that, you know, might be less." Jack felt relieved to stop talking.

"Babe," Thad said, not saying what needed to be said, but then doubled down with, "I won't be able to say this when you land yourself in hot water… so I'll say it now." Jack wasn't sure where this was headed. Thad was direct. "I told you so."

"I know…," Jack man-caved. "I'll speak with them. But I want to at least try. This means a lot to me. I really want to do this. Now's my chance." Emotion stepped forward. "You know…." The "before it's too late" part didn't make it into the physical world, but they both heard it.

Thad grabbed Jack's coffee, put it on the nightstand, and looked at him. "You have my full support. Just promise me you'll be safe." The fear in Thad's eyes was ringing alarm bells. "Promise me."

"C'mon, Thad! Ya… I'll be safe." Jack just wanted him to back up and let him drink his coffee.

The following Monday morning, Jack looked forward to returning to form. A rigid schedule, in an odd way, felt good to him. Like back when he had life goals and a future to dream about. Classes resumed, and Jack stuck to himself and spoke to his classmates as required, but they were in a different place in life. The younger students talked about things that didn't matter to him, and the drama was endless and exhausting. During most of Jack's free time, such as lunch and the occasional break, he'd hang down at the kennel with his new white wolf companion. She had a staid, restrained energy that simmered right above a hair trigger. She was powerful, which was apparent to anyone who came near her. She was not one to over-explain herself; if she had spoken words, they would have carried a hefty weight. Jack sat beside her, pulling out a sandwich for them to share.

"Here," he said, giving her a taste. Then Jack had a thought. *What if I could dial into her energy while I'm doodling?* The thought opened a new possibility, and he found an access point that turbo-charged energy in the mere inspiration of it. He pulled out his books and grabbed a pen but was displeased that he only had regular school paper and ballpoint ink rather than the sheets of texture that he had grown to love because of how they met the charcoal with perfect resistance. It was in that extra oomph that those surfaces asked that made identifying the precise moment of now easier.

Jack closed his eyes, put himself to the side, and then locked into Meheegan's wolf energy; he took up his pen. The shift of the slow began as he worked his way onto the time continuum. He worked the force open and then directed it out onto the paper. Each droplet of ink called to Jack's ear. His blank then received her, "The power in her yin." Jack awed. "This is power." Jack thought. "Yet... it is air. It is lightning without thunder, for she gave that up in exchange for the quick. She is the most powerful energy there is... because... only it creates thusly."

Jack slowed himself, the wolf joining him in the exercise, so they could both hear what was anew. "This is what you write about, Jack," he heard. "Stop and feel this energy. Know this energy. Feel this every day until you can mimic it because then you can generate it." Jack removed himself entirely from his mind to only vibe with what Meheegan was ov. To feel her origins and know her vibration by heart. Jack opened his heart center to know and then allow. His feminine adopted the new and saw the truth of a great spirit such as Meheegan, the white wolf, the divine feminine's might. The dangerous silence. The laser-focused knowing. The deadly silence of her mind. The sensing and not letting ANYTHING be other than what it was. That was her most extraordinary power. Clarity. The white lightning devoid of ick.

Chapter 54

BYWAY

The course halfway done, Jack was managing, but barely. Plus, the instructors had become aware of what Jack could manage, and everyone was working toward the same goal; the instructors could tell how much this meant to Jack. He was in good hands.

It was early December, and the depths of winter meant virtually no daylight entered the student's world. Darkness's only interruption? A few hours of gloaming that failed to materialize into day.

One December evening, after the dog training team had been loaded into the truck and were heading to the base off the grid, Jack had to acknowledge he wouldn't be able to train with Meehegan. Jack looked at the stars and exhaled the day's strive. He had to be honest and knew he would have to wait alone in the vehicle until they were done with their cliff descent before they could take him back. They parted, leaving Jack to neurologically seize up alone in the silence of the Canadian Rockies.

His mind wandered back to when he first started truth-telling to himself. He remembered the exact moment.

Jack walked through his front door after seeing the movie Good Will Hunting. He needed to be alone, and he didn't know why. He couldn't place why that movie so completely undid him. It made no sense to his mind… and yet, there it was, as plain as day. He was fucking devastated.

"Why?" Jack's mind was shut to answers. "Why was it that when the Robin Williams character kept walking toward Matt Damon saying, "It wasn't your fault," did Jack unravel? No answers could be found. At all. And Jack was a basket case for weeks over it. Search as he may, nothing came to him, and he couldn't figure out why he couldn't figure out why. He felt cursed for the immobility and density of a mind that couldn't afford a single

Jack returned to himself and looked into the night; the vast mountain peaks endless, their power enormous. Then Jack felt a twinge. Jack did his best not to react. He had prepared for this. The class had prepared for this, so now he just had to walk through it. He could feel this was going to be a bad event. The resonance and hum were deafening as it cracked open his brain.

Jack detached. He let go. He let himself fall and be thrown.

Jack saw a figure as his vision leveled to the horizon while slipping to the other side of consciousness. A creature. "What…?" Jack said, unsure what side of his mind he was on, unclear if the thing was real. It was a black bird in a tree just a hundred feet away. Weirdly, Jack had the sense that it was Yolo. He didn't know why he was thinking it, but he was, and it was written all over his mind. She had come back! He refocused on her only to notice she wasn't standing on a branch… but hanging upside down from it, like a bat. His queering mind was too spun to make it make sense.

The last thing Jack saw was what he didn't see. He sought to focus more on the thing, but it was as if the creature's silhouette wasn't a thing but a hole or a vacuum. A thing you could see through rather than look at. He saw the tear in the trans-world fabric and reached toward it to connect with it and know it. He threw his consciousness into its portal and learned its vibration as he fell onto the backside of his mind.

On the other side, Jack detached and floated, awake, listening. He hoped to form a thought here. He paused. He could. He remained in curiosity. What else?

Jack had memorized the resonance of the tear he saw in the fabric of the worlds, and he had remembered and adopted it. He sang with it in this place on the other side, and he saw Toby come into view, his soul twin ov light. They smiled in recognition.

"Your time here is almost done, Jack. You leveled through the assignment quickly… but anyone seeing the extra curriculum work in your childhood could see you were serious about leveling up."

Jack smiled, knowing the truth in what was said. "There's more to know. It doesn't stop here. You have only just found the trailhead."

Jack thanked Toby, who clarified before leaving him. "You now have the understanding of the density of your youth. That's a tough assignment you chose. Why?"

Jack smiled at the universal download that was being shimmer-shown to him. A data dump from beyond clarified in his mind that we simply come to give. Just that simple fact, when held correctly, changes one's everything.

"We come to our earth assignment to give, a fact we fully comprehend coming into this existence. However, when we get here, we forget. We forget that we are ov love and have elected to be here for this singular purpose. And it is, without question, the greatest source of pain for so many." Jack leveled and said the barest truth of the thing. "Children are given to their mother and father to benefit the parents' soul journey. Not the other way around. We come here as infinite love and have no understanding of want or need until we are human tadpoles. Then, the mind becomes blind. We want and need and hurt from its lack." Jack allowed this to join his truth. "Any thought to the contrary will result in massive pain."

Jack reviewed his parents in his mind. The love in the birthday cards that he had made for them. His childish ideas and wonder from beyond. Jack saw and knew in an instant the million points of light he brought into the world to model for his parents, and he felt blessed for the give in his journey.

As Jack connected to the new information, he was grateful that his parents were his journeymen. He got it. He understood it. Jack knew what he was looking at, and he named it. Said it as low and free of latent meaning as possible because it had to be clean. It had to be free from any ick because awful doesn't burn clean, and Jack demanded its fester be turned to ash. He would unshackle himself and say, "I did this. I did this for love because what I am is good and decent and loving."

He stared at his twin; his reflection was remarkable, and Toby's eyes were amazing to Jack. That he could look into his twin's face and see wholeness. A full deck stacked in the right direction tee'd up for success with a silver spoon in his mouth. But that wasn't Jack, and it wasn't his story, and when he got really honest with himself, he was grateful for his scars, dark and purple soul, story, and experiences. They all meant something to him, and he knew he was better for it all.

Jack free-floated through space, humming with birds. He couldn't seem to tear his vision from the reflection of his twin. The whole one. The undamaged one... the less interesting one... and then Jack laughed. He laughed because he saw that he wasn't just whole but divine.

Jack grew further into the in-betweens and knew that to be in the presence of your holiness can be terrifying, but to have that in you requires knowing it on your deepest level, naming it, and then claiming it as your most authentic truth. To know that you're accessing and communicating with the off-grid and knowing that we as a race must evolve. Jack looked and saw that in him, in them. He looked at himself and said, "I'm in. All the way." He steadied himself with the enormity of it. "Let's see how far we can take this...." He doubled down, saying. "All the way. To change the world."

Jack closed his functioning eye, fully understanding what that meant and its responsibilities. It meant he had to say goodbye to who he existed as now. He had to enter the maze of information and bear witness to his death; there was no other way. He leveled up terrified and with tears in his eyes. "I'm ready." It was a threshold. The threshold one meets when they touch the off-grid. He exhaled deeply, acknowledging that he was done playing small. Jack was going to write his truth, but he also was going to do it on his terms alone. No input from Thad. His clarity only.

He returned to the vision of the black-winged one hanging upside down in the distant tree. The rip in time had healed. The trainees and dog were on their way back, and he had shit his pants and couldn't move, yet somehow, in that moment, he had never felt so capable.

Chapter 55

Sojourn

Thad collected his lover in the room where they had arranged for a school medic to meet them. Jack remembered none of it. There were swirls of painful light and mind-cracking sounds that seared scars to his mind but nothing more. Nothing tangible because his mind had leveled to near flatline conditions.

The following day, Thad did his best to work Jack back to him, but his partner's ability to function was a slinky going downstairs. The more he reached for it, the further it shuffled away. Eventually, they had to move Jack to be under full-time observation in medical care. Thad had feared this was where they'd end up. He held Jack's detached hand as they strapped him to the ambulance gurney, and then the medics helped Thad into the back of the vehicle.

The ride to the emergency room was cold, dark, and bumpy. Jack had a single moment of being able to access English, so he smiled at Thad, who they had strapped into a wheelchair against the van wall for transport. He quietly rasped, "Well, we're a couple of swells." A pop of life registered behind his functioning eye. Thad smiled and reached for Jack. Their meeting point was Thad's hand on Jack's thigh. It's as far as he could reach from behind their strapped condition, but at least they had that.

A few days later, a decision was made that Jack had to stop. He was going to kill himself if he kept up this schedule. They arranged meetings with the school as Jack overheard conversations that were in progress of ending his dream. Accepting it was devastating to Jack, but he knew this next part, the handicapped part, would require grace. A task he would fail at despite doing his level-human best.

In all, Jack spent four days under medical care trying to revive and jump-start his mind, but with each try, he'd disconnect again and be gone. On the day he was set to be returned to their hotel room, Jack was depressed and without air to the tire of his life. He detached and free-floated. He merely wanted to exchange his pain for nothing. To blank and disconnect from a world he could no longer navigate.

Thad got him in bed and took his hand. "I got you, mate," he said, holding back a well of tears. "I got you...." Then, "Don't leave me!" could be heard in the silence. Jack roused to dim consciousness and smiled, doing his best to understand the confusion of lights and the disorder of sounds.

"Marry me." The information meeting Jack's mind called it into no focus. The gentle shock of love restarted his heart briefly. Then Thad repeated it, trying to garner a response. "Marry me, Jack. I can't take it anymore. I need you." He was crying now. "I fucking need you here. With me." He chose his next word, "Forever." Silence hung in the air tearing his heart. "Please." He cried into Jack's unresponsive form. He heaved sob after sob, negotiating with God.

The following day, Jack was able to sit up and use essential functions. Whatever they had given him at the hospital was trailblazing a lead of functions that lent him chemical hope.

"Morning, handsome," Thad said as Jack managed a focus in his direction. "Here's your coffee." Thad gave him a peck on the forehead. The gentle care of it broadcasted his position.

Thad let Jack meet the day as he was able. All his classes and responsibilities gone, his new nothing of scheduled days now known to Jack's feeble consciousness. He could feel it all slipping away. The hopes of his future being voided. Jack rang with only one message. He looked to Thad, finally speaking. "Now what?"

Thad rushed to him to be as close to his world as possible. "Now, you answer my question." Thad's eyes were big and blinking with intention.

"What?" Jack took in the room as he was able. Thad repeated it.

"You answer my question, Jack. Right now. Will you marry me? I can't take it any longer." His eyes again finding rattled and raw emotions. "Marry me. Marry me now."

Jack fumble-smiled and skirted near bubbly, his eyes matching Thad in hopes and tears. "Of course, Thad," he eventually managed.

Reaching for one another, they were immediately a tumble of love, tears, and hopes and dreams. They rolled and embraced on the bed, knowing how lucky they were for having found one another again.

Again, Jack confirmed, "Yes."

Thad's radiation of joy put the universe on blast that their love was beyond what people could see. Their love was molecular, unyielding, and authoritative. They were a force in the world to behold.

"When?!" Thad asked, all smiles. "Now!"

Jack was still a ramble of incoherence. "Soon." He slowed to try and meet meanings. "Grab a...." Jack couldn't remember the word calendar, but Thad was one step ahead of him. They reviewed the dates and decided on December 21st. The winter solstice.

Thad excitedly tried to make plans, but Jack had to slow his roll. "I need time, Thad." His partner wasn't letting go.

"Okay... we can just hang here for a bit. No rush." It was clear Jack wouldn't be in a condition to move any time soon. Most of it physical, but some of it emotional, and if Jack was honest with himself, it was almost more the depression of not completing his course than anything else. The direction of his life was once again untethered from goals.

Over the week, they finalized plans and decided they'd get married in the Yukon and not try to move Jack. Both men were excited and experienced the unending joy of queer people finally allowed to be united in holy matrimony, which was signed into Canadian law just three years ago. They wanted it known to the world what they were to one another.

Jack made some calls and invited Mellie, Dennis, and Wendy, all of whom said they'd be there. Mellie had other questions.

"Who's going to marry you?" Her question rung with a yet said answer.

"We're just going to the courthouse, Mel."

"The fuck you are, mister." Jack laughed at the unexpected response. "Let me call you right back." Forty minutes later, Jack's phone rang.

"Okay, you guys are set… of course, if this works for you, but Reason has spoken of you often and with kindness. Whatever you two shared was powerful and meaningful to him. He'd like to officiate your ceremony if…."

Jack immediately cut her off, "Seriously?! Oh, wow. MEL." He was a thrill of the moment, and the ceremony suddenly materialized to him entirely anew. Jack saw the power forming around the announcement to the universe that they were forever to be known as one. He felt those clouds now in motion and rolling toward them; their call to the four directions now an unshackled moving force to galvanize them as unyieldingly joined.

The two men set final arrangements and schedules as they spent their days writing their vows and finalizing flowers and location. Not so easy in the furthest reaches of the north in the dead of winter.

"So, where do we do this?" Jack finally managed. A question that sparked a weird giddy into Thad's up. "What?" Jack asked without tone or emotion, indicating he could see his partner was up to something.

"It's all taken care of." Jack thought he should be in on this decision, but he understood he was already doing his best, and he had to let Thad run and do and dream and wish. It was adorable how excited the middle-aged man was over it. Jack let him run with his heart's joy.

The day before the ceremony, Jack was able to return to the gym for a light workout, his faculties and form mostly back to him. It felt good to feel himself working again and the preciousness of time made his efforts sweeter. Returning to the room, Jack had a question for Thad.

"So your vows...." The conversation was on. "How long are you making them? I'm just a few minutes...." Thad swung his thin legs toward him.

"Sounds perfect."

Jack was glad they were on the same page. "I don't need to belabor the point." He had a giggle in him. "You know... just say the basics."

"What are your basics?" Thad was curious.

"You know...," he started laughing, "I love you. Forever. Now stick it in me." Both then laughed more.

"You're going to say that in front of our friends and the officiant?" Thad's aura was brimming with life and love. His enjoyment of his dark partner's essence visible as wonderstruck.

CHAPTER 56

APOGEE

The day of the ceremony was clear, cold, and dark. The stars out at noon were the north's carol that swept out the cobwebs of this solstice day.

It had been a tough morning for Jack. His mind was half-mast, but even that wasn't going to stop his heart from saying what was needed. They dressed at noon for the ceremony, the silent room ringing a serious tone. So much was on their minds, and as they dressed one another, they were on individual shared mental paths. Someone knocked at the door.

"And that'll be Mel." Jack rushed for the door, excited to see her.

"Oh, yay!" Jack thrilled. Mellie looked stunning in white, the color Thad asked everyone to wear. This part was so cloak and dagger to everyone, but the bump and thrill it provided were intoxicating. Jack hadn't even been told the location yet.

They collected everything and set out into the day's night, a gentle peek of red sun showing on the horizon. Thad had to prepare them.

"Okay," he began once they were all in the car. His dark reddish beard was a match for his winter white gothic suit. Jack gazed at Thad as a puppy in love, his soon-to-be spouse dapper and robust. "We're all meeting at the Pacific Arts Building trailhead and walking to lookout point number two. If they hit cliffs, they've gone too far."

Mellie was texting everyone en route while Thad did the same to his guests, including his ex, Robert, and his close friend Rosalyn. They rushed off to get everything ready for the guests and officiant.

Joy was there too, but she never seemed to factor into the headcount – she too looked spectacular in her white dress.

Jack got Thad out of the car and helped him into his walking gear while Mellie grabbed bags of decorations from the trunk. They were set. The merry of the moment was expansive; everyone was excited for the day.

Thad led them up the trail, his hike n' hitch, then match and gain, a testament to the measures he would press on for his love. They slowly made their way to a small glen roughly the size of a big-top tent, and in the middle of the clearing were two impressively tall pine trees. Jack figured they must have been at least fifty feet tall, and they reminded him of the ones they'd have on display in Rockefeller Plaza in New York City. Thad twinkled a mystery in their direction and nodded toward them. Jack and Mellie big-girled in delight. The moment was nothing short of magical.

Thad pulled back the limbs of one tree to show a small pathway under the ensuing branches. Mellie clapped in delight as they bowed to enter the small enclosure. The smell of the dank and earthen air was the first thing Jack noticed. It was different here, but as they walked a few feet down, he could see that the inside branches closest to the massive trunks had all been removed, creating a little room, a clearing between the two huge evergreen spirits. Their celestine presence was alive with Mother Earth's awesomeness. Jack stepped onto the wooden floor that someone had made, giving the space a more formal air, that of weddings and ceremonies.

It was overwhelming to Jack. He wanted so much to be in nothing but awe, but his brain struggles were increasing with the excitement. The body thinking the excitement is stress, created additional problems for Jack's current low-grade storm. He pushed at it and rallied, willing himself to be this-world right.

"How did you find this place, Thad?" Jack asked awonder.

Thad shrugged it off, saying, "It was just luck."

"It's so magical," Mellie said, looking heavenward at the drapes of shimmering electric stars giving way to the blue and green Northern Lights dancing overhead.

"Come," Thad interrupted. "We only have an hour before everyone arrives. Mellie, were you able to get everything on the shopping list?"

"All but the penis sippy-cups." Thad laughed, the dick joke coming from the quiet native girl catching him off guard.

"Ah," he twisted with it. "Yes. Best to save those for later, I suppose." The air was giddy with cheer.

They set out the few chairs and tables someone had previously placed at the permitter. "No doubt Thad's doing," Jack secretly loud-whispered to Mellie so that Thad could hear. Smirks met their faces, and Jack continued, "He does that." Jack started laughing, not being able to get the joke out first. "He lets you think you're helping by picking up a snack or some shit, but in the background, he's party-planned the thing to death." They all laughed as Thad admitted his guilt.

"It's a special day!" Thad laugh-complained.

Within the hour, all were present and waiting to begin the ceremony. Jack's nervous state was laying waste to his abilities, but he made it clear he wasn't going down without a fight. He throttled focus into himself, willing it to bend to his demand.

Reason and the guests met them at the outside entrance, all breathing in the day's cool darkness. Their noble white attire was stark against the green of the trees and the black of the dancing Canadian night. A night where stars were brilliant and clear. It was as if they stood at the backdrop to the open universe. Beyond their horizon was the Milky Way, as clear as with a telescope but available to the naked eye this mid-afternoon's night. The space above them was devoid of light pollution, and the heavens felt so close you could touch it. The magic of the north met them at the moment as the presence in the night remained consciously awake.

Jack ran up and hugged Dennis, while Wendy held their newly born child, his presence essential to the day. Next, he walked up to Reason. The bonds they shared were unbreakable, and it would always be the spirit of Reason that Jack would view when charting challenging waters and very dark nights. *What would Reason do?* he'd ask himself. That was the way forward. Jack always knew this. They held one another in a long silent hug.

Thad greeted his friends and introduced them to Jack, who continued to do his best to be present. He bobbled a bit when he walked, and Jack soon found his right side going offline.

"We should start," Jack encouraged, hiding a level of fear from his voice.

As had been previously discussed, Reason met Jack and Thad in the center of the space as the guests arranged themself in a semi-circle around the "room" to serve as pillars present to impart and relay; they were far from passive participants in the process, each aware of their gifts. However, as Jack tried to make his way to meet Thad, it became evident that the use of his right side was leaving him. Seeing what was happening, not one in attendance fluttered a wrong into the space but held and supported Jack as he could. All in attendance knew that this was how he was supposed to be in the world on this day. They embraced its perfection while Reason grabbed for chairs and brought them to the men who the gods had decided should be married while seated. The three men held each other in a tight circle, Reason kneeling, embracing the perfection he found in them. The Shaman then stood, towering above them seated in their chairs. Next, he put a giant chief arm on each man's back, and they all began to churn, hum, drum on their skins, and chant. It was time to open the sacred space.

Reason standing over the men invoked song and sound. A rattle was heard to shake at the vibration and change the air's course. A drum was heard next to thump at the openings, an invitation to those otherwise awaiting to join them. Reason opened every corner of the space, then the heavens and the earth. Next, Reason invoked a torrent of fieldwork found in off-grid locations. Then he tapped into his personal resonance, his song, his wind-horse. The voice of the eternal flung from the resonance of his lungs into the beyond. The creature arrived, and a stampede of energy ran through the spaces found in-between. The vibration of the sacred marriage space, awestruck.

Next, Jack witnessed the guests gathering their minds and offering their all to the moment. Mellie's sound from her corner was the first in finding air as she too called for her wind-horse to find its reigns. Jack heard her as she grew louder. With more force, she began calling, mother-yowling, and directing. Her native language gave the space even greater air for magic. Jack witnessed as she tuned into what she knew and leveled up her tone and vibration. Jack hadn't realized she was this powerful a medicine woman. It was clear that a beam of power lived in her essence, and her lifetime of work in the matter found a new purchase and hit lift-off. It was pure and known to this land, her land. It was evident to everyone present that she had done the work, knew these songs, and created strength and protection for those around her wherever she was. A mother, a warrior, a guardian, and a protector. THIS was her power.

"Protection of a mother," Jack thought. "That's her purpose." He cried, realizing his friends' angelic role in his life. Something she was most likely called to since the day she first met little Jack. He recognized this for the very first time. Little happy, unscarred Jack. The boy who just wanted to kiss her. He laughed at its reimagining.

Mellie continued with the incantation. Her delight in her song matched by universal reason, both holding the unparalleled power of mothers who have seen too much. In the far corner, Wendy, hearing the song for the first time, knew its tune and joined. She opened herself to adopt this knowing and somehow followed the place of motherliness and awake source-bearers in lockstep. Wendy joined in holding her newborn, knowing what she must now also bring to the world. She needed to protect and love enough into this world to change the space for her newly born queer child. Jack understood that she knew this, for the knowing of mothers is absolute.

The ceremony continued. Reason became quiet-clear and said, "Come." He paused from a quiet mind. "Be present with us." He spoke directly to the gods while he moved his arms in circles on the men's backs while they pause-bowed with arms interlocked, meeting one another on this day, exactly where they were. Thad took Jack's hands, which were non-responsive to his touch, and he cried smiles in Jack's direction, who did the same in return. The gratitude in the hour was unshakable.

Reason continued, "This day is for love, family, and our ancestors. We bow and acknowledge our lessons from the past and our responsibility to future generations. Today is about the love of two people who hold each other dear and choose to dedicate themselves to one another as eternal." Reason slowed his arms on the men's backs, and they sat upright to take one another in. The room hummed in infancy and was pregnant with possibility. "The time is now." The room's vibration hit a new height, and then Rosalyn stood and threw open the curtain of space as a nighthawk's screech met the rumble-thunder of what felt like booming from elephants.

Thad gestured to Jack to watch closely what the Medicine Woman was doing. Rosalyn began to sing an off-grid song. Her voice let loose into the sky a whipper of yips and horns of calls that came from beasts. Jack's awe was struck. He wasn't even exactly sure what he was hearing. Next, her wind-horse charged forth and changed the sky's surface so she could directly access the holy-fire power that she now focused on their love's intent.

Finally, Jack got it. He saw the kernel of what he was doing in terms of tethering to the skies. However, up to this point, he viewed it as opening his chest to meet the world. Not this. Whatever this was. It was science Jack didn't yet understand but seeing this, his curiosity found a new get. In time he hoped she could explain it to him, for based on the expression on his soon-to-be husband's face, Jack couldn't help but wonder if this wasn't one of the reasons she was here that day.

"Remember love," Reason commanded of the space and then turned to the two seated men. "We are ready for your vows."

Thad knew he was up first, so he looked at the officiant and nodded. Thad then addressed those in attendance, but mostly Jack.

"From my family, we have Celtic celebrations… and this is something I've always dreamed of celebrating and saying…." Thad started to get teary-eyed. "It's the Celtic tradition of the Anam Cara, which roughly translates to soul friend." Thad then faced the crowd more openly. "It is said that anyone who enters into a partnership with an Anam Cara, you will be forever joined anciently and eternally." He turned back to Jack in vexed expectation. "With this person whom you most cherish… will you say it with me, Jack? Can we invoke and be eternal?" Jack half smiled and then was quiet as was his way.

"Yes," Jack said. "Let's be eternal."

Reason took the room's attention. His voice reverberated throughout the space. "Come." The air shifted in meaning. "Thad and Jack. Place your right hand over your partner's heart and your left hand over theirs on your heart." They did so, Jack finding it helpful to get physical support from Thad's arms supporting him in his war to remain seated upright. The air in the room was alive and watching.

"Repeat after me," Reason said. "Today, I recognize you as my Anam Cara." The room and heavens rang sonic with the vibration from the invoking words.

"Today, I recognize you as my Anam Cara," the men repeated in unison as the black sky cracked open further. An arc and bend in space in time becoming known and available.

"And ask that you become a part of me in sacred kinship," Reason continued.

The men searched each other's faces and repeated, "And ask that you become a part of me in sacred kinship." The crack of Jack's storm whipped him. He leveled up again to face it and force it to bend. Thad gripped him tighter to help him remain in place.

"With you, I have lost all fear and have found the greatest courage," Reason thundered, his boom slamming into mountain sides miles away.

Again, "With you, I have lost all fear and have found the greatest courage." Words that wildly threw Jack back and forth in his storm.

Reason then whipped the incantation into the men who carried its message forth, saying in unison, "I have learned to love and let myself be loved," the men said boldly, facing the rising swirl of them.

The leveling of the spell holding them and rising within them as Jack could feel the alter-world's call; he, precipice-bound and on the verge of falling through planes… "I have learned to love and let myself be loved."

Reason was now channeling from the night direct, the room bounding, binding, and tethering to spires that wicked information from the day's night.

Jack yelled, trying to hold onto consciousness, meeting Thad with their shared words. "With you! I have found a rhythm of grace and gracefulness." He was awash in the waves of the thing. It's beast something he knew from a very dark place. His mind was clear with one thing, and that was the beautifully dark, a spell's swell that wasn't evil, for in this space, the wizardry was love.

Reason leveled up again to explode above the natural world's rising chatter, "Love has reawakened in my life – a rebirth – a new beginning!"

The wind in the room was swirling and searching. Jack was losing himself to the other side but fighting with every ounce of determination. He cratered from the physical, saying, "Love has reawakened in MY LIFE. A REBIRTH. A new beginning." The men cried a torrent awash in the vortex of energy and devotion.

The men spoke the rune's final line, "With you, my Anam Cara, I am understood. I am home."

Quiet silence returned to the room. The murmur of things felt divine, lit, vivid, and present. The spell had been cast, and its shimmer remained ever-present.

Reason centered, finding his way in the space. "Jack. I know you had a few words prepared as well." Reason then slipped back into the silence as Jack looked into Thad's eyes, crying. Jack began, but soon it was understood that he had no access to the English language. The presence of the room readjusting to what was, they settled then hushed to listen and receive as Jack continued his speech as he was able.

Gibberish fell from his mouth simple and plain yet, even in that, his meaning was as clear as a bell on the dark starry Canadian day. Jack's voice rambled in "choocos" and "too-koos" while everyone adjusted to meet his new frequency. It was crystal clear what he was saying even though, at this moment, it wasn't in a known language because what Jack came to say that day was definitive, precise, authoritative, loving, and angry.

Those in attendance heard how his heart was so full of love for this man, and they could hear his wails of frustrations for those who had the gall to look at their love and pervert it. They heard Jack scream to God for more time and more chances, and they heard him state his divine. But they also heard from a very dark place in him.

Jack faced the heaven who was about to meet this man's fury. They heard his demons wail to Mother Moon the frustration of rampant institutionalized bigotry funded by those who said they were on his side. Jack screamed to her holiness in his way. The space hearing a drivel-run of words but the meaning clear 'HOW FUCKING DARE YOU!" Jack's double side sword of evil finding root. Real evil. They understood how it could wick at his will when day after day, his family and friends cheered with rainbow-colored pom-poms while indoctrinating their children in Catholic schools and openly homophobic churches. A stench they thought so freely-washed off and so freely self-absolved… the bigoted idle tendrils of its old ways too ripe for Jack's stomach or mind.

Jack knew this part of himself existed. The push to true evil to kill with his bare white-knuckled hands was clear to the couple's mind that if someone did come for them, there could be a switch thrown. But the question always was, would Jack come back? This held true for Jack in his soul. The type of soul that needs to be granted more mercy and access to an identification where "good" was never the goal. There needed to be a haven for Jack to be his true, loving, inwardly dark self and where that could be encouraged and nourished so he wouldn't shoot up a shopping mall.

"I claim it," they heard as Jack mocked English with off-world words and cried for their lost meaning, unrelenting in the ask that he do this on this day. Jack leveled up and then blasted gibberish into the heavens. Its meaning spread across the continent "WITH ALL THAT I AM, I WILL FIGHT FOR US." He squalled on in tears, his mumble mouth of sounds filled with an energy that permeated from all corners of the room. "AND I WILL FIGHT! GOD DAMN IT!!!" His words became guttural sounds of wounds. "And I will not let this world say that what we are to one another is ANYTHING than what it is!" Jack threw his chest open, leveling the energetic field for miles. "I WILL NEVER STOP THAD." But then he did stop as the room faded back to silent. He finished the thought, "Until I have silenced the hate and judgment toward us."

Jack had a moment of lift. He repeated his gibberish to himself. "Tcho Koko… kay," or as the guests heard, "For our love, I will fight."

CHAPTER 57

ORIGIN

The ceremony came to a close as Jack slipped to the other side. Thad and Reason thanked the guests and saw them off as Jack's body laid procumbent and unmoving in the center of the space. His unmoored being still as it connected to everything and yet nothing. He was free-floating in the in-between, beyond the click.

Dennis asked if he could help get Jack down the mountain, but they insisted they had taken care of it. Only half of their tasks had been completed this day, and they had hours of work yet to accomplish. Mellie, the last guest of the night, took the dog as a serious quiet came over the newly vacated space.

The men refocused on the work, Reason in prayer, and Thad holding Jack so he wouldn't be alone. Many hours later, Jack returned to them, feeling more rested than foggy this time. He wormed his wiggles awake, his breathing returning to that of a conscious person. He looked around the room to see that everyone had gone. It was still midday night, Jack figured, but then realized how does one tell such a thing when the place offers no day.

"What time is it?" Jack asked.

Thad already had his phone and checked, "Almost midnight, my husband." Thad kissed him on the forehead and stood as Reason came to join at his side. Jack remained lying on the floor, shifting the mood to brand new notions.

Jack let be what may, and he surrendered to the floor. Thad then looked to Reason standing next to him and then back to Jack lying on the floor looking up. He noted an exchange of confirmation that he was not expecting. Thad then asked softly, "Why are we here?"

The particles above Jack shone shimmering and warm. The in-between spaces still humming and fizzing with pops of color and illusions from the other side. The two men's silhouettes were beautiful to Jack, and he saw and knew the register of what met both his eyes. He recognized the voice and the gait of the words at once. Thad asked another question, making everything clear.

"Jack?" Pause. "Are you there, Jack? Tell me why we're here. Teach us."

In that instant, Jack understood what this was, and he wanted to bolt… but didn't know why. Knowing what he was seeing and knowing was too big and much too impossible. Surely it couldn't be! Jack's breath escaped him with the discovery because he knew the thing, and he knew from first-hand account. The vast impossibility of the realization made him stutter as he replayed the voice again in his head. The way it would always appear. The way it always started… only now he knew it wasn't just a voice in his head. He did have guides, and it was them! It was them all along.

"Are you there, Jack? Why are we here?" Pause. "Teach us." Their black shadows set against the stars above his dystonic melding vision.

Jack had bells ringing inside him that he didn't know how to hear. He scattered into lenses, searching for clues yet fearing somehow that what he knew, despite being impossible, he knew. Finally, his clear upper mind yelled into his being, reassuring, "You know what this is, Jack. Stand. Name it!" Jack didn't know why floods of tears felt like they had waited his entire life for his next thought, but his heart-based consciousness saved him by showing him what this was ov. What its origins are. What stuff behind the stuff is it made of, its barest truth told in the least amount of words, free from latent meaning, ick, or ego. "Name it," Reason and Thad encouraged.

Jack laughed, noting an interesting inkling, and he then spoke it into the Akashic Record. "The advanced class." It was done. It was real, and Jack was washed anew while the two men knelt on either side of him to confirm the fact of who they were. Thad continued asking, understanding that Jack needed time to formulate the riddle.

Jack stopped and took a simple, quiet moment for himself. It was a moment that would change the trajectory of his life because he knew in claiming the thing that he'd then be responsible for its requirements.

"Teach us, Jack," Thad continued. "Tell us what you know."

"I know who and what I am. I know. It's in how I know my name. I know its truth. I am in the advanced class and will step and level up because we are out of time. I know this comes with much responsibility, and I accept that. I accept that it's up to me. No one is coming to save us. No one. It's up to us… and I say yes to creating as much of that change as possible in one simple task: providing clarity to conversations I witness. In that, I can change the world. I can call a thing by its barest thing, void of any latent meaning, and by laying it bare for all to see its truth."

The next thought was new for Jack. "The empaths can win the war. That's how we kill the thing. We unveil it by standing in purity, and they fall in that contrast. We use the power of every person on the planet to level up their ability to call clarity to every conversation that takes place before us. When people belong to and fund institutionalized bigotry, name it. Name it. Lay who they are bare. That's how we force change. That's the power behind the Feminine Divine." Jack then sought its clearest clear. "The empath's weapon, the weapon without ego, is clarity."

He understood the information he was receiving and the message and intention to help build a new earth. He might not be able to change it all, but what if he could? What if he changed ten minds? Then Jack got honest with himself. He knew the process would torch him and destroy his personal ick, burning it to the post, leaving nothing but the bare. He foresaw it and felt its truth.

"Jack." Pause. "Are you there, Jack? Why are we here? Do you understand it now?"

Jack looked into Thad's eyes, understanding the flex of the matter. "I do." Jack smiled. His wedding day joke lightening the moment. Jack exhaled and answered what had been asked of him. "We're here today to say goodbye."

Thad rushed in to take him in his arms. Reason waving over them, the air a rustle of specks. "Yes," Thad said. "Tell me more. Teach me."

Jack listened for his truest truth, then said it out loud. I have to say goodbye to my physical body. I know the time has come. We all knew this day would come."

Thad remained listening with curiosity. "Say more...."

Jack laughed to himself, knowing he was being caught. Thad was so in-tune to him that he knew to prompt for more. That there was more truth to tell. He looked to Thad, "I have to witness my death, and it terrifies me." The warble of his words was a cry of acceptance. Thad kissed and held him.

"Yes." Thad's face was so proud. "You can see that."

"I can." Jack cried silently, knowing these were his last few seconds of being him. He felt it all. Jack had learned to love and celebrate who he was and the mile after mile of angst and drudgery, which made him tired. Jack felt in his bones the weariness of it all. *All this work to come to love me as I am only to watch it die.* That was the true clear of it, but Jack was ready. He knew it was time to level up and let go. The breaking point was coming, and there was too much at stake. Jack sat up as the other two men took him in their arms. The whir of the moment immediate and pulsing new life into them.

Thad cleared the space around them as Reason took care of the celestial. Thad began in prayer. "Creator. We understand our brother and my spouse as he is. We ask that you lay your hands upon him so he may be guided beyond today. Jack releases his body and his attachment to it. He rests in the hands of our heavens and is cradled by Mother Earth. We ask that you keep him comfortable and that he never has to be anything other than he is in the moment. We ask for his clarity, and he may follow our lead if needed. Help is always available, and he is safe. Give us consciousness to see and know it as it is, in its barest form. We call on the Feminine Divine for her strength and clarity. We surrender Jack. We surrender him."

The moment rang as still and hallowed. Energy exchanging in coils. Jack then moved to stand. The men, each one on either side. Jack leveled up, stood with assistance, then looked into the stars and said, "I am learning what you are… AND I AM COMING FOR YOU!" He stopped to check the resonance of his following words. "And I know with all that I am that I have to say goodbye to this person who I am today. But I'm ready for that, and I am prepared to witness my death to see how far I can take this thing." Jack's voice was trembling. "I know that's the deal… I get it… and it's me." Jack's conversation a wonder, "It's this dumb version of me in exchange for…?" Jack knew the answer was a feeling and not a word. A sense of divine truth telling.

"To change what I'm ov." He thought about it. "To reformat who I am to the Akashic record." His next words were a confession. "To change the world." Jack understood the trade. The old, worn and comfortable for the glorious secrets that he was finally ready to hear.

Jack had a new vision of what his future would look like. He would be very different for the upcoming process of telling his truth, and he was willing to exchange the physical for other realms. Still, it doesn't make it any easier or make witnessing his death less terrifying. This is why it's so rarely done. The ask is too great.

The three men stood interlocking and solid as Jack reached into his human chest for one of the very last times. "I release it. I choose to be new, different, and true to who I am in this life… and if that path is for the nonverbal or handicapped, I choose it. I wish it." Jack searched the stars to tell them and screamed. "I CHOOSE IT! I CHOOSE THIS PATH OF PHYSICAL DEATH BECAUSE I KNOW WHAT YOU ARE… and in knowing such…," Jack reduced to a bobble, "I will know who I am." He looked to Thad. "What we are. Together." Thad took Jack's face and kissed him deeply, the way newlyweds do for the mere expression of what they now were to each other and the world.

The men lowered Jack back to the floor, and then Reason knew it was time to take his leave. They said fond farewells then Thad scooted under his husband to hold him as had become customary.

"Proud of you," Thad said, looking into his beloved, who was a mingle of mess, Jack's brain levels now barely tracking to the physical. He just wanted Thad near him. "We can do it, Jack. Together. I got you."

Thad undressed Jack, and for the first time as husband and husband, they made love where they once again found that they couldn't get close enough. They both wanted more of being in the same shared space. A oneness with the divine that puddled their hearts.

On the final moments of the solstice day's cusp, they lay naked under a quilt made of past life memories, and as Thad held Jack close, he could feel the rattle that rambled his all.

Thad eventually whispered to his love. "Handicapped, together. It's okay. I got you. You're okay. It's okay to let go." At the corner of what was and what beautifully comes next, Jack knew it wasn't saying goodbye to the physical that would be so tough, but rather it was knowing that in the process of tearing open his world's truth and putting his everything out there to be ridiculed, that he would be forever changed. That goodbye would be the hardest, but he knew Thad would be there at his side every step of the way, and he recommitted himself to his love while taking in the last sights and sounds of this physically functioning Jack.

A version of a human they both held love for... but it was time. It was time to discover life beyond the physical.

About the Author

Dale Allen-Rowse always knew he was a creator and a storyteller. However, it wasn't until Celine Dion hired him as an original cast member for her show 'A New Day' that he understood his calling. During the almost year-long creation of Celine's Las Vegas show, Dale's vision for storytelling, narrative, and fantasy emerged. He worked for three years under the direction of Dion's  director, Franco Dragone, the creative genius behind many of the Cirque de Soleil shows. From that relationship, Dale discovered his voice.

In 2005, Dale left Celine's employment, ending an eighteen-year professional theatre performing career to pursue a new life in real estate. Within three years of becoming a real estate agent, Dale was awarded top honors for individual sales volume for RE/MAX and opened a brokerage firm.

After a twenty-year career as an agent and real estate coach, Dale is adding new passions to his interests, including his spiritual life as a shamanic practitioner and student of core shamanism.

Dale channels his books using 'Automatic Writing,' which he discusses on YouTube.com/DaleAllenRowse channel — as well as many of the topics covered in his books, such as personal evolution, spiritual energy work, core shamanism, manifesting, and evolving. Plus, his talks are set to a disco beat, and that's not nothing.

Dale and his husband John live on a five-acre ranch in Mountain Center, California. They currently have five dogs with a miniature donkey possibly in their future. Other things that keep Dale occupied are his quilts — you can see his work online as the Quilting Cowboy — and his day job as a real estate sales educator and coach.

9 798987 397107